BLUE LONESOME

BILL PRONZINI

WALKER AND COMPANY
NEW YORK

For Rocco,
who is anything but blue lonesome

Copyright © 1995 by Bill Pronzini

All the characters and events portrayed in this work are fictitious.

First published in the United States of America in 1995 by Walker Publishing Company, Inc.; first paperback edition published in 1999.

Published simultaneously in Canada by Fitzhenry and Whiteside, Markham, Ontario, L3R 4T8

Library of Congress Cataloging-in-Publication Data

Pronzini, Bill.

Blue lonesome / Bill Pronzini.

p.   cm.

ISBN 0-8027-3268-2 (hardcover)

I. Title.

PS3566.R67B55   1995

813′.54—dc20   95-13049

CIP

ISBN 0-8027-7561-6 (paperback)

Printed in Canada

2 4 6 8 10 9 7 5 3 1

What is hell? Hell is oneself,
Hell is alone, the other figures in it
Merely projections.

—T. S. Eliot

The devil ain't sorrow,
The devil ain't fear,
The devil he ain't even sin or stress.
The devil, I'll tell you, he's loneliness.

—Elma K. Lobaugh
The Devil Is Loneliness

BLUE LONESOME

1

MS. LONESOME.

That was the name he gave her, how he thought of her from the beginning. But it was more than just a name because she was more than just a woman alone. She was the saddest, loneliest person he'd ever encountered: pure blue, pure lonesome.

He knew loneliness; every night he slept with it and every day it rode him, burrowed deep, like a tick rides a deer. He'd seen it in a thousand faces other than his own, but never as naked as it was in hers. Part of its essence was pain, the soul-heavy kind that never eases, never goes away. And part of it was . . . sorrow and loss? disillusionment? emptiness? yearning? He couldn't be sure because he could not get close enough to her to judge. She was like a woman encased in glass— you could see her more or less clearly but you couldn't reach her.

Pure blue, pure lonesome. If this were the thirties and he had the talent of Jelly Roll Morton or Duke Ellington or one of the other jazz greats, he would write a ballad about her. And he would call it "Blue Lonesome."

How long had she been coming to the Harmony Café? Not long; he was sure of that. He looked up from his dinner one early June night and there she was, by herself in a nearby booth. The naked loneliness shocked him at first. He could not take his eyes off her. She didn't notice; she saw nothing of her surroundings, that night or any night. She came, she ate, she went. But she was never really *there*, in a café filled with other people. She was somewhere else—a bleak place all her own.

He saw her at the Harmony the next time he came in for supper, and the next. Holly, one of the waitresses, told him she was there every night between six-thirty and seven. Holly didn't know who she was or where she lived or where she'd come from. No one else did, either.

Usually he ate at the Harmony two or three nights a week, not because the food was particularly good but because it was out at the end of Taraval, a short two-block walk from his apartment. The woman changed his habit pattern; he began to frequent the café as often as she did, and at the same time. She fascinated and disturbed him. He didn't quite know why. He had never been attracted to lonely women; they possessed too many of the same problems and insecurities he did; the few women he'd dated since Doris had been the opposite of lonely—extroverts teeming with energy and life who had allowed him, if only for a little while, to feel fully alive himself. Nor was it a physical attraction. She was not a pretty woman even by his noncritical standards. Too thin, too pale, even though her skin had a leathery quality that spoke of years spent outdoors; lusterless ash-blond hair carelessly home barbered; unpainted mouth like a razor slash; large, pale gray eyes that would have been her best feature except for the pain and the way they stared, flat and empty, like the eyes of someone almost but not quite dead. No, it wasn't attraction but rather a kind of seductive bewilderment. No one is born that hurt, that blue lonesome. Something had happened to make her this way. Something so terrible that he couldn't even imagine what it must be.

It was three weeks before he screwed up enough courage to approach her. He was a shy man, nonaggressive, uncomfortable in social situations: one of the reasons for his own loneliness. The fact that he approached her at all was a measure of the depth of his fascination. He stopped beside her booth, feeling awkward and uneasy and oddly driven, and cleared his throat and said, "Excuse me, miss."

She had already been served and was eating; she chewed and swallowed a mouthful of food before she lifted her head. The flat, hurting eyes flicked over him, acknowledging his existence—and then denying it again a second or two later as her gaze returned to her plate. She didn't speak.

"It's crowded tonight and I wondered . . . would you mind if I sat here with you?"

Still she didn't speak. At any other time, with any other woman, he would have walked away. Now, here with her, he sat down, slowly and a little stiffly. His skin felt moist. She went on eating without looking at him. Hamburger patty, lettuce and tomato garnish, fruit cup, black coffee—the same meal she ordered and consumed every night, without variation. The dish came with cottage cheese too, but she never took so much as a taste of it. That was one of the things about her that disturbed him. Not so much the fact that she had little if any interest in food, as the fact that she didn't care enough to ask for a substitute for the cottage cheese, or to have it left off the plate entirely.

He cleared his throat again. "My name is Jim," he said tentatively, "Jim Messenger."

Silence.

"Have you just moved into the neighborhood? I ask because—"

"It won't do you any good," she said.

Her voice, more than the words themselves, took him aback. It was low-pitched, so husky as to be almost a rasp—and as unnatural as any generated by a computer. No emotion, no inflection. Utterly lifeless.

"I'm sorry, I don't know what—"

"I'm not interested," she said.

"Interested?"

"In you or anything you have to say."

"I'm not trying to pick you up, if that's what—"

"Doesn't matter if you are or not. I don't want company. I don't want to talk. I just want to be left alone. That all right with you?"

"Yes, of course . . ."

"Good-bye."

She had left him with nothing else to say, nothing to do but to retreat. She hadn't looked at him during the exchange and she didn't look at him as he backed away; she went on eating as if he'd never been there at all. He sat down in another booth. His cheeks felt flushed, but inside he was cold.

He watched her finish her dinner, put her coat on, pay her check, leave the café. She didn't glance his way as she passed him. She didn't look at the cashier. He had the impression that she didn't even see the summer fog that swirled around her, robbed her of dimension and definition, then allowed her to disappear altogether.

My God, he thought. My God!

———

TWO NIGHTS LATER he followed her home.

He didn't plan to do it. The thought never entered his mind. He arrived at the Harmony at almost the same time she did, was served and finished eating at almost the same time. Stood in front of her at the cashier's desk and opened the door for her when she left. The door might have opened automatically for all her awareness of him. Outside she turned toward the ocean. He paused for a moment, watching after her; then, instead of turning the other way, toward Forty-fourth Avenue where he lived, he set off behind her.

They had gone half a block before he fully realized what he was doing. At first it made him angry at himself. Weirdo behavior, for Christ's sake; and illegal besides under the new stalking laws. But the anger didn't last long; rationalization diluted it. He wasn't a rapist or a psycho—he meant her no harm. Just the opposite. He was curious, that was all. He was a kindred spirit.

He was a damn fool on a fool's errand.

Yes. All right. He kept on following her just the same.

At the end of Taraval she turned right onto Forty-eighth Avenue, and before long, right again into the foyer of an old stucco apartment house that faced the ocean. By the time he reached the entrance she was gone inside. The building stood almost three stories, wind- and salt-eroded to a colorless hue, containing six small units—three front and three back. From the sidewalk he could make out a bank of inset mailboxes in the narrow foyer; he went in to them. Each box wore a Dymo label. These told him that five of the apartments were occupied by more than one person, married couples and sharing singles. The one exception was 2-B, second-floor rear.

Janet Mitchell.

That had to be Ms. Lonesome. *I don't want company. I don't want to talk. I just want to be left alone.* She wouldn't share her living space with anyone, male or female. Not her.

So now he knew her name and where she lived. Janet Mitchell, 2391 48th Avenue, Apartment 2-B, San Francisco. And what good was this information? What could he do with it? It was irrelevant, really. The questions that mattered to him were inaccessible, closely guarded inside her glass shell.

Who was Janet Mitchell? What had made her the way she was?

The prospect of never knowing was like a splinter at the edge of his mind.

JUNE BECAME JULY, July became August. Ms. Lonesome continued to come to the Harmony every night, without fail. Continued to eat the same dinner and to speak to no one except her waitress. She grew thinner, more gaunt—or so it seemed to Messenger. As if the hamburger patty and tomato and lettuce garnish and fruit cup were the only meal she ate each day. Or could afford to eat? He didn't think that was the case. She must have some money; her clothes were not shabby and her apartment, even in that old stucco building, must cost at least $800 a month. No appetite for food: no appetite for life. A woman who simply did not care anymore.

He tried to stop himself from making the Harmony his only source of supper, managed at one point to stay away for three consecutive evenings. But she kept drawing him back, like an iron filing to a piece of magnetized iron. He didn't try to approach her again. He didn't follow her again. All he did was show up between six-thirty and seven and eat one of the specials and watch her eat her meal—and wonder.

Obsessive behavior. Unhealthy. He knew it, chafed at it, but couldn't seem to free himself from it. The one saving grace was that his obsession was mild, low-grade; away from the Harmony, at work or alone in his apartment, he thought about her only now and then, for brief moments; he lost no sleep over her. But it worried him just the same. His was not an obsessive-compulsive personality; nothing like this had ever happened to him before. It was even more frustrating because he couldn't understand what it was inside him that made him react to a stranger in this fashion. Their only common bond was loneliness, and yet hers, so acute and evidently self-destructive, repelled him as much as it fascinated him.

One clear Saturday afternoon he went walking on Ocean Beach, something he often did for exercise and because he enjoyed the sea air and the company of young lovers and children, the exuberance of dogs chasing sticks thrown into the surf. On the way home he caught himself taking a detour that brought him past Ms. Lonesome's building on Forty-eighth Avenue. Would she be there, shut up inside her apartment, on a bright, sunny day like this? Yes, he thought, unless she works Saturdays. If she even has a job. What kind of job would a woman like Janet Mitchell be able to hold?

While he was thinking this, he stepped into the foyer and laid his finger against the bell button above her mailbox. But he didn't press it. He stood for almost a minute touching the button and not pressing it. Then he swung around, stiff-shouldered, and walked away without looking back.

What could he say to her? Please tell me your troubles, I'm a good listener, I know what it's like to be hurt and lonely, too? No. No. There was nothing he could say, no words to help or comfort her.

All he could offer Ms. Lonesome was more loneliness.

WHAT DID HE have, really, to offer anyone?

Name: James Warren Messenger. ("I hope you never bring me any bad news," a joking client had said to him once, "because then I'd have to kill you. You know—kill the Messenger?")

Age: 37

Height: 6 feet

Weight: 178 pounds

Eyes: Brown

Hair: Brown

Distinguishing features: None

Distinguishing physical characteristics: None

Background: Born in Ukiah, a small town a hundred miles north of San Francisco. Father owned a hardware store, mother worked in a bakery. Both dead now. Both missed, but not deeply so; it hadn't been a close-knit family unit. No siblings. Average childhood, but none of his boyhood friendships had survived his moving away to attend college. No high points in those first eighteen years. No low points, either. And therefore few memories and fewer conversation pieces.

Marital status: Divorced. The marriage had lasted seven months seventeen years ago, while he and Doris were students at U.C.–Berkeley. "It just isn't working, Jimmy," she'd said to him one night. "I think we'd better end it right now, before things get any worse between us." Not long after they separated, he found out she'd been sleeping with a prelaw member of the track team for more than three months.

Employment: Certified public accountant with Sitwell & Cobb, Business and Personal Financial Consultants, Income Tax Preparation and Strategy.

Length of employment: 14 years

Annual salary: $42,500

Possibility for advancement: Nil

Interests: Jazz, all kinds, with a slight preference for the old New Orleans style—stomps, rags, cannonballs, blues—of Armstrong, Morton, Ellington, Basie, Kid Ory, Mutt Carey. Reading, broad range of subjects. Old movies on tape. Travel. (He had never been farther east than Salt Lake City, farther north than Seattle, farther south than Tijuana. Someday he hoped to visit Hawaii. And the Far East. And Europe.)

Hobbies: Collecting old jazz records. Building a comprehensive private jazz library.

Activities: Occasional outings to one of the Bay Area jazz clubs, and a long weekend every other year at the Monterey Jazz Festival. Occasional baseball games at Candlestick and the Oakland Coliseum (though the recent greed-based strikes had pretty much destroyed his enthusiasm for the game). Walks on the beach. Running (but he didn't do that much anymore because of his knees).

Special skills: None

Future prospects: None

Mr. Average. Mr. Below Average.

Mr. Blue Lonesome.

AUGUST MELTED INTO September. And on the third Sunday of that month, Ms. Lonesome didn't come to the Harmony for supper.

Messenger waited until a quarter past eight, drinking too much coffee and watching the door. Her failure to show up bothered him much more than it should have. Maybe she was ill; there had been a strain of Asian flu going around the city. Or maybe she'd gotten sidetracked somehow. In any case it was nothing for him to get worked up about, was it?

She didn't come the next night.

Or the next.

Or the next.

He *was* concerned by then. Relieved and concerned at the same time. He didn't want her in his life, yet he'd allowed her to become a small part of it—a part that he missed. Eating his supper at the Harmony was not the same without her. In some perverse way her absence made that segment of his day emptier, more lonely.

He wondered if she was ever coming back. For reasons of her own she might have decided to eat her evening meal elsewhere. She might have moved to another part of the city or another city altogether. Suddenly here, suddenly gone . . . didn't that hint at a transient existence? Lonely people didn't always stay in one place. Sometimes need and restlessness turned them peripatetic. She hadn't seemed to be looking for anything—just vegetating. But maybe he'd misread her and she'd been biding her time, waiting to end her suffering in some other place. Waiting to find a new beginning.

When she didn't come again on Thursday evening, he left the café at seven-thirty and walked the three blocks to her apartment building. The space on the 2-B mailbox where her name had been Dymo-labeled was now empty. Moved out, then, he thought with a brief, sharp feeling of disappointment. Where? The manager might know; the label on the box marked 1-A—D. & L. Fong—also bore the abbreviation *Mgr*. He hesitated. Did he really want to know where she'd gone?

No, he thought, I don't.

He rang the Fongs' bell.

There was no admitting buzz at the door. But after half a minute a thin, middle-aged Asian woman appeared in the lobby and peered out at him through the door glass. His demeanor wouldn't have alarmed even the most paranoid individual—the woman opened the door almost immediately.

"Yes?"

"Mrs. Fong?"

"Yes. The apartment isn't ready for renting yet. Next week, could be."

"I'm not here about an apartment. I . . . well, I'm wondering about Janet Mitchell."

Mrs. Fong's eyes narrowed. Her lips pinched together in tight little ridges. "Her? You know her?"

"Yes, I know her," Messenger lied. "Can you tell me where she went?"

"Where?"

"Or at least why she moved out."

"Moved out? You don't know?"

"Know what?"

"She's dead."

"Dead!"

"Sunday night. Sit in bathtub, cut her wrists with a razor blade." Mrs. Fong rolled her eyes. "My building—killed herself in *my* building. Terrible. You know how terrible it is to clean up so much blood?"

2

HE SAT IN his living room with the lights off, a glass of brandy warming in his hands. He'd poured the brandy when he first came in, but he hadn't felt like tasting it yet. He sat watching patterns of light from occasional passing cars flicker across the drawn window curtains. From the stereo turntable, the melodic contours and rhythmic innovations of Ellington and his band swelled and ebbed. One of the Duke's original thirties recordings, this one. "Perdido," with Cootie Williams's trumpet growly sweet and low-down blue.

Perdido. Lost.

Like Janet Mitchell: low-down blue and lost.

Why?

The question throbbed in him to the beat of the music. She'd left no note, Mrs. Fong had told him. Given no warning. And the police had found nothing among her meager effects to hint at a motive. What about her past? he'd asked. Who was she, where did she come from? Mrs. Fong had no idea. Showed up one day five months ago, rented the apartment on a month-to-month basis. Paid two months' rent in advance, plus a cleaning deposit, all in cash; paid each subsequent month's rent in cash. Where did she work? Mrs. Fong shrugged. Self-employed, private income—that was what Janet Mitchell had told her and she hadn't bothered to ask for references. No need for references, not when you were handed several hundred dollars in good green cash in advance and then promptly on the first of every month. Visitors? No visitors, before or after her death. Just him, today. The police hadn't come back, which meant they'd been satisfied that her death was in fact suicide. They wouldn't care otherwise; she was another statistic to them. Mrs. Fong didn't care; to her Janet Mitchell was nothing more than an annoying mess to clean up. Had *anybody* cared that she'd ended her life? A relative—had the authorities found one to claim the body? Mrs. Fong didn't know about that, either. Mrs. Fong was tired of answering questions. Mrs. Fong politely but firmly shut the door in his face.

He felt dull and empty, sitting here now in the dark—almost the same way he'd felt when first his father and then his mother died. But they'd been his parents; he'd loved them, even if he hadn't been close to them. It made no sense that he should feel some sense of loss over a woman he had spoken to once in his life, who hadn't even known he existed.

Or did it?

The blues, he thought. One blue lonesome individual empathizing with the plight of another. But it was more than that. In jazz there were two forms of the blues: a simple, direct, personal sadness, the sadness of remembrances past and of the deep darkness of the unconscious; and the other kind, a deterioration and decline of the personal spirit, a kind of resolution downward to plaintive, desperate resignation. Ms. Lonesome had had the second type. Perdido. Lost. He wondered if maybe he did, too. If this entire business with her was symptomatic of an approaching downward spiral in his own existence. More than just a midlife crisis; a rest-of-his-life crisis, in which he descended gradually into a void of utter passivity.

The possibility worried him, yet he wasn't frightened by it. Perhaps that too was symptomatic. If you think you might be on the edge of a breakdown, you ought to be terrified of the prospect—and if you're not terrified, then isn't that in itself a sign of something clinically wrong? Utter passivity: a synonym for despair. Like the kind of despair Ms. Lonesome had been suffering from?

No. The difference was, he wasn't suicidal. *Sit in bathtub, cut her wrists with a razor blade.* He simply wasn't made that way. He could never commit an act of self-destruction.

Maybe she hadn't believed she could, either. Once.

Why did she do it?

What drove her into the depths?

The Duke's arrangement of "Blue Serge" was playing now, a piece even more reflective of plaintive resignation than "Perdido." Messenger listened, let himself be folded into the music for a minute or so—and then popped out again, back into bleak awareness. He sipped some of the brandy. It tasted bitter: bitter heat. He set the snifter down. Outside, a motorcycle raced past with its engine cranked up, momentarily drowning out Ellington's band. A sudden siren sliced the night, close by; white and then blood-red lights flashed across the curtains and were gone. The room, he realized, was chilly. He ought to get up and put on the furnace. But he didn't do it. He did nothing except sit, thinking and trying not to think.

After a while, when the record ended and quiet pressed down, he said aloud, "She shouldn't have been alone. Nobody should have to die that much alone."

He sat there.

"Lost, wasted life."

He sat there.

"Ms. Lonesome," he said to the darkness, "why did you use that goddamn razor blade?"

IT WAS WARM in the coroner's office on Bryant Street. Too warm: Messenger could feel the sweat moving on his face and neck. Another of life's little illusions shattered. He'd always thought places like this would be dank and cold from top to bottom. And a bare, antiseptic white, presided over by sepulchral types in starched uniforms. Maybe it was that way down in the basement, where the morgue and autopsy room were, but up here was a straightforward business office paneled in wood; and the male clerk who waited on him was young and brisk and nattily dressed in a dark blue blazer and gray slacks.

"Janet Mitchell," the clerk said, and tapped out the name on his computer keyboard. He studied the file that came up on the screen. "Oh, right. The Jane Doe suicide last week."

"Jane Doe? Does that mean her name *isn't* Janet Mitchell?"

"Evidently not."

"Then her body hasn't been claimed yet."

"Not yet. It's still here, in storage."

"Storage," Messenger said.

"In cases like this cadavers are frozen immediately after autopsy. Do you think you might be able to identify the deceased? If so, I can arrange a viewing. . . ."

"There's no point in it. I knew her as Janet Mitchell."

"I see."

"How long will you keep her body here unclaimed?"

"Thirty to sixty days, depending on space available."

"And then?"

"We'll make arrangements with the Public Administrator's Office for cremation or burial. But in this case, at least, the city won't have to assume the cost."

"Why is that?"

"She left more than enough money to pay for it."

"How much money?"

"I'm afraid I can't give you that information."

"Can you at least tell me what's being done to find out her real identity?"

"No, you'll have to discuss that with the officer in charge of her case."

"If you'll give me his name . . ."

"Inspector Del Carlo," the clerk said. "Second floor, main building."

INSPECTOR GEORGE DEL Carlo was sixtyish, heavyset, with black-olive eyes that seldom blinked. He was neither friendly nor unfriendly, but still he made Messenger feel uncomfortable, as if he thought his visitor was behaving in a way that was socially if not criminally suspect.

"You say you hardly knew the woman, Mr. Messenger. Then why are you so interested in who she was and why she took her own life?"

"I keep asking myself the same question. I suppose it's because she was a . . . solitary person and so am I. I looked at her and I saw myself."

"Did you have a relationship with her?"

"Relationship?"

"Date her. Sleep with her."

"No. I told you, I hardly knew her."

"But you did talk to each other."

"Only once, for about a minute."

"Did she tell you anything at all about herself?"

"No. Nothing."

"You try to find out on your own?"

"No."

"So you don't know anybody else who knew her."

"No."

"Where she came from, why she was in San Francisco."

"No."

"What led her to commit suicide."

"She was lonely," Messenger said.

One of Del Carlo's eyebrows rose. "There're a lot of lonely people in this city, Mr. Messenger. It's not much motivation for suicide."

"It is if you're cut off from the rest of society, if you exist in a kind of vacuum of despair."

"Vacuum of despair. Nice phrase. And that's the way this woman lived?"

"I think so, yes."

"By choice, or did something drive her to it?"

"I don't know. But I can't imagine anyone living that way by simple choice."

"Running from something or somebody?"

"Either that, or running from herself."

Del Carlo said, "Uh-huh," and leaned back in his chair. "Well, there's not much I can tell you, Mr. Messenger. She didn't leave a note and there was nothing among her effects to tell us why she did the Dutch. We did find a photograph in the bathtub with her body; must've been looking at it before or after she slit her wrists. Too badly water- and blood-damaged to be identifiable, but our lab people say it was of a child."

"Boy or girl?"

"Couldn't be sure. Sex or age."

"What about her effects? What happened to them?"

"Building manager still has them, with instructions to keep everything until further notice. No place left in the property room here for a Jane Doe suicide's stuff. But like I said, there's nothing there to help us. No driver's license, no Social Security card, no credit cards—no ID of any kind."

"Fingerprints?"

"We filed them with the Department of Justice's CID computer, along with X rays and as much other physical data as her body could give us. No record of her anywhere. No match with any missing persons report. We also ran the name Janet Mitchell through various local agencies; that got us another zero. Doesn't seem to be much doubt that it was an assumed name."

"What about money? Didn't she have a bank account?"

"No," Del Carlo said. "What she did have was a safe deposit box at the Wells Fargo branch on Taraval. Stuffed full of cash—better than fourteen thousand in hundred-dollar bills."

"My God, that much?"

"That much. Bank keeps those little slips they make box holders sign when they come in. She dipped into her box once a week, on Friday afternoons, regular as clockwork."

"Which means she paid all her expenses in cash."

"Looks that way."

"You need to provide a Social Security number to rent a safe deposit box," Messenger said. "I suppose she put a phony one on her application."

"Right. And nobody at the bank bothered to check it. Ditto all the other information she supplied."

"She sounds like a criminal of some kind. But I can't believe she was. Not her."

"Well, you could be right," Del Carlo said. "People adopt aliases for a lot of reasons, legal as well as illegal. Same goes for hiding out, squirreling away a large amount of cash and living off of it."

"I don't suppose there's any question that her death really was a suicide."

"Not as far as I'm concerned. Wasn't a shred of evidence to suggest foul play."

"Then it's a closed case."

"Except as far as the money is concerned. That went into an escrow account in case a relative shows up and puts in a claim. Minus whatever it costs to bury or cremate her remains."

Messenger said, "And if nobody claims the balance after seven years, it goes to the state."

"How did you— Oh, right, you're a CPA."

"If it really was her money, it should go to her family."

"Sure, assuming she had a family. But the way it looks now, we'll never know."

"I guess you're right. The way it looks now we never will."

3

HE WAS AN hour late getting back to work. Not that it mattered; no one said anything to him about it. After fourteen years with Sitwell & Cobb, he had a certain amount of leeway where his time was concerned. It didn't make any difference to Harvey Sitwell where the work got done, office or home, or how much time it took to do it as long as an employee kept his billable hours up. In that respect, and in terms of base loyalty to his people, Sitwell was a good man to work for. The problem was that he was tightfisted and inflexible in his opinions. Prying an annual raise out of him was always a chore; and once he'd made up his mind where you fitted in the office pecking order, that was where you stayed. It had taken Messenger five struggling years to find out that his slot was some-where in the middle, and that no matter how hard he worked, no matter what he did, he'd still be in that same slot in ten, twenty, thirty years.

More than once, early on, he'd thought about leaving the firm and hooking up with another that offered a better chance for advancement. But he'd never quite gotten around to doing it, and now he no longer even considered the idea. Apathy, sure, but it was apathy motivated by complacency. The job here was secure; he got along well with Sitwell and with his fellow wage slaves; his salary was more than adequate for his modest needs; and his annual vacation time was three weeks, plus odd days here and there whenever he finished an account ahead of schedule. It was only once in a great while—like today—that he chafed at the job, that his little slot seemed too tight, too confining, and he yearned for something more. Or at least for something different.

He found that he was having trouble concentrating. His mind kept shifting gears, replaying his conversations with the coroner's clerk and Inspector Del Carlo. The fourteen thousand dollars bothered him the most. Whether it was legally Ms. Lonesome's or not, and where she'd gotten it. If there was somebody somewhere who was entitled to it, who needed it far more than the state of California, and soon.

At four-fifteen he quit trying to work and packed the Sanderson tax account into his briefcase. He'd get his head into the figures at home later, with the aid of Kenton and Dizzy Gillespie.

"Leaving early, Jimmy?"

He looked up. Phil Engstrom. Fellow wage slave; slot or two higher than his but also not going anywhere. Thin, bald, and determinedly optimistic. His best friend in the office.

"Might as well," he said. "I can't seem to concentrate this afternoon."

"Anything wrong?"

"No. Just one of those days."

"You need a vacation, son. Still have two weeks, right?"

"Right. End of October."

"Made up your mind yet where you're going?"

"Not yet, no. Hawaii, maybe—if I can afford it."

"Good choice. Plenty of eligible women in the islands. And I don't just mean one-night stands."

"Sure."

"Speaking of which," Phil said, "what're you doing tomorrow night?"

"Friday?"

"Friday. Start of the weekend. Any plans?"

"No, no plans. Why?"

"How'd you like to go to a party with Jeanne and me?"

"Oh, hell, Phil . . ."

"Now don't say no until you've heard the particulars. Jeanne's brother, Tom, is an artist, remember? Well, he just sold one of his paintings through the Fenner Gallery for eight thousand bucks—his first big sale. So he's throwing a party to celebrate. His studio in North Beach. The place is a cavern—it'll hold more than a hundred. That's how many he's invited, more than a hundred."

"He didn't invite me," Messenger said. "I don't know him."

"No problem. You'll be Jeanne's and my guest. It's a good chance to meet people, Jimmy. Artists, writers. And there's sure to be more than one unattached female."

Phil was always trying to socialize him, fix him up with dates and opportunities to meet single women. He'd given in a few times, without enthusiasm and without much success. Had a brief fling with a divorced social worker in her twenties, but it had died of inertia: all they ever talked about were her clients. ("I had this one Latino couple, my God, what a pair *they* were! He got himself arrested one day for exposing himself to three teenage girls from Mercy High School. And you know what *her* reaction was? 'Nobody's supposed to see that thing but me.' That's what she said, I swear to God. She wasn't outraged that he'd committed a perversion, she was outraged he'd whip it out in front of anybody but her. . . .")

"I'm not much for parties, Phil," he said, "you know that. Crowds make me uncomfortable."

"Sure, I know. But you don't have to stay if you're not having a good time. Just come for an hour, have a couple of drinks, check out the action."

"Well . . . maybe. See how I feel tomorrow after work."

"No kidding, I think it'll be worth your while."

"Sure," he said. "Sure, you're probably right."

TWO SIPS OF the bourbon and water he made for himself convinced him that he didn't want a drink after all. He put on a Stan Kenton CD and tried to work. That was no good either. Still couldn't concentrate. And the apartment felt stuffy, almost oppressive.

At six-thirty he put on his topcoat and walked over to the Harmony Café. Crowded, as usual. Familiar faces—and total anonymity. When he scanned the menu, his gaze held on the "Lite Meals" listing for hamburger patty, cottage cheese, fruit cup. He ordered the meat loaf special. But when it came he found he had no appetite. He picked at the food, finally pushed the plate away. He paid the cashier and went back into the cold wind from the ocean.

MRS. FONG WAS not pleased to see him again. She frowned over a pair of reading glasses, holding the foyer door open a scant few inches. "What you want now? More questions?"

"Not exactly, no. I came about Janet Mitchell's belongings."

"Belongings?"

"Clothes, personal effects. Inspector Del Carlo told me you have it all here."

"Boxes in the basement. Not much."

"Yes, that's what he said."

"No jewelry, no valuables. Cheap clothes."

"Would you mind if I look through them?"

"What for?"

"I'd like to know more about her."

"Nothing there to tell you. Police already looked."

"I know. But I just . . . would you mind?"

"Better not," Mrs. Fong said.

"I won't take anything, I just want to look. You can stand by and watch—"

"Better not. Police wouldn't like it."

But she didn't shut the door. She stood peering at him over the rims of her glasses—a waiting pose.

Oh, Christ, he thought. He said, "The police don't have to know. Suppose I pay you to let me look?"

"How much?" she said immediately.

"Twenty dollars."

"No. Not twenty."

"You name a price, then."

"Fifty dollars."

"Forty." He took two twenties from his wallet, held them up for her to see. "Cash. All right?"

She said, "All right," and opened the door wide.

THERE WERE THREE cardboard cartons, one large and two small, a small overnight case, and a larger suitcase. That was all. Mrs. Fong left him alone with it all, in one corner of her dusty basement; now that she'd been paid, she didn't seem to care if he walked off with anything. Or maybe she just didn't want to know.

He stood looking at the meager pile, feeling irritated at himself and vaguely foolish. Forty dollars to paw through a dead stranger's belongings. What was the point? The chance of his finding anything enlightening was slim to none. Jerking himself around, that was all he was doing. Why couldn't he simply let go of her, forget that their paths had ever crossed?

He knelt and opened the largest of the cartons.

Clothing. Underwear mostly. Two sweaters, both of which he recognized from the Harmony Café. A Western-style shirt with fake-pearl snap fasteners in place of buttons. Three blouses. A stained suede jacket.

The second carton yielded half a dozen tattered paperback books, a skimpy collection of cosmetics (but no perfume or toilet water), a street map of San Francisco, a half-full box of saltine crackers (inexplicable that Mrs. Fong would have put stale crackers into the carton), an old-fashioned, inexpensive pocket watch with a scratched cover and an imitation gold chain flecked with greenish oxidation, and a torn and dusty child's panda bear minus one of its shoe-button eyes.

The third carton: A pair of worn and badly scuffed boots that bore a scrolled cowboy design. A pair of sandals and a pair of flat-heeled shoes. Two skirts, one pair of slacks, one pair of Levi's jeans.

The small overnight bag was empty. The larger suitcase contained the thin cloth coat Mrs. Lonesome had worn to the Harmony most evenings, and nothing else.

Pathetic lot. Remarkably so for a woman who'd had fourteen thousand dollars in cash in a safe deposit box. Looking at it spread out on the basement floor made him feel sad, depressed. The only personal items, really, were the pocket watch and the bear.

He picked up the watch, worked the stem. The hands moved but the winding mechanism was broken. He slid a thumbnail under the dust cover and flipped it up. Words had been inexpertly etched on the casing inside, as if with a homemade engraving tool. Letters and portions of letters were worn away, but the full inscription was still distinguishable when he held the casing up to catch the light from a naked bulb overhead.

To Davey from Pop.

Davey. Husband, lover, brother, friend? There was nothing to give him a hint—to Davey's identity or to the reason why she'd kept the watch.

Same with the panda bear. It looked old: hers, from her childhood? Or had it belonged to a child of her own? He remembered the damaged photograph Del Carlo had told him about, that she'd taken into the bathtub with her for the last few minutes of her life. Did a child have something to do with her suicide—the loss of one, maybe? A little boy named Davey? Davey's watch, Davey's panda?

The depression was heavier in him now. He told himself to put everything away, get the hell out of here; the toy bear's one remaining eye seemed to be staring at him, for God's sake. Instead, compulsively, he unfolded the San Francisco map to see if there was anything written or marked on it (there wasn't), even poked inside the box of saltines before he dragged over the half dozen paperbacks.

One of the books was poetry—*A Treasury of American Verse*. Three were thick historical romances, all set in the South before or during the Civil War. The fifth: a Western novel with a cover even more lurid than those on the romances. The sixth: a nonfiction self-help book called *Coping with Pain and Grief*. Odd assortment. But the last might be significant, he thought. Grief and loneliness went hand in hand, especially if a child was involved. So did grief and suicide.

Messenger thumbed through the self-help volume. No dog-eared pages, no underlining, no personal annotations; and nothing tucked in among the pages. He riffled through each of the other five books, not expecting to find anything in them, either. But on the last page of the verse treasury, something caught his eye—stamped words in faded red ink.

Beulah Public Library.

Beulah. A town, or possibly a county. But in either case not in California; he'd never heard of the name before.

He went through the other books again. None bore a similar stamp. The one didn't have to have any direct connection to Ms. Lonesome then. Books travel in different ways, sometimes go through many hands. And this edition had been published in 1977, a lot of years ago. She might have picked it up anywhere, some place far away from Beulah, wherever Beulah was.

He wondered if Del Carlo had noticed the stamp. Even if he had, chances were he'd had similar thoughts and dismissed it. Worth discussing with him? Worth stopping first at the main library, to see if he could locate Beulah—?

No, he thought. Dammit, no.

Thousands of towns spread across the U.S., some so tiny they weren't even on most maps; if Beulah was one of the little ones, it could take days of research. And for all he knew, more than one Beulah existed— four, five, or six of them. And even if he found just one, what then? He didn't have the resources to follow up on such a slender lead. Del Carlo did, but like all big-city cops, he was overworked. He wouldn't care enough to waste any more time or public funds on a simple suicide case. You couldn't blame him for not caring enough.

The whole idea was an exercise in futility. Just as paying forty dollars for a look at these pitiful memento mori had been.

Enough, Messenger. The obsession ends here, tonight. Ms. Lonesome is dead and you're alive—get a grip before it's too late and you really do have a breakdown, before *you* wind up existing in a little vacuum of despair.

Quickly he scooped the books and bear and watch and the rest of her things into the cartons and cheap suitcases. Then he stood, turned away.

But he didn't leave just then. Not for another minute or so.

Not until, in spite of himself, he'd turned back to the cartons and found the copy of *A Treasury of American Verse* and hidden it inside his coat pocket.

4

THE RED-HAIRED WOMAN'S name was Molene. Molene Davis. He asked her about it after she introduced herself, to make sure he'd heard her correctly, and she spelled it for him. No, it had nothing to do with the town of Illinois, which was spelled differently anyway. Her father had been a poet, she said. As if that explained it.

He'd noticed her shortly after his arrival with the Engstroms. Jeanne's brother, a bearded bear of a man who was high on either ego gratification or some chemical substance, had whisked her and Phil away, leaving Messenger to fend for himself. There were sixty or seventy people already in the cavernous, paint-spattered North Beach loft, and more arriving every minute; the crush of people, the too loud voices and too hearty laughter, made him edgy—would eventually, if he stayed too long, make him claustrophobic. Crowded rooms always had that effect on him. Not enough space, not enough room to breathe.

But he was here to have a good time. Meet people—meet a *live* woman who interested him, if he was lucky. And from a distance the redhead had struck him as interesting. Tall, as tall as he, and he was nearly six feet. Very thin, almost hipless, but lithe in her movements, sinuous, as if she might be double-jointed. His age, or maybe two or three years older. Dressed in black jeans and a black tunic top, the red hair tumbling in tight curls halfway down her spine. Long, narrow face and big, dark, restless eyes. He watched her for five minutes or so as she got herself a glass of wine, nibbled at canapés. When he was satisfied that she was alone he forced aside his natural reticence and approached her.

He half expected to be blown off, but she surprised him. Quick smile, quick appraisal, quick connection. Up close, her eyes struck him as shoe-button—like the one eye on Ms. Lonesome's toy panda. No, he thought immediately, not like that at all. Hers were real eyes: bright, intelligent. Alive. Yes, and interested in return.

"I'm an artist," she said. "I create mobiles. Mobiles by Molene. Alliterative, don't you think? I work mainly in the fourth dimension— explore the fourth dimension, you might say. You know what I mean? Not exactly? Well, there's the dimension of length—that's one. The dimension of breadth is the second. Depth is the third. Well, what I do in my mobiles is to geometrically extend the lines in each of those three dimensions to create a fourth, to artistically and visually *enter* the fourth dimension. . . ."

She enjoyed the sound of her own voice. But that was all right. What she said was engaging enough, if not wholly explicable, and she talked with a great deal of energy and intensity. Besides, her monologues saved him from having to think up words to fill the usual conversational lulls that develop between strangers. He was poor at the game of small talk. But if there was one social amenity he was good at, it was listening attentively.

Still, she was not one of those individuals who view others as little more than sounding boards. Nor was Molene Davis the only topic of fascination for her. "Tell me about Jim Messenger," she said before long. And when he did, briefly, she didn't seem to consider being a CPA a dull and boring profession, as so many people did. "You sound like a very stable guy, Jim," she said.

"I like to think I am."

"Personally as well as professionally?"

"Yes. I'm pretty conventional."

"Not married, are you?"

"No."

"Ever been?"

"Once, in college. It didn't last long."

"Neither did mine. I was married too young, too."

"Sins of our youth, I guess."

"Brian and I didn't have any kids. I didn't think I wanted any, then or ever. Now . . . well, I'm not so sure. I can hear my biological clock ticking."

"Not in this crowd, you can't."

Molene laughed. "How about you, Jim? Any kids?"

"No."

"Regret it?"

"Once in a while. Not very often, I have to admit."

"Why is that?"

"I'm not sure. Maybe I just wasn't cut out to be a father."

"An everyday kind of father, you mean. Changing diapers and feed-ings at three A.M. and all that."

"Right."

"Well, I can understand that. Most men aren't, and too many make the mistake of thinking they are. How about being a husband? Do you miss that?"

"Sometimes."

"I don't mean sex," she said. "I mean living alone . . . you do live alone?"

"Yes. An apartment out near Ocean Beach."

"Living alone, not having someone to come home to every night. Do you miss that, Jim?"

He hesitated before answering. What did she want him to say? Yes, I'm lonely and I really would like to be married? No, I'm content being single, living my life as I see fit, without family responsibilities and encumbrances? He didn't even know himself what the true answer was.

"I don't really miss it, no," he said at length. "I guess you could say getting married again isn't a central ambition in my life."

"It's not even a minor one in mine," Molene said. "Once is enough, thank you. I'm too damn set in my ways to put up with a male underfoot day after day." She shrugged and finished her wine. "How's that for brutal honesty?"

"I like people who are honest," Messenger said.

"So do I. We're going to get along fine, aren't we, Jim?"

"I hope we are."

He brought her another glass of wine and some more canapés on a napkin. They talked about random subjects, mostly impersonal. Or rather, she did most of the talking and he did most of the listening. The party swirled around them, the big loft getting more and more jammed until it resembled, at least to Messenger, the party scene in *Breakfast at Tiffany's*. If it hadn't been for Molene he would have fled by now. As it was, he longed for space and quiet and fresh air.

She seemed to sense this need in him. Either that, or she felt the same claustrophobic effect. "Jim, why don't we get out of here?" She had to lean close and half shout to make herself heard above the babble. "All this noise is giving me a headache."

"I was about to suggest the same thing."

"My apartment is just a few blocks from here."

He felt a stirring of excitement. "Fine."

"I want you to see my mobiles."

"I'd like to. Your etchings, too?"

"What?"

He shook his head. Poor attempt at humor. He liked Molene, found her sensual and attractive, and he very much wanted to go to bed with her; he hadn't been with a woman in what seemed like a very long time. Don't blow it by being trite, Messenger.

"I'd better tell the people I came with that I'm leaving," he said against her ear. "Otherwise they'll wonder what happened to me."

"I'll meet you in the hall."

"Five minutes."

It took him that long just to find Phil Engstrom. When he said that he was going, Phil winked and asked him if it was with the redhead he'd been talking to. He said yes. "Cute," Phil said, "if a little too skinny for my taste. Didn't I tell you coming along tonight would be worth your while?"

"You told me."

"What's her name? What's she do?"

"Too noisy in here. I'll tell you Monday."

"Details too, Jimmy." Another wink. "Blow by blow."

Messenger moved away without answering. Some men, and Phil was one of them, never outgrew the boy's locker-room approach to physical intimacy. How far did you get? What did she do? What did you do? How was it? He himself didn't understand the need to cheapen and dehumanize sex. A personal relationship wasn't a game, and it shouldn't be fodder for somebody else's childish jokes and analysis.

Molene was waiting in the hall. Out on the street they paused to drink in the cold night air. Then she took his arm, held it tight against her small breast as they walked uphill on Green Street. Her apartment was on Reno, she said, a little alley off Green. Just a couple of blocks.

Her building turned out to be a converted Victorian, the second-floor

apartment small and cramped. Mobiles hung everywhere, either indi-
vidually or in what appeared to be some sort of interconnected pattern—
free-form bits of wood, metal, and pottery, some with brightly
hand-painted designs, others in their natural state. Walking around and
among them was like traversing an obstacle course. To Messenger they
made the apartment seem chaotic. Living here, he thought, would be
like living in the midst of an unsettling dream.

Molene poured glasses of wine for each of them, then sat close to
him on a huge, cracked-leather beanbag settee: a refugee of the sixties.
Her perfume was musky, not unlike cloves. The heat in his loins fanned
and grew.

She asked him what he thought of her mobiles. He said they were
fascinating—but he kept his eyes on her so he wouldn't have to look at
them. She talked about art and the fourth dimension for a time, using
phrases that meant little or nothing to him. Then she set her glass down
and took one of his hands in both of hers. Almost solemnly she asked,
"Jim, have you had an AIDS test?"

"AIDS test? No," he said, "I haven't."

"Don't you think you should?"

"Well, I'm not . . . I don't sleep around much."

"Neither do I. But I had one to be safe."

He didn't know what to say.

"You really should, you know," she said.

"I suppose you're right."

"Will you, then? For me?"

"All right. Yes."

"Good. Oh, that's good." She smiled close to his mouth. Hers was
very red, very wet. "What about other tests, Jim?"

"Other . . . I don't know what you mean."

"A fertility test. Have you had one of those?"

"No."

"Well, we can talk about that later. Tonight . . . tonight we'll just be
careful and enjoy ourselves. You have a condom?"

"No."

"No problem. I have some. But I like it better without, don't
you? So much nicer that way." She smiled again, sloe-eyed now,
and when she stood up among the mobiles her red curls seemed to
become a misshapen part of one of them. She still had hold of his

hand; she tugged on it gently. "Come to bed, Jim," she said.

He understood the truth by then, with too sharp clarity. All the fire had died quickly and the attraction was being smothered under the ashes. He went with her anyway, in a gesture of bitter defiance. But it was a fool's mistake. The defiance soon changed to shame, as he should have known it would. He didn't stay long in her bed. Or in her cramped, surreal apartment. And when he left, both of them knew he would not be coming back.

With Molene he was impotent.

He couldn't have sex with her because she didn't look at him as a person or even as an instrument of pleasure. She didn't see *him* at all.

What she was after was a baby. Just that, a baby.

He had been nothing more to her from the first than an adequate sperm donor.

SATURDAY MORNING, half an hour past dawn, Messenger put on his sweats and an old pair of Reeboks and drove to Golden Gate Park. A couple of years ago he'd gotten into running on a regular basis—early mornings before work and on weekends. Twice he'd entered the twenty-six-mile Bay to Breakers endurance race, and the second year he'd actually finished near the head of the pack. But then his knees and the tendons in his legs began to weaken; he'd cut back, on advice from his doctor, then quit running altogether and settled for aerobics as a much less painful method of keeping himself in shape. He hadn't been out on a run in six months now. Hadn't felt the need until this morning.

He parked near the boathouse at Stow Lake and set off on the easy route, half around the lake and across its little wooded island, with a detour partway up steep Strawberry Hill that rose in the islet's middle, and then back along the lake on the other side. He made three circuits, each one using a little more speed. His legs seemed to be holding up all right, so he took to the roads that completely encircled Stow—a run of more than a mile, a larger portion of it uphill. That route tired him badly. His legs were on fire and he was all but hobbling when he got back to the boathouse.

Nor did he feel any better mentally than he did physically. No sense of exhilaration—the runner's high he'd experienced on his best days and in the second Bay to Breakers race. Just weariness and a sense of wasted effort.

Back at the apartment he showered and rubbed ointment into his aching leg muscles. By the time he finished a light breakfast it was nine o'clock. The rest of the day stretched out long and empty ahead of him. How to fill it? There must be something he felt like doing.

Sure there was. One thing.

Aloud he said, "Shit," and went into the bedroom to get dressed.

At nine-thirty, with an uneasy mixture of anticipation and resignation, he was in the car again and on his way to the main library at Civic Center.

BEULAH WAS IN Nevada.

An old mining town in the southwestern Nevada desert, north of Death Valley and 150 miles or so from Las Vegas. Population, according to the 1990 census: 2,456.

It took him the better part of three hours, using the library's supply of state maps and almanacs, to locate it and to determine that it was apparently the only place in the country with that name. If Beulah, Nevada, had a library, the paperback edition of *A Treasury of American Verse* must have come from there. But what about Ms. Lonesome?

He remembered the leathery texture of her skin, as if she had spent a lot of time outdoors in a hot climate. He remembered the Western-style shirt with the fake-pearl snap fasteners, and the stained suede jacket, and the Levi's jeans, and the boots with the scrolled cowboy design. Well, maybe. If not Beulah, then someplace not too far away. It *was* possible.

He consulted a recent telephone directory for the section of Nevada that included Beulah. There was a listing, all right, for Beulah Public Library; he wrote down the address. Also listed was a single Mitchell— David M.—but it was in a town fifty miles away. He copied it down anyway, even though Janet Mitchell had almost certainly been a fictitious name.

Aimlessly he flipped through the yellow pages. Half a dozen businesses carried Beulah addresses; one was a mining supply outfit. This led him to the library stacks and a handful of Nevada guidebooks and history texts. Not too much in any of them about Beulah. The town had come into existence in the late 1880s, as a supply point from which mule teams had hauled machinery and tools and food to mines in the surrounding hills. One of its founders had named it after a favorite mule. Twice in the early years of the century it had come close to dying, when the gold-bearing veins in the mines petered out and they were abandoned. During World War II a tungsten find at nearby Black Mountain breathed new life into it; and in the fifties the U.S. Air Force and the Atomic Energy Commission had begun operating hush-hush government installations in the general vicinity, one of the areas where the controversial open-air atomic bomb tests were conducted. The tungsten mine was still operating, as was a large gypsum mine in the Montezuma range to the west. The town's population had remained more or less stable for the past fifty-plus years, partly because of the producing mines, the government installations, and desert-springs cattle ranches, and chiefly because it was situated on Highway 95, the main road between Tonopah and Las Vegas, with close access to Death Valley and the high-desert country along the eastern slopes of the Sierras.

So much for Beulah. So much for the possibilities.

Now what?

HARVEY SITWELL RESEMBLED nothing so much as a bulldog, particularly when he frowned. There was no sign of a frown on Monday morning; his round face was cheerful, almost serene, which probably meant that for a change he'd broken a hundred in his Sunday foursome at Harding Park.

"Three weeks early?" he said in response to Messenger's request. "How come, Jim?"

"I'd just like to get away sooner, that's all. Truth is, I'm feeling a little burned out and I can use some R and R."

"What's your plan? Lie on a beach somewhere?"

"No. I thought I'd go to the desert."

"Desert? Which one?"

"Down around Death Valley. I've always wanted to visit that part of the state and it shouldn't be too hot this time of year."

"No offense, but I can think of better places for R and R."

"Well, I doubt if I'll spend the whole two weeks in Death Valley."

"Vegas, eh?"

"It's only a few hundred miles farther."

"I wouldn't mind a week in Vegas myself. You're not much of a gambler, though, are you?"

"Haven't been, no," Messenger said. "But I've been thinking that I need a little something to spice up my life."

"Just stay clear of the crap tables," Sitwell advised. "I blew nine hundred bucks on one in Vegas twenty years ago. Madge still brings it up now and then, when she's pissed at me."

"I'll do that. Blackjack's the only game I know."

"Only game worth playing. Better odds."

"So what do you think, Harvey? Can we rearrange my schedule?"

"Well, I don't know." Sitwell leaned back, interlaced pudgy fingers across his paunch: his thinking pose. "It's a fairly slow time of year, no question of that. What shape are your accounts in?"

"Good. Nearly current on all of them."

"How long would it take to bring everything up to date?"

"A week, if I put in some overtime and work into the weekend."

"And you'd want to leave when?"

"Next Sunday. Monday at the latest."

Sitwell considered a while longer. Then he popped his chair forward and showed his magnanimous grin—the one he seldom used when you were asking for a raise, and never when the subject was a higher slot in the firm.

"From what I hear," he said, "Death Valley's an interesting place. Let me know what you think of it, Jim . . . when you come back to work two weeks from next Monday."

5

H E L E F T T H E city early Sunday morning and spent two full days
on the drive to Beulah, Nevada. Taking his time, enjoying the scenery
and the bagful of jazz cassettes he'd brought along for company. There
was no hurry. This wasn't just some quixotic adventure; it was a kind
of healing vacation. Burned out and in need of R and R, just as he'd
told Harvey Sitwell. A day in Beulah, at the most two, and then no matter
what he found out he'd be free of Ms. Lonesome once and for all.

His route the first day was up through Yosemite, then down Highway
395 past Mono Lake and Mammoth Lakes to Bishop. The second day
he took the desert highway from Lone Pine across the Panamint Mountains into Death Valley. Hot there, but not so hot that his Subaru's
air-conditioning had to be cranked up high. Sparse traffic, too. For long
stretches it was as if he had the barren distances all to himself.

He'd heard it said that people are seldom indifferent to Death Valley; that you have one of two distinct reactions to it. Either you find it
unsettling—endless miles of dead, sun-blasted landscape, where on
windless days the utter absence of sound is so acute it creates a painful
pressure against the eardrums. Or it strikes you as an almost mystical
place—a living rather than a dead one—of majestic vistas and stark
natural beauty. In the two hours he spent crossing the bowl of it, his
reaction was overwhelmingly the latter. The monument both awed and
stimulated him—so much so that two-thirds of the way into the Funeral
Mountains that made up the northeastern boundary, he stopped and
stood for a long while in the shade of an outcrop, looking out over the

valley floor, watching the colors of rock and sand hills and salt flats change subtly with the inching shift of the sun. When he got back into the car, it was with reluctance. This was a good place for Jim Messenger, one he would return to. Its vast empty spaces dwarfed his problems, made them insignificant and therefore more tolerable.

It was late afternoon when he reached Beatty, just across the Nevada border. He stopped there for a leisurely dinner, then pressed on. The last fifty miles to Beulah was across open, rumpled desert: low hills spotted with sage and greasewood, cut through by shallow gullies and deeper arroyos. Larger hills shimmered nakedly against the darkening horizon—brown at first, then bright gold, dark gold, purple, and finally black as the sun dipped and vanished.

His first impression of Beulah was of a cluster of winking lights spread across higher ground. He was still fifteen miles away when he first saw the lights, and he thought they must belong to some other town; but until he was within five miles of them they seemed not to grow any brighter, any closer—as if they were moving away from him at the same speed he was approaching.

The terrain grew hillier, more rumpled; the highway eased into a long, gradual lift. More lights, widely scattered, winked and shimmered in the surrounding desert—the cattle ranches he'd read about probably. Then the lights of the town began to separate, to take on neon color and definition. The road steepened more sharply, and at the top of the rise he saw the first motel sign. Before he reached it his headlights picked out another sign: WELCOME TO HISTORIC BEULAH.

The motel was a Best Western called the High Desert Lodge; he turned in to its driveway. A talkative, gray-haired woman named Mrs. Padgett and the inevitable bank of slot machines waited for him inside. He took a room for one night. The place wasn't crowded; if he needed to stay over, a second night's lodging would be no problem.

In the room he unpacked his toilet kit, put a clean shirt and a pair of slacks on hangers, and then lay down on the bed. He had no desire to go out again. Tired from all the driving; and there would be plenty of time tomorrow to look the town over, see what it had to offer, before he asked his questions.

He was aware of a need to draw out his stay here as long as he could, to postpone what was likely a final dead end. That was why he hadn't questioned Mrs. Padgett. As much as he wanted his freedom from

Ms. Lonesome, letting go of her would not be easy. It would be like losing a small part of himself. A nonessential part, a little piece of self-indulgence, but something meaningful just the same.

IN THE EARLY-MORNING sunlight Beulah had a drowsy, mildly schizoid appearance. New, modern buildings standing cheek by jowl with wooden false-fronts, aging brick structures, a three-story gray stone hotel that had to be well over a century old. Traffic lights, dust-dulled cars, and lumbering motor homes parked and passing through, a gaudy, red-neon stallion rearing high above the entrance to the Wild Horse Casino; and meandering among the low, tawny hills that flanked the central part of town, rutted dirt roads that looked as if they would be more hospitable to ore wagons and buckboards than to any twentieth-century vehicle. Beyond the outskirts to the north, the main highway ran straight across empty desert flats, narrowing until it became a pencil-thin line where a pair of black-shadowed mountain ranges seemed to converge in the far distance.

A dry breeze fanned Messenger's cheeks as he walked from the motel to where a two-block-long main drag lanced off to the west. The air was still night-cool, heavy with the scents of sage and dust, but a gathering heat licked hard at its edges; another couple of hours and it would be hot enough to draw sweat. Everything—sky, desert, man-made objects—had a clarity and brilliance that made him squint. But the combined effect of it all was appealing. One of those mornings and one of those places that made you glad to be alive. And made you ravenously hungry too, he was surprised to discover. It was the first time in as long as he could remember that he'd had any kind of appetite before noon.

Mrs. Padgett had told him the Goldtown Café was the best place in town for breakfast. The café was on Main, just off the highway intersection, its plate-glass front window advertising "beer-batter pancakes, Nevada's finest." Inside he found an atmosphere at once similar and dissimilar to that in the Harmony Café. The smells were the same; despite the ever-present slot machines, much of the decor was the same. But there was more conversation, more laughter, more obvious pleasure in eating among the men and women filling the booths and strung out along the counter; and the faces, whether they belonged to locals in

Western garb or travelers on their way to or from Las Vegas, seemed on the whole more cheerful, more open and inclined to make eye contact.

He wondered if the significance of this was that a city like San Francisco enclosed people who seldom if ever left it, weighed so heavily on them and made them so guarded after a while that they closed themselves off without even realizing it—turned into Hemingway's metaphoric islands in the stream. Whereas an environment like this was so big, so unbounded, that it allowed for an expansion rather than a contraction of self. He'd felt such an expansion in Death Valley. Not that you had to live out here to keep the self from shriveling. It was the perspective that mattered, the knowledge that there were places you could go that actually could help to lift your spirits.

He ordered the pancakes and a side of ham. Ate every scrap and took refills on his coffee. When he paid the bill he asked his waitress, a heavy-bosomed strawberry blond whose name tag read *Lynette*, for directions to the library.

She said, "Block south and two blocks east, on Tungsten. But it doesn't open until ten."

"Thanks."

"Sure thing." Her smile was friendly, even a little flirtatious. Nothing closed off about her, either. "You going there to see Mrs. Kendall?"

"Who?"

"The librarian. Ada Kendall."

"No," he said. "I want to return a book I found."

She said, "Oh," without comprehension, as if he'd just spoken in a foreign language. "Well, you have a nice day now. Come back and see us again."

"I will."

A sunburst wall clock and his Timex both read 8:15. He walked back to the High Desert Lodge, picked up his car, and went to explore the rest of Beulah.

There was not much of it: a dozen or so blocks of side streets, the largest buildings on any of them a two-story stone courthouse and a sprawling new high school gymnasium. Private housing seemed to be a mix of mobile homes and mostly older houses built of board and batten or cinder block. A few of the outer streets were unpaved, rocky and serrated like the desert roads and overlaid with a white, powdery dust. Lava dust, he recalled from one of the guidebooks he'd read. The

Subaru's tires churned it up into feathery wisps that seemed to hang suspended in the now still air.

He drove out into the desert on two of the country tracks, one to the east and the other to the northwest. The latter took him past a long-abandoned hillside mine: gaunt head frame, two crumbling shacks, dunelike mounds of ancient ore tailings. Here and there he saw little clusters of buildings, cattle feeding on dry scrub. Hardscrabble places, for the most part. Life out here couldn't be easy for 90 percent of the residents. But he didn't have to wonder why they stayed.

At ten he drove back into Beulah. Tungsten Way was an unpaved side street, the library set at the far end and housed in a metal-sided mobile home, on the front of which a wooden porch had been built. Inside, walls had been removed and stacks erected, close together to accommodate a greater number of both hardcover and paperback books. A brace of ceiling fans stirred the air sluggishly. In the summer the cramped space would be like the inside of a kiln. Even now, with the outside temperature not much above eighty, the fans going, and the front door propped open, it was dustily close in there.

Just inside the door, a thin, colorless woman in her sixties sat at a desk separated from the rest of the library by an old-fashioned bank of card files. A name plate on the desk said she was Ada Kendall. Another woman, fat and raisin-eyed, browsed in a section marked Historical and Romance Fiction. They both looked at him when he came in, casually at first and then with the interest and vague suspicion of small-town inhabitants for strangers who show up in a place strangers aren't expected to visit.

"May I help you?"

"Well, I'm not sure," Messenger said. He'd brought the copy of *A Treasury of American Verse* with him; he laid it in front of Ada Kendall. "Is this one of your books? It has a Beulah Library stamp on the last page."

She frowned at him, frowned at the book. When she picked it up, opened it to the last page, it was with the tips of her fingers, as if she were afraid it might be contaminated in some way. "Yes, that's our stamp. Someone's torn the card pocket out." She said the last as if she thought he might have done it.

"So it's not a discarded book?"

"There's no discard stamp," she said.

"Then I wonder if there's any way you can tell me who checked it out last."

"That would depend on *when* it was last checked out."

"I don't know when, exactly. More than six months ago."

"Whoever it was doesn't seem to care about books *or* other library users. This book is in very poor condition."

"Yes. But I—"

"The person will have to pay a fine," Ada Kendall said. "A *large* fine. Where did you find it?"

"In San Francisco."

"In . . . where did you say?"

"San Francisco. A woman named Janet Mitchell had it. At least, Janet Mitchell was the name I knew her by."

Ada Kendall opened her mouth, closed it again; the frown, fixed now, had narrowed her eyes into a myopic squint. The raisin-eyed woman was no longer browsing. She stood watching him, Messenger realized, with a peculiarly eager intensity.

He asked the librarian, "Do you know anyone—a former resident of Beulah—named Janet Mitchell?"

"No."

"Janet, then. Or Mitchell."

"No Mitchells around here," the raisin-eyed woman said. She moved over closer to where Messenger stood, as if to get a better look at him. It allowed him a better look at her, too; the intense expression was gossip-monger's hunger. "No Janets either. Never has been, that I know of."

"That's what I was afraid of. Just a name she was using, one she made up."

"Why would she use a name that wasn't hers?"

"Well, she must've had her reasons."

"What reasons?"

"I don't know. I'm trying to find out."

"You think she used to live here? On account of that book?"

"It's possible. I thought so, anyway."

"What's she look like, this woman?"

"Tallish, thin, ash-blond hair, striking gray eyes—"

"My God," the raisin-eyed woman said, "I knew it, I *knew* it!" Ada Kendall said nothing, but her thin mouth drew so tight the lips vanished into a crooked line, like a crack in an adobe wall.

Messenger felt a prickling of excitement. "Then you know her."

"San Francisco. So that's where she went. I never would've guessed a place like that, would you, Ada? A desert rat like her?"

"No. No, I surely wouldn't."

"What's she doing there?" the gossipmonger asked him. "What's she have to do with you?"

"She was a . . . she was somebody I knew."

"Was? She leave Frisco, go somewhere else?"

"She's dead," he said.

"Dead? You say *dead*?"

"I'm afraid so. She—"

"How? How'd she die?"

"She committed suicide."

"Ada, you hear that? She killed herself!"

"I heard," Ada Kendall said. "Lord have mercy."

"Lord had His vengeance, you mean. How'd she do it, mister? How'd she kill herself?"

"She cut her wrists with a razor blade."

"Oh my! Wait till John T. hears that!" And the raisin-eyed woman burst out laughing, an eruption of sheer, unrestrained glee.

6

MESSENGER WAS SHOCKED. He had never seen anyone react with such callous pleasure to the news of another person's death. *They hated her, both of them. Sad, broken woman like Ms. Lonesome . . . what could she have done to incite that much hate?*

The fat woman's laughter continued unchecked, rising to an almost hysterical pitch. The sound of it echoed through the close, dusty spaces of the library. It put a coldness on his nape. And for a reason he couldn't define, it caused apprehension to rise in him like bile.

"You stop that, Sally Adams," the librarian said. Her tone was schoolmarmish, as if she were speaking to a naughty child. "What's the matter with you? Don't you have a shred of respect? This is a *library*, for heaven's sake."

Her words had the opposite effect: The gossipmonger's laughter came even harder, in whooping spurts, like the shrieking of a madwoman. Sally Adams broke forward at the middle, gasping and whooping, arms clutched across jiggling fat as if to keep it from shaking loose inside her bright print dress. Tears rolled down cheeks flushed the color of fire-roasted peppers. Visible spasms began to rock her; her buttocks twitched and rolled. It was as though her ferocious mirth had turned sexual and she were in the beginning throes of orgasm.

The look of her, as much as the sounds she was making, drove him out of there.

He opened the Subaru's sun-hot door. All his earlier good-to-be-alive feelings were gone; the undigested remains of his breakfast lay sour in his stomach. He felt confused, not a little incredulous. Ms. Lonesome's suicide was a source of pleasure for Ada Kendall too, he thought. Both of them, two women in a town this size . . . delighted to hear that someone they'd known was dead. It made no sense to him. There was no correlation between their reaction and his knowledge and impressions of Ms. Lonesome. A mistake? Not the same woman after all, despite the description—?

"Mister! Wait, mister—wait!"

His head came up, eyes pinching against the sun glare. Sally Adams had appeared on the library porch. She waddled down the steps toward him, wiping away tear-wet with fingers like brown sausages.

"Don't leave yet," she called to him in a breathless voice. "The details . . . the rest of the details . . ."

Quickly he folded his body inside. He had the engine rumbling when she reached the car; she came around to the front, stood there blocking the way, her mouth moving with words he couldn't—didn't want to— hear. He put the gearshift lever into reverse. The Subaru's tires churned up a blossom of white dust as the car skidded backward. He kept on powering in reverse until Sally Adams was an indistinctly hazed shape in the middle of the street.

THE CHURCH OF the Holy Name sat by itself on a low bluff on the southwest edge of town. It resembled a rectangular box, unadorned and freshly whitewashed, with an ungraded parking area in front, a grave- yard stretched out behind, and a smaller whitewashed building—prob- ably a parsonage—off to one side. Cottonwoods had been planted around the buildings to provide shade. A few more dotted the burial ground, but most of it sat baking openly under the hard eye of the sun.

In place of a steeple was a huge white cross, thrust up above the church's entrance so that from a distance, with sun rays glinting off its surface, it had the look of a brand burned into the smoky blue sky. It was the cross that had drawn him here. That, and the fact that he'd noticed the church on his earlier explorations: it was by far the most prominent of the three in Beulah. He had to have someone to question, and the last thing he wanted was a repeat of the emotional scene at the library. Who calmer than a clergyman? Who knew more about what went on in a small town?

He parked in front of the church. There was no one in sight, although he could see a small Jeep wagon parked in the carport adjacent to the parsonage; the only sounds were the distant ones of traffic and someone using an electric saw. The church's double doors were unlocked. He hesitated before he entered. He was not a religious man, at least not in the sense of embracing formal religion, and the few times he'd been inside a place of worship he'd felt uncomfortable.

Single room, long and narrow, with a high cross-beamed ceiling and stained-glass windows shadowed by the branches of the cottonwoods. Two dozen rows of pews and a plain altar with a bronze crucifix mounted on the wall behind it. Hardwood floors worn smooth in places and scarred in others by the feet of two or three generations of worshipers. The hot, dry silence had an empty quality. In the wall to the right of the altar was a closed door that would lead to the sacristy. He walked down there and knocked on it. No answer.

Outside again, he started toward the parsonage. More of the grave-yard grew visible as he went, and in the same moment he saw movement and heard a sound over that way. Somebody—a young woman wearing jeans and a straw hat—was kneeling on parched ground at the rear of the church, her back to him. He hesitated, then changed direction and approached her.

The cemetery had an austere look in keeping with the desert sur-roundings: not much in the way of grass or other ground cover, most of the markers of wood and, with one exception, all small and simple. The exception was a plot closer to the back wall, near where the woman knelt; it was presided over by a six-foot, white marble angel, wings spread, its surfaces dulled and pocked by windblown sand, poised atop a four-foot block of black granite. The monument was so out of place here it was almost a grotesquerie. Even from a distance Messenger could read the name etched on a bronze plate set into the granite: ROEBUCK.

The young woman was working at a much smaller grave site a few yards from the Roebuck plot, one marked only by a newish wooden cross. Spread out beside her were gardening tools, a nursery planter containing a white-flowered shrub. She was hacking at the dry earth with a trowel, making a hole for the shrub. She must have been there, quiet, when he drove up.

Intent on what she was doing, she didn't hear him. When he stepped around in front of her and said, "Excuse me," her reaction was sudden and defensive; she reared up jerkily and drew the trowel back as if to fend off an attack. Messenger backed up a step. "I'm sorry, I didn't mean to startle you."

"Who are you?"

"My name is Messenger. I'm looking for the pastor here."

"Messenger?"

"Yes. Jim Messenger."

She was tense for another few seconds, staring up at him with her free hand shading her eyes. Then all at once she relaxed; she laid the trowel down and got loosely and jerkily to her feet. Skittish, he thought. High-strung. She was two or three years past her twentieth birthday, slim except for wide hips, very brown. Wisps of hair visible under the brim of her hat were a lustrous blue-black. Indian or Mexican blood. The high, broad cheekbones and dark eyes indicated it, too.

"My father," she said.

" . . . I'm sorry?"

"The pastor. He's my father. Reverend Walter Hoxie."

"Oh, I see."

"I'm Maria Hoxie." She didn't offer her hand. "He's not here right now; he went to do some shopping. He should be back pretty soon."

"I'll wait, if that's all right."

"Better not wait in the sun without a hat."

He nodded. "Hot out here even with a hat."

"Yes, but I'm used to it."

"Are you the caretaker here?"

"Caretaker? No. Well, sometimes. I can't stand it looking so bare and colorless. It should have flowers, plants."

"So you've started planting them."

"When I don't have anything else to do. You're a stranger in town, a tourist. Right?"

"A stranger, yes. A tourist more or less."

"Are you going to gamble at the Wild Horse Casino?"

"I don't think so."

"Good. I don't like gambling, I think it's sinful. John T. laughs at me but it's what I think."

"John T.?"

"John T. Roebuck. He manages the casino. Do you think gambling is sinful?"

"I don't have much of an opinion either way."

"My father preaches against it sometimes." She paused. "Sunday services start at nine o'clock."

"I doubt I'll be here on Sunday."

"You have some business with him? My father?"

"Well, a few questions I'd like answered."

"What questions?"

"About someone who used to live in Beulah."

"Who? Maybe I can tell you what you want to know."

She probably could, but her youth and the way her mind seemed to jump from one subject to another made him reluctant to confide in her.

"Thanks, but I'd better wait and talk to your father."

"All right."

Messenger's gaze strayed to the marble angel atop its four-foot block of granite. "The Roebucks must be important people in this community."

"Why do you say that?"

"The size of the monument there."

"The Roebucks aren't important, even though John T. thinks they are. Nobody's important except God. Excuse me, okay? I want to finish planting this before it gets too hot. The other one I put here died."

"Too much sun and not enough water?"

"It just died," she said.

Messenger said he would wait out front and left her on her knees again, scratching at the hole in the sandy soil with her trowel. He sat in the shadow of one of the cottonwoods, his back against the bole, looking out over the town and the desert beyond. It was a short wait. Inside of five minutes the whine of a car engine cut through the stillness; an old, sun-faded station wagon appeared on the access road, swung over into the carport next to the Jeep wagon.

Pint-sized stick figure; that was his first impression of the man who got out of the station wagon and came forward to meet him. Not much more than five feet tall, so thin his shadow was like a child's line drawing. The cords and bones in his neck and arms protruded in sharp relief; his Adam's apple was the size of a walnut. Thin, graying hair—he looked to be in his fifties—was combed crosshatch-fashion across a liver-spotted skull. Maria hadn't gotten her Indian or Mexican blood from him, or her dark good looks. In fact, it seemed improbable that his genes could have helped create her at all. Stepfather or adoptive father was more likely.

"Hello, there," he said cheerfully, smiling. His voice was the only big thing about him: an oddly rich and resonant baritone. "Waiting for me?

"Yes, if you're Reverend Hoxie."

"In the flesh, what there is of it." He chuckled at his little joke. "And you're—?"

"Messenger. Jim Messenger."

"What can I do for you, Mr. Messenger?"

"Well, it's a personal matter. Some things I'd like to know."

"I'll be glad to help, if I can. Come inside where it's cool."

The interior of the parsonage was overly cool; a noisy air conditioner had been turned up so high, and left on so long, that the large and spartan front parlor was almost chilly. "My daughter," Reverend Hoxie said by way of apology. "You should see our electric bills in the summer. Did you meet her? My daughter, Maria?"

"Yes. She's doing some landscaping in the cemetery."

"Is she? Not even in the house and the air conditioner going full blast." He shook his head again. "Do you have children, Mr. Messenger?"

"No. I'm not married."

"A blessing, to be sure. Children, I mean. But they can also be trying at times. Not that Maria's a child any longer, of course, although sometimes I daresay she acts like one. Well, I'll just turn it down before we catch a chill. Would you like something to drink? A glass of lemonade? I made some fresh this morning. . . ."

"No, thanks. Nothing."

"I'll have one, if you don't mind. Be right back."

Messenger perched on a settee made of some woven material. The rest of the furniture was mismatched, without much color, and seemed to have been chosen at random and with little thought to comfort or esthetics. On one wall was a hammered bronze crucifix; on another, an oil painting of the Last Supper. There were three framed photographs of Maria at different ages, and one of a younger but no less scrawny Reverend Hoxie holding a seven- or eight-year-old Maria in the crook of one arm.

Hoxie returned with his lemonade, arranged himself in an old mohair chair, and leaned forward attentively. "Now, then," he said. "What is it you'd like to know?"

"Whatever you can tell me about a woman I knew in San Francisco, briefly and not very well. She called herself Janet Mitchell but that wasn't her real name."

"Yes?"

"I think she came from Beulah. I'm curious about her true identity, and why she left here and went to San Francisco."

"You say she was using an assumed name?"

"Yes. I have no idea why."

"She told you nothing about herself?"

"No. I hardly knew her, as I said."

"But I don't understand. If you hardly knew her, why have you come all the way to Beulah? Are you trying to find her for some reason? Do you think she's come back home?"

"She's never coming home," Messenger said. "She committed suicide three weeks ago."

Hoxie's smile turned upside down. "Dear Lord."

"She didn't leave a note, nothing to explain why. No one's claimed her body yet. The police weren't able to identify her or trace where she came from; it's sheer luck that led me to Beulah. If she does have relatives here, they should know what happened to her."

"Of course. She should have a proper burial."

"There's that, and also the fact that she left quite a bit of money in cash. Fourteen thousand dollars."

A silence built between them. Messenger saw knowledge seep into the minister's eyes; the man's expression turned doleful. "Fourteen thousand dollars," Hoxie repeated.

"It was sixteen when she came to San Francisco."

"Yes, that's about how much she received. How long ago was it she arrived there?"

"About six months."

"Describe her to me."

Messenger described her.

"Anna," Hoxie said then, and sighed. "Poor Anna."

"Anna?"

"Anna Roebuck. I should have realized it as soon as you mentioned suicide."

Anna Roebuck. The name seemed strange to him; Janet Mitchell somehow fitted her better. No, that was a false illusion, created and colored by his impressions of who and what she'd been. He *hadn't* known her—that was the thing.

"Tell me about Anna Roebuck, Reverend."

"A tragic case," Hoxie said. "She led a hard life, like so many sagebrush ranchers out here. Came from a poor family, and stayed poor even after she married Dave Roebuck. He was a black sheep and a womanizer; she couldn't have made a worse choice. Still . . . such a terrible vengeance. Such terrible acts."

"What acts?"

"She was never tried or convicted, mind you, except in people's eyes. Never even arrested. And of course she maintained her innocence to the day she disappeared."

"Reverend, what acts?"

"The worst of all sins against God's law. The taking of human life."

"*Murder?*"

"Double murder. Her husband, for one. Killed in their barn with a twelve-gauge shotgun."

"My God. Who else was killed? A woman he was with?"

Hoxie shook his head sorrowfully. "If that were the case, she wouldn't have been reviled and driven away. No, the second murder was far more heinous."

"I don't . . . heinous?"

"Her daughter, eight years old. The child's skull was crushed with a rock and the poor broken body put down the well."

7

MESSENGER SAID, "I don't believe it."

"Yes, I know. It's difficult to believe anyone could do such a thing to an innocent child, especially a woman who seemed devoted to her daughter."

"Even if she went crazy . . . what possible reason could she've had for putting the girl's body into the well afterward? The husband's body wasn't moved, was it?"

"No." Again Hoxie sighed and shook his head. "There's something else too, even more bizarre. Tess was struck down near the barn; bloodstains were found at the spot. But before she was carried to the well her clothes were apparently changed."

"Her clothes?"

"Anna swore that when she last saw Tess, the child had on jeans and a T-shirt. When the body was taken from the well it was clothed in her best Sunday dress."

"That doesn't make any sense."

"Very little of what happened does, Mr. Messenger."

He was silent. In his mind's eye he could see the tattered old panda bear; it must have belonged to the little girl. And Tess must have been the child in the photo Del Carlo had found in the bloody bathtub. The pocket watch . . . *To Davey from Pop*. Dave Roebuck's watch. Would a woman who'd murdered her husband and daughter in cold blood have kept mementos like that? Would she have kept a book on how to cope with pain and grief? He couldn't imagine it. Most of what he'd heard the past few minutes was beyond his powers of imagination.

Questions occurred to him, one after another, crowding into the forefront of his thoughts. He had a logical, orderly mind, if not an inventive one, and he was used to devising and asking questions and evaluating the answers he was given. That was a part of his job at Sitwell & Cobb, some of whose clients were anything but logical and orderly, while others skated dangerously on the thin edge of deception and fraud.

"If Anna was a devoted mother," he said at length, "how could people here be so quick to condemn her?"

"No one else could've committed the crimes," Hoxie said. "At least, so it seemed then and still seems now."

"Why not one of Roebuck's women? You said he was a womanizer. A lover's quarrel that turned violent, and the little girl killed because she was a witness?"

"A possibility, yes, but there was no evidence to support it. The only clear adult fingerprints found anywhere belonged to Dave and Anna."

"The operative word being *clear*," Messenger said. "There's also the possibility of gloves."

"Perhaps. But the county investigators and Sheriff Espinosa questioned dozens of people, including the women Dave Roebuck was intimate with. And Joe Hanratty, a ranch hand who had a fistfight with him a week before the murders. They found nothing to incriminate anyone."

"This man Hanratty couldn't have done it?"

"No. He works for Dave Roebuck's brother, John T., and the other hands swore he never left John T.'s ranch that day."

"What about a stranger, a drifter?"

"Highly unlikely," Hoxie said. "Dave and Anna's ranch is far off any main road. When his body was found his wallet was untouched; it contained fifty-seven dollars in cash. And nothing was disturbed or missing from inside the house."

"Well, there couldn't have been any evidence to incriminate Anna, either. Otherwise she'd have been arrested and charged."

"Circumstantial evidence, but not enough to satisfy the district attorney."

"Where did she say she was at the time of the killings?"

"At the old Bootstrap Mine."

"What was she doing at a mine?"

"Looking for gold."

" . . . She was a miner as well as a rancher?"

"It was a hobby with her," Hoxie said. "The Bootstrap has been shut down for thirty years, but there are traces of gold left in it. The mine and most of her ranch are on BLM land, less than a dozen miles apart."

"BLM?"

"Public land. Owned by the Bureau of Land Management. Most sagebrush ranchers around here lease grazing land and grazing rights from the BLM. It's a common practice in Nevada."

"So she went alone to the mine that day?"

"Yes."

"And no one saw her there?"

"No one."

"How long was she away from the ranch?"

"Three hours or so, she claimed."

"And when she returned she found the bodies?"

"Her husband's body. Sheriff Espinosa and one of his deputies found Tess. Anna showed little emotion when she called them, and hardly any more when Tess was found. In public opinion that was another strike against her."

"Shock," Messenger said. "Or she was the kind of person who internalizes pain and grief."

"Perhaps."

"Why was everyone so willing to believe the worst of her? Was she disliked for some reason?"

"Misunderstood, rather than disliked. Anna was a difficult person to know or understand. Except for her family she preferred her own company."

"Lonely. A lonely person."

"Private, in any case. Much more so after the tragedy. She refused to see or talk to anyone, even her sister."

"Sister?"

"Younger sibling. Dacy Burgess."

"Does Dacy Burgess live here?"

"On a ranch not far from Anna's."

"Where would that be, exactly?"

"Salt Pan Valley, west of town. Dacy and her son are alone out there now. Too large a place for the two of them to manage by themselves, really, but they can't afford a full-time hired hand anymore. Times are hard here. As everywhere these days."

"Is she Anna's only living relative?"

"Yes," Hoxie said, "she and the boy. But if you're planning to see her, I'd advise you to go carefully. Dacy's cut from the same cloth as Anna was. She keeps to herself, doesn't trust strangers, and doesn't like to talk about what happened."

"But she does believe in her sister's innocence?"

"At first she did. But when Anna disappeared . . . no, I doubt even she does any longer."

"Does anyone around here believe in it?"

"Jaime Orozco."

"Who's he?"

"A retired ranch hand who worked for the Burgesses for several years. He also did odd jobs for Dave and Anna."

"And he's the only one?"

"Who believes Anna was innocent? I'm afraid so."

"Which puts you in the majority, too."

Hoxie sighed. "I'd like to say otherwise, but I can't find it in my heart to credit any other explanation. Not now."

"Why not now?"

"Anna's suicide, of course. Wouldn't you say that was an admission of guilt, Mr. Messenger?"

"No," he said, "I wouldn't. It's just as possible she killed herself because she was innocent."

THE ROAD LEADING from Beulah to Salt Pan Valley was one of the two graveled ones he'd taken earlier. He drove past the crumbling hillside diggings, out into the desert another mile and a half until he came to a Y fork. Hoxie had told him to take the left branch. He did that, jounced up onto higher ground over a series of low ridges spotted with yucca trees. Dust boiled up behind him, so that he was able to see little else when he glanced into the rearview mirror—as if he were towing a parachute on invisible wires. Sand and gravel thrown up by the Subaru's tires peppered the undercarriage.

Two miles of this, and the road dipped again into a wide bowl-shaped valley bounded by tawny hills that seemed taller and had sharper edges. The valley floor was flat, thickly covered with sagebrush and greasewood and scattered clumps of cactus, scored here and there by shallow washes. In the distance, where the land dipped low, a patch of white shimmered and glinted under the harsh sun: a sink full of salt deposits that had given the valley its name. Barbed-wire fences were strung along here, and power lines angled in from the south. Lean black and brown range cattle grazed in the washes and around the sage and greasewood scrub.

Off to his left he could make out a jumble of ranch buildings set within a grove of cottonwoods. A graveled access road veered off that way. When he reached the intersection he saw a closed gate inside a square wooden head frame, a burnt-wood sign on the head frame's crosspiece that said ROEBUCK in the same style lettering as on the cemetery marker. Old Bud Roebuck's ranch, according to Hoxie. Dave and John T.'s father. It had been willed to John T. alone, evidently because of some falling-out between the old man and his youngest son. Hoxie hadn't been inclined to elaborate.

Messenger drove on. A few hundred yards beyond the turnoff to John T. Roebuck's ranch, the road surface worsened. Instead of gravel there was sand-coated hardpan, washboarded and spotted with chuck holes. He reduced his speed to less than thirty for fear of damaging something along the Subaru's underbelly.

After another mile an unmarked track cut away to the right, past a weathered wooden storage shed. He went on past by fifty yards, then on impulse braked and reversed through hanging plumes of dust to where he could turn onto the track. He sat for a few seconds, making up his mind. The side road led to Anna Roebuck's ranch. Dacy Burgess lived another mile and a half along the main road, at the far end of the valley where the tawny hills rose bare and rough-edged against the hazy sky.

"Nothing to see at Ms. Lonesome's except ghosts," he said aloud. "What's the point?" But he made the turn anyway. *Admit it, Messenger: It was in your mind to do this all along.*

The track led him over bumpy ground, around a hillock, then for three-quarters of a mile through a shallow canyon. When it climbed out of the canyon there was rusty barbed-wire fencing on his right. Past another turn, more fencing stretched away on the opposite side; and at the top of a short rise the roadway ended at a closed wood-and-wire gate. He parked and stepped out into a windless hush. Motionless hush, too: It was like being confronted with a desert hologram, everything three-dimensional yet not quite real. Still Life with Ghost Ranch. The stillness was so complete the click of the car door as he shut it had a loud, brittle quality.

The gate was secured with a length of heavy chain and a padlock, both relatively new. A hand-lettered sign on the gate post read: NO TRESPASSING. KEEP OUT OR ELSE! A hundred yards beyond, in a hollow that ran out into a sage flat, were the ranch buildings: small, squatty house shaded by tamarisk trees, a low-roofed structure with a wire enclosure at one end, a shed not much larger than an outhouse (maybe it *was* an outhouse), and at the edge of the flat, a barn and the remains of a corral, a windmill, and a huge galvanized water tank. The windmill lay broken on its side, collapsed or blown over or pulled down. He couldn't see the well from up here; it must be behind the house.

The heated air was thick with sage spice and the creosote odor of greasewood; it ignited a burning sensation in his lungs. Breathing shallowly, he climbed over the gate and made his way down the track, his shoes creating little scraping sounds on the hard earth. Halfway down something startled him by jumping out from behind a yucca tree and darting away through the desert scrub. Jackrabbit. He saw it stop, its great ears lifting and falling like semaphores, then run again and vanish.

The ranch yard was littered with tumbleweeds and wind-gathered debris; he crossed it slowly toward the house. Board and batten, with a roof of weathered shingles, a narrow porch across the front, a tangled growth of prickly pear at one end. If it had ever been painted, the last vestiges of the paint had long ago eroded away. All of the glass in the front windows had been broken out. The front door hung lopsidedly inward on one hinge; one of its panels was splintered, as though it had been rammed or kicked in. The entire facing wall was riddled with holes, but it wasn't until he was within a few yards of the porch that he recognized them as bullet holes. Somebody—more than one somebody—had fired dozens of rounds at the house, handgun or rifle or both. As if trying to kill it.

The bullet holes, the eerie stillness, the lifelessness of the place opened an odd hollow feeling inside him. Sweat ran down into his left eye, smearing his vision; he wiped it away. The sun was like a weight on the top of his bare head, the back of his neck. He wished he'd had the sense to stop at one of the stores in town and buy a hat of some kind. He wasn't dressed at all right for this country. Stranger in a strange land.

The boards creaked when he stepped onto the porch; the rusted hinges creaked when he pushed the door farther inward so he could pass through. The living room was empty of furniture, the bare-wood floor littered with dust and drifted sand, broken glass, rodent droppings, and dead insects. A quick look into each of the other four rooms told him the house had been completely stripped. All that was left were a few shelves, a broken chemical toilet, and an ancient claw-foot tub in the bathroom. Vandals? John T. Roebuck? Dacy Burgess?

Outside again, he heard the faint, faraway throb of a car engine on the valley road. Except for his footfalls as he walked around to the rear, it was the only sound. White noise that enhanced rather than disturbed the stillness.

The well was a circle of native stone set between two of the trees. A hand-operated pump had been used in place of a windlass; but the pump had been torn loose and battered with something like a sledgehammer until it was a mangled lump of metal. Scattered around it were bits of stone and mortar that had been beaten off the well itself. He moved a few steps closer. A fitted wooden cover still sat in place over the well opening.

His stomach began a faint kicking. The cause was not what had been done to the well but what he'd been told about the murder of Tess Roebuck and its aftermath. Heinous, Hoxie had called it. God, yes. Heinous and inexplicable.

He turned away, went across the rear yard. The low-roofed structure had been a chicken house; dried droppings and feathers lay strewn over the hardpan inside the wire enclosure. He passed the privylike shed. Its door had been pulled off and tossed aside; inside he could see a raised platform, a jut of bolts and tangle of wires. Generator, probably. They'd had electricity, and the power lines that serviced John T. Roebuck's ranch didn't extend out this far into the wilderness. The generator had been taken away along with everything else.

He tried to visualize what it had been like living here, in conditions that were only a step or two removed from the primitive. Tried to fit Ms. Lonesome into these surroundings; to envision her happy, laughing, mothering and playing games with a faceless child of eight. He couldn't manage that either. *She was a stranger, dammit. All you knew was the shell of a woman, a walking piece of clay. She could have been a monster and you know it. Good people don't have a monopoly on loneliness.*

He approached the barn. It and what was left of the corral fence were aged-silvered, tumbledown. The barn's wide double doors sagged open; bullet holes studded them too, just a few, like afterthoughts. Beyond he could see more holes pocking the galvanized surface of the water tank. And the windmill . . . it looked to have been dragged down with ropes attached to the back of a car or truck; an end-frayed length of hemp trailed from a section of the windmill's frame. Outrage at the killings. Mindless attacks on inanimate objects that had had nothing to do with the taking of two human lives. Teenagers, maybe. It was somehow worse to think that adults had been responsible.

Messenger paused at the barn's entrance. Dark inside, a thick gloom that stank of dried manure and rotting leather and Christ knew what else. Better not go in. Snakes . . . the desert was full of rattlers, and this was just the kind of place where they nested. Nothing to see anyway. Coming here had been a mistake, an exercise in morbid curiosity—

Something smacked into the barn wall, head high, a couple of feet to the right of where he stood.

He swung around that way as sound broke suddenly through the hush, a flat cracking like a distant roll of thunder. But the sky was clear—

Singing buzz, and dust spurted from a spot on the ground near his right shoe. The cracking noise came again, echo-rolling this time. He stiffened, bewildered, just starting to comprehend what was happening.

Another buzz, another spurt of dust even closer, another flat crack. It burst in on him then, full understanding that carried with it an adrenaline surge of fear and astonishment.

Rifle shots.

Somebody's shooting at me!

8

THE ONLY PLACE for him to go was into the barn.

He twisted around, got his feet tangled together, stumbled, and went down on all fours, jamming his left knee. His shoulders hunched; he could feel the skin bristling along his back. But there were no more shots as he scrambled inside, to safety around one of the sagging doors.

He flattened himself on bare, lumpy earth near the front wall. He was slick with sweat; he smelled himself along with the sour stink of the barn's interior. His breathing had a labored, stuttering quality. He opened his mouth wide, made himself take in air in shallow inhalations so he wouldn't begin to hyperventilate.

His mind was a clutter of disconnected thoughts. One of them: Seventeen years he'd lived in San Francisco, with all its urban threats and terrors, and he'd never once been attacked, mugged, burglarized, or bothered by anyone more dangerous than an aggressive panhandler. Now, all the way out in the Nevada desert, abandoned ranch in the middle of nowhere . . . somebody with a rifle, for God's sake, shooting so close to him he'd heard and felt the bullets' passage. It was as if it were happening to somebody else. As if part of him were standing off and watching some other poor schmuck hugging the floor of a barn. Stage set, scene in a John Wayne or Randolph Scott Western . . .

An awareness crowded in: Outside, it was quiet again.

With an effort, he forced his thoughts into a semblance of order. He couldn't just lie there and wait for whoever it was to come in after him. Move—that was the first thing. He put his hands under his chest and pushed up, then over on to one hip. The shadows were thick, clotted in corners and among the rafters, but enough smoky-looking light penetrated through gaps in the walls and roof to let him see how the barn was laid out. Stalls along the far wall, an enclosed feed bin. Hayloft above, with an opening into it but no ladder for access. No windows, no other doors. Trapped here. And nothing he could see to use as a weapon; the barn had been stripped of machinery and tools and anything else it might have once held.

The postshooting stillness remained unbroken.

Several more deep breaths and then he crawled over against the wall, to where a missing piece of board provided an eyehole. His thin imagination, heightened and wild-running, led him to expect more than one armed man. What he saw made him suck in another ragged breath, as much in confusion as in relief. A woman, alone, walking alongside the house toward the barn. Short, wiry, youngish, wearing a wide-brimmed cowboy hat, khaki clothing, scuffed boots. Carrying a rifle waist high, at the ready, with the ease and competence of long familiarity. Nothing else moved anywhere except for watery sun-shimmers.

He remembered the car engine he'd heard. It hadn't been over on the valley road; the car must have been on the access track by then—her coming here. He watched her walk slowly to within thirty yards of the barn. When she stopped she shifted the rifle slightly and stood in an attitude of listening. Then—

"Hey! You in there! Come on out where I can see you."

Hard, angry voice. A woman used to giving orders and having them obeyed. He stayed where he was, watching her.

"I'm not gonna shoot you. If I'd wanted that, I'd've put the first round into your hide instead of the wall."

He didn't move.

"Better get your ass out here if you don't want any more trouble. It's too damn hot for a Mexican standoff."

Still he didn't move.

"I'll give you two more minutes. Then I'll disable your car and go for the sheriff, and by God I'll press charges against you for sure."

Now he was convinced. He got shakily to his feet. His respiration and pulse beat had returned to normal; the fear-grip had left him and his mind was clear again. He stood for a moment to compose himself. Then he limped around the door and out into the yard.

"About time," the woman said.

He shaded his eyes with one hand so he could see her better. "Why'd you shoot at me like that? You scared the hell out of me."

"That was the idea. Can't you read, mister?"

"Read?"

"Sign on the gate, big as life. No Trespassing. Keep Out."

"I saw the sign."

"But you came down anyway. Where's your camera?"

"My . . . what?"

"Camera. Tourist, right? Looking for something real quaint to take pictures of?"

"No." He reached down to rub his sore knee. "I'm not a tourist."

"Then what in the hell're you doing here?"

"I came . . . I wanted to see this place. Anna Roebuck's place."

The woman scowled and advanced a few paces. The muzzle of her rifle remained centered on his chest. She appeared to be in her early thirties, cured by sun and wind to a creased-leather brown; too thin, all bone and sinew. But not unattractive and not dried out. Juices flowed hot in her—that was plain enough. A woman of mood and temper and passion.

"What do you know about Anna Roebuck?"

"Not very much. I didn't have the chance to know her well."

"Where'd you meet her? You're not from around here."

"San Francisco."

"When?"

"Not long ago. A few months."

She stood stiff-backed and flat-footed now. A film of moisture like a pale mustache had grown on her wide upper lip. "What's your name? Who are you?"

"Jim Messenger. I'm not anybody, just a man who's interested in Anna and her past."

"Everybody's somebody."

"And you? Who're you?"

"That any of your business?"

"Are you Dacy Burgess?"

"She sent you here, is that it?"

"Please," Messenger said. "Are you Anna's sister?"

"All right, I'm Dacy Burgess. Anna send you or didn't she?"

"No, no one sent me. She's . . . I'm sorry, I wish I didn't have to tell you this, but Anna's dead."

" . . . Say that again."

"Your sister's dead, Mrs. Burgess. She committed suicide three weeks ago in San Francisco."

She stared at him without moving. There was no expression on her brown face; no hint of what she was thinking or feeling. All she did was stand there, still and straight, her mouth parted slightly and the film of sweat beginning to break and slide down around its corners from her upper lip.

"I'm sorry, Mrs. Burgess, truly sorry. I—"

She turned on her heel, in a kind of jerky about-face, and hurried away from him.

He was startled enough to stand rooted, with more words caught tight in his throat. She didn't look back; walked faster, until she was almost running as she passed the patch of prickly pear. His motor responses finally sent him in pursuit. He tried to run himself, but his sore knee twinged and threatened to buckle the leg on him; all he could manage was an awkward hobble. By the time he came around to the front of the house she was all the way uphill at the gate.

"Mrs. Burgess, wait. . . ."

If she heard him, she gave no indication of it. She climbed quickly over the gate, disappeared from his view until he'd hobbled to the top of the rise. Parked fifty yards downhill was an open-sided, canvas-topped Jeep; she was just sliding in under the wheel. The engine roared, hammering echoes across the desert wastes. She reversed into a skidding half-turn that boiled up dust like pallid smoke. He heard the gears grind as she shifted into low, then the Jeep bucked ahead and was gone into an expanding funnel of dust.

He didn't think about pursuing her; he just did it. The powdery grit was like an abrasive in his already dry mouth and throat, making him cough steadily as he started the Subaru and turned it around. The hanging dust half obscured the track's surface all the way to the valley road. He couldn't do much more than crawl along. From the intersection the Jeep's dust trail extended in caterpillarlike segments west toward the burnt hills. Heading home, he thought.

It took him more than ten minutes to reach her ranch, which put him at least that many minutes behind her. The fine white powder was settling in the ranch yard and he had a good look at the place as he drove through the open gate, past another warning sign: PRIVATE PROPERTY. KEEP OUT.

The Burgess ranch was a little larger than Anna's, its buildings set against the fold where two naked hills came together. The spring that had dictated its location must have been a fairly large one; there were twice as many trees here, cottonwoods and tamarisks, and grassy spots and a vegetable garden that looked as if it got enough water. The house was of wood and native stone, with a broad chimney at one end and a covered porch along the front. The sun struck fiery glints from a squat silver Airstream house trailer set on blocks at an angle between the house and barn—an arrangement, planned or accidental, like the three points in an isosceles triangle. In a pole-fence corral adjacent to the barn, three lean horses stood languidly in the barn's shade. Beyond was a pasture that contained cattle pens. And behind the house, chickens scratched inside a coop's wire run and more sun glints came off windmill blades and a galvanized water tank like the one on Anna's property.

The fences and the buildings were all well made, had once been well cared for, but there were signs of recent erosion and neglect: sagging fence poles that needed replacing, a broken windmill blade, a cracked and tape-repaired house window. Reverend Hoxie: *She and her son are alone out there now. Too large a place for the two of them to manage by themselves, really, but they can't afford a full-time hired man anymore.* He wondered if the former hired man, Jaime Orozco, had lived in the Airstream trailer. He couldn't see any reason for its being here except as a kind of one-man bunkhouse.

The Jeep was parked in front of the house. Messenger drew up alongside it. There was no one in sight, but he could hear a dog barking furiously inside the house. He started past the Jeep to the porch.

"That's far enough, mister. Hold it right there."

Male voice, young, and as hard as Dacy Burgess's. Messenger stopped, turned slowly toward the sound of it. A gangly kid of fourteen or fifteen, sweat-stained cowboy hat shoved back on his head to reveal a mop of sun-bleached brown hair, had come out at the far corner. The rifle in his hands was similar to the one the woman had carried, and he held it with the same competence and authority. The sight of it and its aimed bore didn't bother Messenger as much as it would have before the shooting at Anna's ranch. He thought: Gun-happy people. Then he thought: No, that's not fair. If I lived alone in a place like this, and had the recent history they've had, I'd be leery of strangers and keep a weapon handy, too.

The kid said challengingly, "What's the idea chasing after my ma?"

"I wasn't chasing her. Just followed her home, that's all."

"What happened? What'd you do to her?"

"Nothing. Didn't she tell you about it?"

"Didn't tell me anything. Just drove in all lathered and went inside." His mouth worked as if he were about to spit. Instead he said, as though explaining something, "She's never lathered."

"I gave her some bad news."

"Yeah? What bad news?"

"Lonnie," Dacy Burgess said, "leave him be. I'll handle this."

She had come out onto the porch, was standing there in that ramrod posture. Her hands were empty now. She'd shed the broad-brimmed Stetson too; her hair, short and windblown from the open Jeep, a thick lock jutting like a topknot, was the same sunbleached brown as her son's.

The boy, Lonnie, said, "Handle what? What's going on?"

"Your aunt Anna's dead."

"What?" Nothing changed in his face. "When?"

"Three weeks ago in San Francisco."

"So that's it." Then, flatly, "Well, good."

"Lonnie. She killed herself."

"Did she? Who's this guy?"

"Never mind that now. Go on back to your chores."

"You okay with him?"

"Yes. Go on now, I mean it. We'll talk later."

No argument from Lonnie. He lowered his rifle, slow-walked toward the barn without looking back.

Messenger said, "He must really hate her."

"Well, he's got cause. He loved his cousin."

"Tess."

"That's right, Tess."

"Do you hate Anna, too? Even now?"

"No. Maybe I should, but I don't." She ran a hand through her hair; the topknot bounced back up again. "I shouldn't have run off on you that way."

"It's all right. I understand."

"Do you?"

"The news hit you pretty hard and you needed time to recover." Time to cry a little, too: Her eyes looked red and a little puffy, even though she'd washed her face afterward. "You'll want to hear the rest of it. That's why I followed you."

"Might as well know. Come inside."

She led him into the house. On one side of a narrow hallway was the kitchen, on the other a living room with plain furniture, Indian rugs, books on homemade shelves; no television set, but a home computer on a desk. The computer seemed out of place, anachronistic in these surroundings, though of course it wasn't. He wondered what she used it for.

It was not quite as hot in here; a noisy rooftop swamp cooler stirred the air sluggishly. Over the rattle of the cooler, the dog's frantic barks seemed to thud like solid things hurled against a wall. "That's Buster," she said. "Doesn't like strangers any more than we do. Go on into the kitchen. I'll settle him down."

The kitchen had an old-fashioned look that appealed to him, dominated by a huge black cast-iron cookstove—the kind that sold in Bay Area antique stores for upward of two thousand dollars. A bulky refrigerator-freezer was the only newish appliance. A dinette table sat next to the window with the cracked pane; as he drew out one of the three chairs, the dog's barking cut off into a shrill whine and then silence. Half a minute later Dacy Burgess reappeared.

She took glasses from a cupboard, a jug of ice water from the refrigerator, and brought them to the table. "You look dry," she said. "Help yourself."

"Thanks."

She sat down and watched him drink thirstily, not touching the glass he'd poured for her. Up close and without the broad-brimmed Stetson, she bore a faint resemblance to Anna. The same facial bone structure, the same pale gray eyes. But her eyes were full of life, even dulled as they were at the moment. He wondered if Anna had been a woman of mood and temper and passion once too, long ago, and decided that she probably had.

"I'm sorry about your sister, Mrs. Burgess."

"You already said that."

"I want you to know I mean it. Really very sorry."

"So am I. Now Lonnie's all the family I've got left."

"What about your husband?"

"I don't have a husband."

"Lonnie's father . . . ?"

"Him. Long gone, and good riddance."

He started to say, "I'm sorry," again, bit the words back. Meaningless. And she wouldn't want to hear them anyway.

She pinched a pack of Marlboros from her shirt pocket, lit one and coughed out smoke, grimacing. "Shit, that tastes awful. I've been trying to quit but it's not easy. Not when you've had the habit more than half your life."

"No, I guess it isn't."

"Don't smoke yourself?"

"Never have, no."

"Smart," she said. Then, "What was Anna to you?"

"Somebody I wish I'd known better."

"She didn't make friends easy."

"We weren't friends."

"Bed partners?"

"Not that, either."

"No, you're not her type. Only man she ever wanted was that son of a bitch she married."

"Dave Roebuck."

"God's gift to women, to hear him brag on it. We sure could pick 'em, Anna and me." She sucked in more smoke, made another face and exhaled gustily. "So you met her in Frisco."

"We lived in the same neighborhood. Ate every night at the same café."

"Surprised me at first, to hear that's where she went."

"You had no idea she was living there?"

"Before you told me? No. Not a word from her since she up and left here. I figured she'd gone somewhere in Nevada or Arizona. Born and raised in the desert—desert rats usually stay close to home. More I think about it, though . . . makes some sense that she'd head for a city. Get as far away from here as she could, in miles and surroundings both. Frisco was the only city she ever visited that she liked."

That isn't why she went there, Messenger thought abruptly, with an insight so clear he had no doubt it was true. Contraction of self in the city: easier there to wrap loneliness and despair and resignation tight around yourself, weave a smothering cocoon of it all; easier then to put an end to the pain. Anna either thought that out or intuited it at some level. In any case, she went to San Francisco to die.

"Just how well did you know her, Jim?"

"Hardly at all," he admitted. "I tried to talk to her once but she didn't want any part of me or anyone else. She'd cut herself off from all human contact."

"Never even had a conversation with her?" Dacy Burgess squinted at him one-eyed; smoke from her cigarette had closed the other one. "Then why'd you come here? Beulah's a long drive from Frisco."

"It's on the way to Las Vegas. I'm on vacation and I thought . . . I wanted to find out about her, her real name, some idea of why she took her own life. And if she had any relatives."

"What do you mean, her real name?"

"She was living under an assumed name. She died alone, without leaving a note, no explanation of any kind, and the police weren't able to trace her. That's why you weren't notified of her death."

"How'd *you* trace her, if the police couldn't?"

"There was a book with a Beulah Library stamp among her effects."

"Yeah? How'd you get a look at her effects?"

"If I tell you that you'll think I'm crazy."

"I about half think it already."

"She fascinated me," he said, "from the first day I laid eyes on her. I've never seen anyone sadder or lonelier."

"And you just had to find out what made her that way."

"Yes. Her death bothered me more than it should have. I talked to the police and then I went to see the manager of the building where she lived. Her belongings are stored there. I . . . well, I paid to look at them."

"Paid?"

"I told you you'd think I'm crazy."

She studied him for a time. "Not married, right? No kids, no woman?"

"What does that have to—"

"Takes lonely to know lonely," she said.

Yes it does, he thought. And we're both sitting here looking at loneliness, aren't we? Anna's sister in more ways than one.

"Well, now you know the truth about her," Dacy Burgess said.

"Some of it, anyhow. People in town told you all about the killings, right? Must have, for you to find your way to what's left of her ranch."

"I went to see Reverend Hoxie at the Church of the Holy Name."

A mirthless smile bent her mouth at the corners. "The good Reverend. He doesn't know the whole story. Good thing for him he walks around with blinders on half the time."

"What do you mean?"

"You meet his daughter? Maria?"

"Yes, I met her."

"Pretty little thing, isn't she?"

"Yes, she is. . . ."

"Dave Roebuck thought so, too."

"Oh," Messenger said. "So it was like that."

"Just like that. Maria Hoxie and half a dozen others I could name. That bastard would've humped a snake if somebody'd held its ears. Can't blame Anna for blowing his head off with a load of number two shot. Not *him*, you can't blame her for. Tess is another story. What she did to Tess . . . she'll burn in hell for that."

"You're convinced she was guilty of both murders?"

"Guilty as sin."

"But she never stopped claiming she was innocent."

"No. Swore it to me on a Bible."

"Jaime Orozco believed her. Why didn't you?"

"You talk to Jaime?"

"No."

"What do you know about him?"

"Only what Reverend Hoxie told me."

"Which was what? Jaime's the only person in Beulah who never doubted her for a minute? Well, that's right. He's got a heart big as a bucket and he never had a bad thought about anybody, except Dave Roebuck. He's known Anna and me all our lives. He doesn't believe she did it because he doesn't want to believe. Just like you, huh?"

Messenger said, "What I can't believe is that a mother, a caring mother, would crush her daughter's skull with a rock. And then put different clothes on her and the body into the well. And then swear her innocence and grieve so hard she could barely function."

"Well, maybe you never heard of catathymic crisis."

"No. What's that?"

"Term in forensic psychology. Describes a person who kills some-body they're close to and still grieves for the victim, same as if they were innocent. Doctor I know in Tonopah told me about it. Catathymic epi-sodes start with anxiety and depression over emotionally tense relation-ships and end up with a belief that the only way out is murder. Could be that's how it was with Anna."

"Where her husband's murder is concerned, yes, I can see that it might be. But her daughter? Her relationship with Tess wasn't emotion-ally tense, was it?"

"Oh, hell, she could've thought so. Part of the same psychosis."

"It still doesn't seem right to me."

Dacy Burgess stabbed out the remains of her cigarette with enough force to make sparks and ash fly. "Okay, then, here's another explana-tion. She went plain old batshit crazy and afterward she repressed the whole thing. Couldn't remember doing any of it, couldn't face up to it in her own mind, so she convinced herself she didn't do it."

"Your doctor friend provide that theory, too?"

"That's right. And if that's the way it was with Anna, then maybe it all came back to her in Frisco. She couldn't live with it so she killed herself."

"I can think of another possibility," he said.

"For killing herself? What else is there except guilt?"

"Innocence. She couldn't live with the pain of her loss, or the knowl-edge that whoever did murder her husband and daughter would go unpunished."

"They why'd she run in the first place?"

"Guilt isn't the only thing that makes people run."

"Right. Cowardice is another."

"And hopelessness is a third," Messenger said. "She might not have seen any hope in staying and fighting alone. From what I've gathered, the people around here didn't give her any hope."

"Me being one of them."

"I'm not trying to lay any blame on you, Mrs. Burgess. I'm only doing what you've been doing, offering a possible explanation."

"You're offering bullshit, as far as I'm concerned." She was angry again; the inner fire made her eyes shine and sparkle like sunlight on glass. "Anna was guilty and you coming around and saying otherwise isn't gonna change the fact. You don't know a goddamn thing about her or me or what it's like to live and die in this country. Go on back to the city—that's where *you* belong."

"I didn't mean to upset you—"

"Did a good job of it, mean to or not. Go on, get out of here. You and me are finished talking."

"Not quite. There's something else you should know."

"Yeah? What's that?"

"Your sister had quite a bit of money when she died. Fourteen thousand dollars. The authorities impounded it when they couldn't trace next of kin."

"Blood money," Dacy Burgess said. "Dave's and Tess's life insurance policies. Company had to pay off when no charges were filed against Anna. And now you're gonna tell me I'm entitled to it, right?"

"That's right."

"Well, I don't want it. Lonnie and me don't want it, you hear me?" She was on her feet, the cords in her neck bulging, the bones in her upper chest as sharply defined as hatchet blades. "You tell the authorities to keep it, give it to the homeless, do whatever they want with it. Tell them Dacy and Lonnie Burgess don't want a dime of Anna Roebuck's fucking blood money!"

9

SLOW, HOT DRIVE back to Beulah. He spent it brooding about Anna, Dacy Burgess, the situation he'd walked into here. Logically, what he ought to do now was to check out of the High Desert Lodge and then drive on down to Vegas; he'd get there in plenty of time for a little blackjack, dinner, perhaps a show. What more could he do in Beulah? He'd found out what he'd come to find out, fulfilled his good-citizen's obligation to Anna's family. The only responsibility left to him was to notify Inspector Del Carlo of the Jane Doe suicide's true identity, and he could make that call from Vegas today or tomorrow.

Yet there was a reluctance in him just to walk away from what he'd learned. His curiosity was far from satisfied. There were too many questions, too many puzzling elements; they presented the same sort of challenge as a knotty tax problem, stimulated his desire to work toward a solution, create order out of a certain amount of chaos. Facts were like numbers—shift them around, add and subtract, multiply and divide, try different equations, and sooner or later you could be certain you had the correct answer.

Was Anna Roebuck guilty or innocent of double murder? That was the central question, the central problem. His feeling that almost everybody in Beulah was wrong about her guilt was groundless, even foolish; he had scanty facts and little or no concrete knowledge of the people involved. And yet it remained strong and persistent. Seventeen years as a CPA had taught him to trust his gut reaction to a given situation; in tax and financial matters, at least, it had seldom proven wrong.

The child's body in the well was its core. He could accept the brutal murder of an eight-year-old, a type of atrocity that happened too often in these violent times; he could accept a mother committing such an act as part of a psychotic episode triggered by the shotgun slaying of a faithless husband. But the rest of it simply did not ring true to him as a mother's crime. Kill a husband and leave him lie in his own blood, yes; kill a daughter and reclothe her and then drop her body into a well, no. Somebody had done those things, somebody had had a reason no matter how bizarre or insane, but not the woman who'd kept a one-eyed panda bear, her husband's boyhood watch, and a book on coping with pain and grief. Catathymic crisis be damned; repressed memory be damned. Not Ms. Lonesome.

All right. Then what harm could there be in spending another day or two in Beulah, talking to others who'd known Anna and the circumstances of the crimes? Talking to Dacy Burgess again, or at least trying to. Despite the fact that she'd taken those potshots at him, he found her almost as compelling as her sister, and for some of the same reasons. Product of a place and a way of life so far removed from his own that they might have been from different cultures, yet there were similarities, too, that put them on a mutual level of understanding. Loneliness was one, but he sensed others as well. He felt he would like to know her better. So why *not* stay and make the effort? It couldn't be any more unfulfilling than throwing money away on a blackjack table, ogling bare-breasted showgirls on a stage, or trying to find a one-night stand that would only make his loneliness more acute, whether he succeeded or not.

Once he'd made the decision, he felt better. A sense of purpose always buoyed him. In town he stopped at a Western clothing store on Main and bought two shirts, a pair of Levi's jeans, an inexpensive pair of high-topped hiking boots, and a flat-crowned, dun-colored Stetson. When in Rome. He was enough of an outsider without continuing to look like one. Besides, he would need proper clothing if he intended to return to Death Valley and go tramping around other desert locales.

Thirst tugged at him when he left the store. There were a brace of taverns on this block, but instead he entered a package liquor store and bought two iced cans of Bud. A cool shower and the air-conditioned privacy of his motel room held more appeal than the company of strangers.

A blob of red flickered in the room's half-light when he let himself in: the message light on the bedside telephone. It surprised him, but not very much. The air conditioner was turned down low and the room was stuffy; he put the unit on high, then opened one of the cans of beer and drank a third of it before he called the office.

Mrs. Padgett answered. "Oh yes, Mr. Messenger. Yes, I have a message for you. Message for Messenger." She simpered a little, as if she were nervous or keyed up. "It's from Mr. John T. Roebuck. You know who he is, I'm sure?"

"I've heard the name."

"Well, he called about one. He'd like to see you at the Wild Horse. That's the casino on Main—"

"Yes, I know, I saw the sign."

"He'll be in his office until five."

"Thank you, Mrs. Padgett."

"You're certainly welcome. Ah, Mr. Messenger . . . ?"

"Yes?"

"Is it true about Anna Roebuck? That she killed herself in San Francisco?"

"It's true."

"Opened her veins with a butcher's knife? That's what I heard. Is that how she did it?"

There was a note in her voice that made him think of a vulture poised over a piece of carrion. He said, keeping his tone level, "No, you heard wrong," and broke the connection.

They really hate Anna, he thought, dead as well as alive. The whole town. You couldn't blame them if she was guilty, but she'd never even been arrested, much less charged with the crimes. Judged and tried and convicted by all her neighbors except one, without benefit of even a hearing. Condemned, too, willfully if not in fact, and now that the death sentence had been carried out by her own hand, they were gloating over the bits and pieces of her remains. Like the knitting women smiling and watching heads roll in *A Tale of Two Cities*.

He finished the beer, tossed the empty can into the wastebasket. His watch said that it was a few minutes past three. Plenty of time: there was no need to rush to see John T. Roebuck. He was pretty sure he knew what Roebuck wanted—the same thing Mrs. Padgett and Sally Adams and Ada Kendall and the rest of them wanted. He'd go give it to him eventually, before five o'clock; he was curious about the Roebuck family and about John T., the big fish in the local pond. But there was someone else he wanted to talk to first: Anna's only other champion, Jaime Orozco.

In the bathroom he ran the shower until he had a temperature that suited him. He spent ten minutes under it, soaking away the desert grit and trying to work the last of the soreness out of his bruised knee. Dressed again in his new clothing, he had a look at himself in the bathroom mirror. Not too bad. In fact, much better than he'd expected. Not every city dweller could wear Western garb without looking like a refugee from a dude ranch, or just plain ludicrous, or both.

After a brief debate with himself, he left the Stetson in the room when he went out. No use in overdoing it.

L O C A T I N G J A I M E O R O Z C O took a little time and effort. There was no listing for him in the local telephone directory. Mrs. Padgett might know where he lived, but Messenger was reluctant to deal with her again after their phone conversation; he thought it would be better to ask strangers. The first one he asked, a surly attendant at a nearby gas station, either didn't know or wouldn't bother to tell him. He made his second stop at a *taquería*, but the waitress and cook there were equally uncommunicative—probably because *he* was a stranger, and an Anglo at that.

It was the clerk in the Western clothing store where he'd bought his new outfit who finally told him: Jaime Orozco lived with his daughter, Carmelita Ramirez, and her family on Dolomite Street. "That's on the south flats," the clerk said. "Down past the new high school. I don't know the number. You'll have to ask one of the people down there."

Messenger found the street easily enough. It was unpaved, part gravel and part rutted hardpan, and flanked by a haphazard collection of wood frame houses and small trailer homes, all of them sun-flayed and poor-looking. Chickens and goats and dogs were visible in most yards. All of the faces he saw were Mexican. This was what once, not so long ago, would have been called Mextown or Spictown by the white establishment. Now, with racism forced into a more euphemistic existence, it was "the south flats, down past the new high school" and "the people down there."

A woman carrying a market basket pointed out the Ramirez home: one of the newer trailers, set inside a neatly fenced yard; a roofed arbor extended out to the rear. In the yard a chubby boy of six or seven was playing fetch with a black-and-tan mongrel puppy. He stopped the game when Messenger opened the gate and walked through; stood peering round-eyed, a well-chewed tennis ball poised in one fist.

Messenger smiled at him. "Hi there. Can you tell me if Jaime Orozco lives here?"

The boy just looked.

Didn't speak English? No, it was probably just that he was shy. Might be easier to talk to in Spanish. Messenger had had two years of elective Spanish at Berkeley; he dredged around in his memory for long-stored words and phrases.

"Por favor, niño. Es esta la casa de Jaime Orozco?"

That produced a tentative grin. "Sí. Mi abeulo."

"Esta aquí ahora?"

"Por ahi fuera." The boy gestured. "En el patio."

"Gracias, niño. Muchas gracias."

Messenger went around to the rear of the trailer. A pair of weathered, picnic-style tables with attached benches and two mismatched lounge chairs were arranged under the arbor. A man sat propped on one of the chairs, reading a newspaper; there was nobody else in sight. When he saw Messenger he lowered the paper, folded it carefully, and set it on a nearby table—all without taking dark, sad eyes off his visitor.

"Señor Orozco? Jaime Orozco?"

"Yes, that's me."

Messenger had expected a much older man: Reverend Hoxie's use of the word "retired," the chubby little boy saying Orozco was his grandfather. The man on the lounge chair was no more than fifty-five, lean and fit-looking, with eyebrows like clumps of black brush and cheeks and forehead crosshatched by dozens of lines and furrows, as if a bas relief map of a section of desert landscape had been graven there.

"Sit down, Señor Messenger."

Messenger went to a bench connected to one of the picnic tables. "I guess I'm getting to be well known in Beulah. Even dressed like one of the natives."

"I thought you might come," Orozco said gravely. "Anna Roebuck had no other friends here."

"So I've been told."

"Were you her friend?"

"I wanted to be. I tried to be."

"But it was too late when you met her."

"Much too late."

The trailer's rear door opened, releasing the aroma of cooking meat and peppers; a heavyset woman in her late twenties stepped out onto a tiny stair landing. Orozco introduced her as his daughter, Carmelita. She acknowledged Messenger with such thin-lipped disapproval that he felt she'd been watching and listening at the curtained window beside the door.

"A cool drink?" she asked him. "Beer, water?"

"Nothing, thanks."

"Papa?"

"No." When the woman had gone back inside, shutting the door harder than was necessary, Orozco shook his head and said, "Not even Carmelita."

"Not even . . . oh. She doesn't agree with you that Anna was innocent."

"We have had arguments." Orozco shifted position, wincing slightly, and Messenger realized that his right leg was stiff, the foot— encased in a slipper—oddly bent inward at the ankle. When Orozco saw him looking at the leg he reached down to rub it with his fingertips. "No one told you about this, eh?"

"No. What happened?"

"An accident. Nearly two years ago. My horse stepped in a rabbit hole while I was chasing a stray cow. He broke a leg, I broke an ankle. He was the lucky one, I think."

"Lucky?"

"They shot him. Me they took to the hospital."

"I'm sorry."

"God's will," Orozco said, and shrugged. "Have you talked to Dacy Burgess?"

"This afternoon. She doesn't agree with you, either."

"Yes, I know. But at least her heart isn't filled with hate. Did she cry for Anna?"

"She cried. A little, anyway."

"Good. I cried too, a little."

"Why are you the only holdout, Señor Orozco? What makes you so certain she was innocent?"

"She came to see me after it happened. She swore her innocence with her hand on the Bible. Before God in the mission church, she swore. She wouldn't have lied to God."

I wish I could believe in God, Anna's innocence, anything at all with that much absolute certainty.

"Does it surprise you to hear that she was religious? She was, in her own way, even though she didn't go to church. Even though she . . ." Orozco shook his head and left the sentence unfinished.

Messenger finished it mentally: Even though she committed suicide. Mortal sin in the Catholic faith. Take your own life and you're forever denied entry into the Kingdom of Heaven. If there *was* an afterlife, he hoped the Catholics were wrong and God was big enough to forgive an act of desperation by an already tortured soul.

He asked, "Then who is guilty? Who murdered her family?"

Orozco shrugged. "Dave Roebuck had enemies, more than most men."

"The women he had affairs with?"

"Men as well as women. He was a bad one."

"Bad how? Drinking, fighting?"

"And stealing."

"What did he steal?"

"Horses, cattle. Two hundred dollars in cash, once."

"Was he ever arrested, prosecuted?"

"Arrested, yes, several times. Punished, no."

"Who had the biggest grudge against him, the best motive for wanting him dead?"

Another shrug and a spread of the hands, palms up.

Messenger asked, "What about Joe Hanratty? I was told he and Roebuck had a fistfight a week before the killings."

"Hanratty is a violent man when he's had too much whiskey. But he was at John T.'s ranch that day, working with Tom Spears."

"Spears and how many others vouched for that?"

"Only Tom Spears."

Which wasn't quite what Reverend Hoxie had told him. "And I'll bet the two of them are friends."

"Yes. But the sheriff and the state police were satisfied that they told the truth."

"What was the fight about? A woman?"

"Hanratty's sister."

"One of Dave Roebuck's conquests?"

"Yes," Orozco said, "but Hanratty knew about it weeks before the fight. Lynette made no secret of it."

"Lynette. There's a Lynette who works as a waitress at the Goldtown Café."

"Lynette Carey. She is Hanratty's sister."

"Did Hanratty provoke the fight with Roebuck?"

"Those who were there say he did."

"What set him off?"

"No one knows. He walked into the Hardrock Tavern, called Dave Roebuck a dirty son of a bitch, and punched him in the face."

"Hanratty wouldn't tell why?"

"No."

"Not even to the law?"

"He said he was protecting his sister."

"From what, if the affair was common knowledge?"

Orozco spread his hands again. "It was finished by then. Lynette had stopped seeing Dave Roebuck."

"Why?"

"She wouldn't say."

"Is it possible she killed him and Tess?"

"No, it wasn't Lynette. She has a child of her own, a year older. She would never harm a child."

"One of Roebuck's other women then. Maria Hoxie?"

"The daughter of a man of God? No."

"Maria did have an affair with Roebuck?"

"So he claimed. It may have been a lie. The girl is a good Christian. Reverend Hoxie taught her to embrace God from the first day he brought her here."

"Brought her?"

"She was an orphan. His wife couldn't have children, a great sadness in his life. When she died he brought Maria from the Paiute school in Tonopah and raised her as his own."

Messenger watched Orozco shift position another time. Then he said, "You don't think it was any woman, do you?"

"No. Not a woman."

"Why? Because of what was done to Tess?"

"One reason."

"But if Roebuck was shot by an angry lover and Tess was a witness . . ."

"Women had cause to spit on him, but not to take his life. He promised them nothing—bragged about it. He would say, 'I don't have to make promises to a woman to fuck her. She knows from the start what she's getting into, and so do I.'"

"Still, it's possible one of them decided she wanted more from him than just sex."

"He had no more to give," Orozco said. "Not love, not friendship, not money—nothing."

"Why did Anna stay with him?"

"She had nowhere else to go, she said."

"She and Tess could have moved in with the Burgesses."

"Dacy offered many times. Anna wouldn't leave. She believed Dave Roebuck would change, settle down, learn to be a proper husband and father. Until his death she believed it."

Self-delusion. "She must've loved him in spite of it all."

"She did. Anna was —"

He broke off because the trailer door opened again and Carmelita put her head out. The spicy-meat aroma was stronger now—strong enough to remind Messenger that he hadn't eaten since breakfast. "Papa," she said, "Henry will be home any minute. We'll eat as soon as he comes."

"Yes, Carmelita."

"Bring Juanito with you when you come inside. And don't forget to chain the dog."

"I won't forget." Orozco waited until she'd reshut the door before he pushed stiffly to his feet. He asked, "Will you have supper with us, Señor Messenger?"

"Thanks, but I don't think your daughter would like me as a guest at her table."

"There are many things my daughter doesn't like. I'm fortunate she still likes me." His mouth quirked wryly. "Until I forget once too often to chain my grandson and bring the dog with me when I come inside to supper."

Messenger realized then, only then, what he should have known two minutes into their conversation. Jaime Orozco was another member of the fraternity. Jaime Orozco was a very lonely man.

10

THE WILD HORSE Casino was like a squared pie cut into three more or less equal wedges. One wedge was a restaurant called the Wild Horse Grill ("Prime Nevada Beef—24 oz. T-Bones our Specialty"); the second was an open bar–lounge with a small stage and dance floor ("Now Featuring Beulah's Own Jeri Lou Porter, the New Queen of Country"); and the third was the casino itself, all machine noise and blazing neon, populated by less than a dozen low rollers at this hour. Messenger threaded his way among the banks of modern electronic bandits: progressive slots, video 21 and Joker Is Wild poker games. These were getting the most play. The dozen or so traditional blackjack, roulette, and craps layouts sat neglected, three-quarters of them shrouded by dust covers.

The cashier's cage was at the rear. He asked one of the women inside for John T. Roebuck's office; she directed him to a locked and barred door nearby. A security guard took his name, made him wait while he used a telephone, and then admitted him and conducted him up a flight of stairs and down a hallway to an open door at the far end.

The office he walked into was an odd mix of functional and casual-comfortable. A pair of gunmetal-gray desks, each bearing a computer terminal, and a cluster of gunmetal-gray file cabinets shared the space with a massive leather-and-wood wet bar, a grouping of leather chairs, and a couch almost as large as a double bed. A man and a woman stood close together in front of the wet bar, each holding a drink. They didn't move, waiting for him to come to them, taking his measure as he approached. John T. Roebuck and his wife, Lizbeth. Neither of them smiled as the introductions were made. This suited Messenger; he kept his expression as neutral as theirs.

The Roebucks seemed as mismatched as the room. She was tall, almost statuesque, no older than thirty, with platinum blond hair and heavy breasts that strained the low-cut yellow dress she wore. Her eyes were a pale violet color, hard and shiny and shrewd; one up-close look into them and Messenger knew the dumb-blond appearance was pure facade. John T. was four inches shorter, fifteen years older—lean and dark, salt-and-pepper hair cropped short to minimize the fact that he was going bald. His black eyes were even shrewder than his wife's, set deep under craggy brows. They didn't blink much. His stance and his manner, like those of many small men, were aggressive. The take-charge, no-nonsense type. His handshake was iron hard. The some-thing-to-prove type, too.

"Expected you some time before this, Jim," he said. "Lizbeth and I were just about to go have supper."

"I didn't get your message until after four. Then I had a few things to do."

"Sure you did. How is Jaime these days? Been a while since I've seen him."

"Well enough, for a man with a bad leg."

"You don't seem surprised I know you been to see him at his daugh-ter's trailer."

"I'm not," Messenger said. "From what I've heard, there's not much happens in Beulah that you don't know about."

"That's right, Jim, there isn't. Not much at all. Drink?"

"Not for me, thanks."

"Single-malt scotch, sour-mash bourbon? Even got soda pop, if you prefer that."

"Nothing."

"Not a drinking man, Jim?" Lizbeth Roebuck asked. Sexy voice, husky and intimate. And just a little slurred.

"Not much, no."

"That's too bad. Liquor's good for what ails you, and fine for cele-brations. Tonight's a whoop-up night for sure."

"Special occasion?"

"Very special," she said. "The long-awaited death of a murdering bitch." She raised her glass. "Here's to the soul of Anna Roebuck, may it rot in hell."

There was a silence.

John T. said, "You don't like that toast, eh, Jim?"

"That's right, I don't."

"How come? That's just what Anna was, you know. A murdering bitch."

"Seems to be the consensus."

"But you don't think so."

"I have my doubts."

"Why is that? Anna tell you she didn't do it? Cry on your shoulder?"

"I didn't know her that well. It's just a feeling."

"A feeling," John T. said. He took a tooled leather cigar case from his pocket, extracted a long, thin Mexican cheroot. He sniffed it appreciatively before he spoke again. "You drove all the way from San Francisco to Beulah, spent an entire day stirring folks up, because of a *feeling*?"

"No, that isn't why I came. I never intended to stir anybody up. I still don't."

"I'm listening, Jim."

"I came to find out about her. And if she had any relatives, to notify them of her death."

Roebuck lit his cigar, blew aromatic smoke in Messenger's direction without being deliberate about it. "Job for the police, isn't it?"

"The police weren't able to trace her. She was using an assumed name."

"But you traced her. How was that, Jim?"

"Luck," Messenger said. "Just luck."

"What'd Dacy have to say when you talked to her?"

"I think you know what she said."

"And that's not good enough for you? Anna's own sister believing she was guilty?"

"It isn't good enough for Jaime Orozco."

"Jaime's a sentimental old fool. You know those three monkeys, Jim? See no evil, hear no evil, speak no evil? Well, that's Jaime in a beanpot."

It had been in Messenger's mind, on the way to the casino, to tell John T. Roebuck about the fourteen thousand dollars impounded in San

Francisco. If Dacy Burgess truly didn't want it, then Anna's dead husband's brother was next in line. But now that he'd met Beulah's big fish, he wouldn't say a word to him about the money. He didn't like John T. Nor Mrs. John T., either. Let Dacy tell them if she felt like it. Or Inspector Del Carlo, once he was notified.

"Fact is, Jim," Roebuck said, "the murders of my brother and his baby girl were the worst thing that ever happened in this town. Even in the old hell-roaring mining days, wasn't anything as terrible. It hit us hard and it hurt us bad. You can understand that, can't you?"

"Of course."

"So it's only natural we're happy the woman who did it is dead and gone to hell where she belongs. All we want now is to put the whole ugly business behind us, try to forget it as best we can. But we can't do that if a man who knows nothing much about the crimes, nothing at all about our people and our ways, goes around making wild claims about Anna's innocence."

"Suppose she *was* innocent," Messenger said.

Lizbeth Roebuck said, "Oh shit, we know she wasn't. We *know* it, you hear?" She finished her drink, went to the wet bar, and poured herself another.

"That's right," John T. said. "Anna did it, no question. That's why she killed herself. Innocent people don't slice their wrists and bleed themselves to death."

"They do if they're driven to it."

"Meaning by us, her friends and neighbors? We drove her out of town, drove her to suicide? Well, I hope we did. Better that than what might've happened if she'd stayed."

"What would've happened?" Messenger was angry now. The Roebucks' cold and bitter self-righteousness was like an abrasive on his nerves. "You'd have taken the law into your own hands? Gone out to her ranch some dark night and lynched her?"

"You been watching too many Western movies, Jim. We're real civilized out here these days. Got indoor plumbing and everything. The last lynching in this county was more than ninety years ago."

"How about the last accidental shooting death? The last sudden unexplained disappearance?"

John T. didn't like that. He pointed his cheroot at Messenger and said thinly, "That's just what I meant before. About stirring folks up, making wild claims."

"I'm not claiming anything. Except that I don't believe Anna killed your brother and her daughter. I'm sorry if that bothers you, but I don't see any reason to keep quiet about it."

"Man's entitled to his opinion. Question is, what're you planning to do about it?"

"I don't know. Maybe nothing."

"And maybe something. How long you fixing to stay in Beulah?"

"I don't know that either."

"I wouldn't stay too long, if I was you. This is a tight little town and it can be pretty uncomfortable for an outsider hellbent on rubbing salt in healing wounds."

"Is that a threat, John T.?"

"Threat? Lizbeth, you hear me make any kind of threat?"

"No." Ice rattled in her glass; her hand was no longer steady. "All you did was tell him not to keep pissing against the wind or it's liable to blow right back in his face."

"Got a way with words, don't she?" Roebuck said. "Tell you what, Jim. Have yourself a T-bone and a couple of drinks in the Grill, on me. Then go on back to your motel, think things over, and maybe you'll decide the best thing for everybody is to head out in the morning after all. Drive on down to Vegas. Hell of a lot more attractions down there, by a wide margin. It's a friendlier place, too."

"I don't doubt that."

"How about it, then?"

"I'm not in the mood for steak tonight," Messenger said, "and I doubt I'll be in the mood for Vegas tomorrow. Beulah's got all the attractions I'm interested in right now."

"Then you better learn how to duck. That's my best advice, Jim: Learn how to duck real quick."

HE WONDERED, as he drove back to the High Desert Lodge, if he'd been foolish to provoke John T. Roebuck the way he had. If he might be getting himself in over his head. Small towns were bad places to make enemies, especially of the local honcho; he understood that from having grown up in one. And John T.'s thinly veiled threats hadn't struck him as idle. Stick around, keep asking questions, and he was inviting more trouble than he was equipped to handle.

Maybe he *should* pull up stakes tomorrow morning. What did he know about playing either detective or the standing-tall hero? One man pitted against an entire town—familiar theme in mysteries and Westerns both, and not a role for somebody like him. He was a CPA, for God's sake. He led a quiet, nonviolent, disciplined existence. He was so far out of his element in Beulah, Nevada, that he could blunder around here for the next two weeks and even if he stayed out of harm's way, find out little more than he knew right now.

Still, he was reluctant to let go of the opportunity. He may be a passive individual, but that didn't mean he ought to let himself be pushed around by men like John T. But it went beyond that. It even went beyond the question of Anna's innocence or guilt, the challenge of systematically trying to prove an equation true or false. What he had developed was almost a compulsion, as if he were being manipulated into finishing what he'd started. Not by outside forces, but by forces within himself—the same forces that had led him to do what he'd done here so far.

Male menopause, he thought. Jim Messenger's own private hot flashes. But it wasn't funny. In a way it was crucial. A kind of rebellion, perhaps, against the slow downward spiral into resignation and despair that had claimed Ms. Lonesome, and that one day, if he allowed it, might claim him as well.

IN THE COLD hour before dawn, he awoke to the moaning melody of a rough desert wind blowing outside. Blowing riffs, high notes and low, like a hot-licks horn man improvising at an all-night jam. He had been dreaming about Doris, and he lay there thinking about her—both for the first time in years. Lay remembering another cold, windy night four months after their marriage: Candlestick Park, Giants versus Astros, early May.

Doris loved baseball. She had a man's feel for the game, an enthusiastic appreciation of strategy and statistics as well as for its subtleties, its fluidity and grace. When he'd voiced this perception to her she made a face and accused him of being sexist; but he hadn't meant it that way at all. His own interest in baseball was not quite as keen as hers, particularly when it came to going to the 'Stick or the Oakland Coliseum for games; he was just as content to be a couch-potato TV spectator. But she craved the live atmosphere. Games were more exciting in person, she said. Besides, she loved hot dogs, peanuts, all the other ballpark trappings. They went to a lot of Giants and A's games that first year—thirty or more.

He hadn't wanted to go that May night because of the weather. Doris nagged him into it. Pleasing her was important to him then; it had been important to him, for that matter, right up until the day she'd told him, "It just isn't working, Jimmy. I think we'd better end it right now, before things get any worse between us."

The wind-chill factor at the 'Stick must have been close to zero—a raw wind so frigid it might have swept down from the Arctic wastes. Less than 2,500 other hardy souls were scattered through the stadium, most clustered in the lower deck behind home plate. Doris preferred to sit in the upper deck, the higher the better on the first base side; she thought you had a better perspective on the whole field from up there. As empty as the park was, they had an entire section to themselves: nobody above them, nobody within twenty rows below. Two castaways in the center of an island of empty seats, huddled and shivering beneath a heavy wool car blanket . . . he remembered that image crossing his mind at some point during the evening.

It wasn't much of a game. The Giants scored six runs in the bottom of the first and after that it settled into a dull pitchers' duel. By the sixth inning he was bored and numb from the cold. The wind penetrated coats, sweaters, mittens, the blanket; not even body heat or hot coffee from the big thermos they'd brought kept the cold at bay. Twice he suggested leaving. But she was such a diehard fan she wouldn't hear of it. "I don't want to miss anything, Jimmy. You never know what might happen."

In the seventh a gust of fog-laden wind made his teeth chatter loud enough for Doris to hear. She snuggled closer. "Are you really that cold?" she asked.

"Well, my nose quit running ten minutes ago and now I've got icicles hanging out of it."

"I'll bet I can warm you up."

"Nothing could right now except a hot shower."

"I know a better way than that."

"What way?"

Her hand slid along his thigh, stroked tight into his crotch.

"Hey! What're you doing?"

"What does it feel like I'm doing?"

"Cut it out, Dorrie."

"Why? Don't you like that?"

"You know I like it. But we're not home."

"No kidding."

"I mean this is a public place. . . ."

"And we're under a blanket and nobody's near."

He tried to push her hand away. She resisted. She'd worked her mitten off; he felt her slim fingers tugging, heard the faint rasp of his zipper. The fingers insinuated themselves inside, icy cold, making him jump when they touched bare flesh.

"Mmm, that's one place you're warm."

"Dorrie . . ."

"How about if I get right down there under the blanket and *really* make you warm?"

"No."

"Hand or mouth, big guy, your choice."

"No!"

Her breathing had quickened; it was warm and feather soft against his ear. In the privacy of their apartment, that would have excited him. In the privacy of their apartment, the touch and manipulation of her hand would have given him an immediate erection. Here, there was not even a stirring in his loins. He felt nothing except nervous embarrassment. He tried again to dislodge her fingers, his gaze jerking up and down, from side to side.

"Dorrie, for God's sake . . ."

"What's the matter?"

He heard himself say, "TV cameras."

"What?"

"Game's being televised back in Houston. There're cameras all over the stadium."

"So what? They're focused on the field, not on us."

"Sometimes they pan around the stands, you know that. One of them might be on us right now . . . all those people out there watching . . ."

"Jesus," she said.

"When we get home . . . can't you wait until then?"

She drew away from him, removing her hand at the same time. "I doubt I'll be in the mood when we get home," she said. "You just took me right out of it. I was getting pretty horny, too."

"A public place, a baseball stadium . . ."

"That's what made me so horny."

"I don't understand that."

"No, I guess you don't. Not you, Jimmy."

"What does that mean?"

She wouldn't tell him then; she sat stiffly for the rest of the game, staring at the field, not saying a word. It wasn't until later, in the car on the way across the Bay Bridge, that she told him.

"The trouble with you, Jimmy," she said, "is that you're afraid to take risks. Any kind of risk. You want everything to be nice and safe."

"That's not true. . . ."

"It's true, all right. No chances, no risks—not even little ones like tonight, the kind that make life more interesting, give it an edge. A safe life is a dull life, you know? I don't think people were meant to live that way."

You want everything to be nice and safe. No chances, no risks—not even little ones. A safe life is a dull life, Jimmy.

He hadn't understood then, or in all the years afterward. But he understood now, here in this motel room in Beulah, Nevada. What Doris had said to him that night was part of the reason—perhaps the main reason—she'd begun the affair with the prelaw track star and then put an end to their marriage. It was also the reason he was a lonely man. And the reason there was so little substance in his life . . . his nice, safe, dull, empty life. And at least part of the reason for the compulsion, the rebellion that had taken root and was growing inside him.

The time had come to take risks.

The time had come for his life to have edges, even if he ended up hurting himself on one.

11

H E W A S O N his way to the Goldtown Café, walking as he had the previous morning, when the car drifted over alongside. He didn't hear it at first because of the wind, still blowing in dry, humming gusts; didn't see it because he had his head ducked down to keep the blown grit out of his eyes. The sound of its horn—a single sharp toot—made him aware of it angling into the curb in front of him. Blue-and-white cruiser with flasher panels on the roof and a sheriff's emblem on the door.

He stopped, still hunched against the wind. The man who rose up out of the driver's side was big and bulky in his khaki uniform. He motioned Messenger over to the cruiser, said when he got there, "Mr. Messenger? I'm Sheriff Espinosa, Ben Espinosa. Like to talk to you for a minute."

"All right."

"Talk better in the car, out of this wind. Slide in."

Messenger slid in. The cruiser's interior smelled of sweat, leather, gun oil, and a sweetish pipe tobacco. The tobacco aroma came off Sheriff Espinosa as well; a blackened pipe bowl was visible under a shirt pocket flap, like a Cyclopean rodent peering out. He was in his mid-thirties, high-cheekboned, flat-eyed. The clipped mustache he wore lay like a black anthracite bar across his upper lip. The flat eyes were steady, measuring. He didn't offer to shake hands.

Messenger said, "I was planning to pay you a visit later this morning."

"That right?" There was no particular inflection to the words, but Messenger sensed a hostile undertone just the same. "Why didn't you pay your visit yesterday?"

"I didn't see any official urgency, Sheriff."

Espinosa said, "Maybe you didn't. But I'd've liked to hear about Anna Roebuck's suicide from you, instead of half a dozen locals."

"My mistake. But it isn't as if she was a fugitive."

"Might as well've been, disappearing the way she did. It left a bad taste in my mouth."

"Why is that?"

"Why do you think? The murders were still under investigation. She was still under investigation."

"Did you warn her about leaving Beulah?"

"No. Too much time had gone by for that."

"Then she had every right to leave, didn't she?"

The flat-eyed stare had a little heat in it now; he met it steadily. "What puts you on her side, Mr. Messenger? From what I hear, you claim you hardly knew her out there in Frisco."

"I saw her often enough. She was in a lot of pain and I don't think guilt was the cause."

"You don't think. Just a gut feeling, then."

"Just that."

"You know about the murders before you came here?"

"No, not until yesterday."

"Anything at all about her past?"

"No."

"Why come here then? What do you figure to get out of it?"

"Nothing, except my curiosity satisfied."

"Sure it's not some of the money you're after?"

"What money?"

"The insurance money, what was left of it. Fourteen thousand dollars, isn't it?"

"If you think I'm angling for a reward, you're wrong. I told Dacy Burgess about the money yesterday because she has a right to know as next of kin. She said she didn't want any part of it and neither do I."

"You didn't tell John T. about the money."

"No, I didn't."

"Why not?"

"We didn't get along very well. And he's not related to Anna Roebuck except by marriage."

"Still should have told him. He had to hear it from Dacy later on."

"And you heard it from him right after that."

Tight ridges of muscle appeared along Espinosa's jaw. "Tell you something, Mr. Messenger. I don't think we're going to get along any better than you and John T."

"I'm sorry to hear that. I'm not trying to make enemies."

"No? Well, you're up to something and I don't like it. Whatever it is, I don't like it."

"Are you going to tell me to get out of town by sundown?"

"You trying to be a smart-ass?"

"No, sir. I just asked a question."

"You haven't done anything to make me come down on you. Yet. But I'll be watching you. The whole town'll be watching you. If I were you I wouldn't step out of line. I wouldn't jaywalk or spit on the sidewalk. Or do too much pissing against the wind."

"You've made yourself clear, Sheriff."

"Sure hope I have. All right, go on about your business."

Messenger stood looking after the cruiser as Espinosa wheeled it away. Two warnings in less than eighteen hours. No—the same warning issued twice, in almost the same words. John T. Roebuck not only ran Beulah, it looked as though he had a hand in running the local law as well.

HEADS TURNED WHEN he walked into the crowded Goldtown Café. Eyes stared; voices murmured. There was one vacant booth in the section presided over by Lynette Carey. He sat down there and pretended to read the menu, pretended to ignore the staring eyes even though he could feel them crawling like insects on his skin.

Lynette Carey wasted no time in waiting on him. She was plump-breasted and heavy-hipped in her beige waitress uniform, the strawberry-blond hair teased and sprayed into a style two decades out of fashion. Thirty or so, and pretty enough in a puffy, cynical way. Cornflower-blue eyes were her best feature; he looked for hostility in them and didn't find any. Just a natural wariness, and a curiosity that was close to being avid.

"What'll it be?"

"Pancakes and coffee."

"Juice? Side of ham or bacon?"

"Just pancakes and coffee, Lynette. Lynette Carey, right?"

"How'd you know my last name?"

"Jaime Orozco mentioned it."

"He did, huh? What'd he say about me?"

"Nothing bad. I guess you know who I am."

She glanced around at the staring eyes, but not as if they bothered her; she didn't seem to mind being the center of attention. She leaned a little closer. "Everybody in here except the tourists knows who you are. How come you're still hanging around town?"

"Some unfinished business."

"You want my opinion, you're wasting your time. Anna Roebuck was guilty as hell. Nobody'd have blamed her much if it was just that no-good bastard of a husband she blew away. But little Tess . . . ah, who could forgive a thing like that?"

"I'd like to talk to you, Lynette. Would you mind?"

"Talk? Isn't that what we're doing?"

"I mean in private. Later today."

"What for?" She was wary again. "Nothing I can tell you."

"I'd still like to have a talk. I won't take up much of your time."

"Well, I don't know. . . ."

"I could come to your home, or—"

"No. I don't know you, mister, and I got a kid of my own."

"A public place, then. Anywhere you say."

The tip of her tongue made a slow wet circuit of her lips. "Let me think about it."

She hadn't made up her mind yet when she returned with his coffee. When she brought the pancakes she said, "I'm not so sure it's a good idea to be seen in public with you." Still on the fence but leaning his way a little.

"You don't strike me as a person who's worried by what people think."

"Well, that's right, I'm not. They think what they want to anyway."

"Ten minutes of your time, that's all."

She smiled suddenly. She had a nice smile, broad and sunny; it smoothed away most of the cynicism. "Tell you what. I get off work at four and I like a cold beer afterward. Over at the Saddle Bar in the next block, usually."

"What kind of beer do you drink?"

"Heineken draft, unless I'm buying my own."

"I'll have one waiting for you."

H E H A D H I S first look at Buster as he drove into the Burgess ranch yard. Seventy-five pounds of snarling black and brown, tied to a long chain that allowed the animal to roam from the barn around in the front of the house. He didn't know much about dog breeds but he thought that this one might be a rottweiler or a rottweiler mix.

Buster hurled himself at the end of the chain, barking furiously, as Messenger parked twenty yards out of range. Fangs and flying slobber glistened in the harsh sunlight. There was no other sign of life, and no sign of the canvas-topped Jeep. He stepped out into a sudden gust of wind that spun grit into his eyes. He had to duck his head and rub hard to clear them. The wind seemed to be behaving oddly out here today: It gusted so sharply for short periods that he'd seen half a dozen dust devils swirling across the desert plain, then stopping with the same suddenness, as if someone had turned off a wind machine, and a dead calm prevailed until the next flurry. It was a phenomenon that would take some getting used to.

Squinting, he saw that Lonnie Burgess had emerged from a shed attached to the barn. A long, metallic object hung from one hand. As Lonnie closed the distance between them, yelling at Buster to shut up and settle down, Messenger recognized the object as a wrench spotted with grease. Grease also streaked the boy's hands, arms, and the coveralls he wore.

The dog subsided into a series of whines and yelps, sat back on its haunches, and grew silent when Lonnie reached down to rough its ears and scruff. But Messenger could see the animal quivering as it watched Lonnie move away. He had no doubt that at any threat to its people, the rottweiler had the strength to break loose from the chain and the nature to tear out an enemy's throat.

"You again," Lonnie said, but there was no animosity in his tone or expression. Matter-of-fact and reserved, nothing more.

"Me again."

"Bought yourself some clothes."

"How do I look?"

"Like a city man in Western duds."

"That's what I was afraid of. Is your mother here?"

"Out mending fence."

"Some job in this wind and heat."

"Well, I would've done it but the damn pickup quit running again. I'm better with motors than she is." He shrugged and then spat into the dirt. "Trucks and fences," he said. "Always something."

"Don't you go to school?"

"Not this term. Maybe next, if Ma has her way."

"What grade are you in?"

"Junior. She wants me to graduate, go on down to UNLV."

"But you don't care?"

"I care, sure. I always wanted to study veterinary medicine."

"Why don't you?"

Lonnie shrugged again. "No money for it. And no time. There's too much to do here."

"Does seem like you could use some help."

"Can't afford that either, right now. Not with the tight new BLM quotas."

"Bureau of Land Management. Right?"

"Right. They own most of our grazing land; we lease it from them. They tell us how many cows we can run, how long they can stay on public land, how many new calves we can add each year."

"Ecological reasons?"

"Too many wildlife species headed for extinction on account of livestock grazing on public land—that's what they say. So they regulate the number of cows on a parcel by how much grazing *they* figure the land will support, no input from us. Shit, this is sagebrush desert. Cattle couldn't do any real ecological damage in country like this if every rancher out here ran five times as many head."

"The BLM must know what it's doing."

"That's what you think." Sore subject; Lonnie changed it with a question: "So what do you want this time?"

"Want?"

"With my ma."

"A little more talk, that's all. I guess she told you about our conversation yesterday."

"She told me," Lonnie said. "You got her all lathered again before you left."

"I didn't mean to. That's another reason I'm here: I want to apologize to her."

"Yeah, well, the best way you can do that is to go away and leave us alone. We got enough grief to deal with."

"Adding to your grief is the last thing I want, Lonnie."

"Maybe so, but it's what you're doing. *She* killed them. Why do you want to make out she didn't?"

"What makes you so sure your aunt was guilty?"

"She's the only one who had enough cause to do it. My uncle deserved killing, he sure as hell did, but she didn't have to hurt Tess, too. It wasn't Tess's fault."

"What wasn't Tess's fault?"

"That she had a son of a bitch for a father."

"You hated him," Messenger said. "Why? All the women he cheated with?"

"That's one reason."

"What's another?"

"I don't want to talk about him. He's dead. They're all dead now and Ma and me just want to forget about it. Why don't you let us do that, huh?"

Messenger let the question pass. How do you explain a need and a conviction like his to a fifteen-year-old? He couldn't explain it even to himself.

He said, "Where's she mending fence, Lonnie?"

"Old mine road."

"Where's that?"

"West. First left up toward the hills."

"The road to the Bootstrap Mine? Where your aunt hunted for gold?"

"Not enough gold left in that mine to fill two of your teeth."

"But she did go prospecting there. She could've been there the day of the murders, just as she said."

"She was home killing Tess that day."

"Were you here? Did you see her pass by at any time?"

"I wasn't here, I was in school. Ma was away, too. All right? *She* killed them and nobody was here to stop her. I wish to God I had been!"

The sudden angry outburst set Buster off again, barking and lunging at his chain.

"Lonnie, I'm sorry if I—"

"I've got work to finish," Lonnie said. He turned toward the shed. All the way there he swung the wrench in short, chopping air blows, as if it were a weapon being wielded at an enemy's head.

He knows something, Messenger thought.

The feeling was as clear and sharp as the insight he'd had here yesterday about Anna's move to San Francisco. It wasn't actual knowledge of the crimes; Lonnie's belief that his aunt had committed them seemed genuine. Something else. But what? What *could* he know?

12

THE OLD MINE road was little more than a half-formed series of ruts that hadn't been graded or repaired since it was built. A metal arrow sign, rusted and bent and bullet-pocked, said BOOTSTRAP MINE, with a mileage figure that had been worn away. Bullet holes in the center of the two O's in *Bootstrap* made them look like a pair of dead, staring eyes.

Messenger saw the Jeep and then Dacy Burgess less than a minute after he turned onto the ruts. The terrain here was rumpled, just beginning to rise into the stark, sunburnt hills. A narrow arroyo, steep-sided and strewn with fractured rock, angled down from the higher elevations, and where it paralleled the road for fifty yards or so the Jeep was drawn up in the meager shade of an overhang. On the far side of the wash, barbed-wire fencing stretched upward in an irregular line—obviously put there to keep cattle from straying into the wash. That was where Dacy was, standing now with her back to the fence, watching as he drove up behind the Jeep.

He walked to the edge of the wash. "Morning."

She said, "I figured it was you soon as I saw the dust. Lonnie tell you where to find me?"

"Yes."

"He's a good kid but he talks too much."

"All right if I come over where you are?"

"Better not—you're liable to bust a leg. I'll come over there. I'm done here anyway."

At her feet was an open tool kit. She closed and hoisted it, then made her way quickly and agilely down into the arroyo and up the loose-shale bank to where he stood. The look she gave him was neither friendly nor unfriendly. Tolerant, he thought. A little speculative, too, as if she were seeing something in him that she hadn't noticed yesterday.

"What happened to the fence?" he asked.

"Wind blew a section down. Happens all the time. Damn soil is too loose to keep a post down tight."

"Hard work, repairing it?"

"Not so hard, if you don't have to string new wire. I didn't, this time." She put the tool kit into the Jeep, shed the heavy work gloves she'd been wearing. "Why'd you come back?"

"For one thing, to apologize. I didn't handle our talk very well yesterday."

Dacy shrugged and adjusted her sweat-stained Stetson. "No need. I didn't handle it very well, either. What else?"

"To give you this," and he handed her the paper he'd written out before leaving the motel earlier.

"Who's George Del Carlo?" she asked after she'd glanced at it.

"Police inspector in San Francisco. He's the one to contact to identify Anna. He'll explain the procedures to you."

"What procedures? I told you yesterday, I don't want Anna's blood money."

"You don't have to keep it, but you might think about claiming it. This seems to be a fairly poor county; give it to charity here. Otherwise, it'll go to the state of California, and that's not right."

She seemed about to argue, changed her mind and said, "Maybe it isn't. All right, I'll think about it."

"You'll have to make arrangements for burial or cremation, too. Del Carlo will put you in touch with whoever handles that in the coroner's office."

"Christ, they still have her in the morgue?"

"Yes. Frozen storage."

One corner of Dacy's mouth twitched. "Well, I can't afford to have the body shipped back here for burial. Even if I wanted to, which I don't. Put her in the damn ground out there."

"That's up to you. But at least give her a marker with her real name on it. She deserves that much."

"Does she? If you think so, why don't *you* pay for a headstone?"

"Maybe I will, if you don't."

She shook her head, tight-lipped, and tucked the paper into her shirt pocket. "Now if that's all, how about if you head out to Vegas or wherever you're going and let me get on with my work."

"I'm not going anywhere just yet," he said.

"No?"

"No. You know it, too. You saw John T. after I did last night and he told you I'm staying."

"How do you know I saw John T.?"

"Sheriff Espinosa. He looked me up this morning."

"That baked apple. John T. sic him on you?"

"Seemed that way to me," he said. "Baked apple?"

"Brown on the outside, white on the inside."

"Is that the kind of man Espinosa is?"

"A lot of people think so, most of them brown."

"Does John T. run him too, along with everything else around here?"

"John T. doesn't run me or mine." She paused and then said, "Ben does what he pleases about half the time. And John T. doesn't like you worth a damn. What'd you say to rile him up last night?"

"Didn't he tell you?"

"No. He says you're a fucking troublemaker—his words."

"Do you agree with him?"

"No. I think you're probably a damn fool."

"Why? Because I refuse to accept your sister's guilt?"

"Because you'll end up getting people mad as hell at you if you try to prove different. Mad enough, maybe, to do you a meanness."

"Hurt me?"

"That's what the expression means."

"What if I'm right, Dacy? You don't mind if I call you Dacy?"

"Why should I mind. It's my name."

"What if I'm right? What if Anna didn't do it?"

"You're not right. But if by some miracle you were . . . I guess it'd depend on just how right."

"I'm not sure I understand that."

"On who did it. Nobody liked Anna much; they can all live with her being a murderer. But if it turned out to be one of Beulah's select citizens instead . . . well, you wouldn't be doing the town any favors."

"Why didn't people like Anna?"

"Same reason they don't like me," Dacy said. "The Childresses have always kept to themselves and we do things our own way. Plus there's the fact that our old man was a pretty shrewd horse trader. He once screwed John T.'s old man out of some land, or so old Bud Roebuck always claimed. If the Roebucks don't like you, nobody likes you."

"Dave Roebuck must've liked Anna."

"Sure. And that made John T. dislike her all the more."

"Did he get along with his brother?"

"No. Never did. It got worse after—"

"After what?"

She hesitated. And shrugged and said, "Dave hit on John T.'s wife once. John T. threatened to horsewhip him if he did it again. But don't try to make anything out of that. It happened four . . . no, five years ago."

"Maybe it happened again, more recently."

"Uh-uh. Too many women said yes to Dave for him to keep after the ones that said no. He hit on me once too; I told him I'd rather screw a snake and he never bothered me again."

"Isn't it possible Lizbeth changed her mind and went after him?"

"Not hardly. You don't know Lizbeth. She's got her faults—booze, for one—but she knows who's buying and buttering her bread and she doesn't play around. Besides, she's a cold fish. In bed, I mean. Wouldn't think it to look at her, would you?"

"How do you know she's cold?"

"John T. let something slip once."

"Well, what about him? Does *he* play around?"

"If he does he's damn discreet about it."

"You don't like him much, do you."

"I don't like him at all. He's a user and a first-class son of a bitch. All the Roebucks were and are. They either get their way or they make you pay for fighting them. Sometimes they make you pay even if you don't fight them. But not in blood, if that's what you're thinking. Ruining people is John T.'s way, not killing them. And family means a lot to him. He didn't get along with Dave, maybe even hated him, but he fought like hell more than once to protect him."

Messenger asked, "You have much trouble with John T.?"

"Some. Now and then."

"Then why do you keep living here, this close to him?"

"Now that's a stupid question, Jim. Why do you suppose? It's my home. Where else would I go?"

"You could always make a new home."

"Like Anna did?"

"That's a different thing and you know it. She didn't want to leave; she was forced to."

"Well, I don't want to leave either. And nobody's forcing me out. I wouldn't give John T. the satisfaction of leaving after what happened with Anna, and I'm sure as hell not going to do it now."

"Did he try to force you out then?"

"He took a couple of shots at it."

"What kind of shots?"

"Ones that didn't hit anything. That's all I'm going to say about it. My business and his, nobody else's."

He nodded, glanced up along the road to where it vanished into the heat-hazed hills. "How far is the mine from here?"

"The Bootstrap? Why?"

"I thought I'd take a look at it."

"Why?"

"No particular reason. I just want to look at it."

"You won't find anything to prove Anna was there the day of the killings."

"I don't expect to. How far?"

"About a mile and a half." Dacy lifted her chin in the direction of his Subaru. "But you won't get there in that."

"Bad road?"

"Bad enough. Four-wheel-drive country up there. You'd have to quit a mile below the mine or risk busting an axle."

"Could I walk the last mile?"

"Sure, if you don't mind an uphill climb most of the way. And these hills are full of rattlers, so I wouldn't recommend it."

Messenger said, "Your Jeep has four-wheel drive."

"So?"

"Would you let me borrow it for an hour or so?"

"You're something, you are. No, you can't borrow it. Nobody drives that Jeep but Lonnie and me."

"Will you take me up to the mine?"

"Take you? You think I got nothing better to do? I don't play at ranching, I work at it."

"Drive up, quick look around, drive back. It wouldn't take very long."

"Long enough."

"I'll pay you for your time. . . ."

It was the wrong thing to say. Anger kindled in Dacy's eyes. "Ranching, that's *all* I work at. I'm not a guide or a goddamn chauffeur."

"I didn't mean to insult you. Will you do it as a favor?"

"I don't owe you any favors."

"No, you don't."

Her gaze moved over his face, as if seeking an understanding of how the wheels and cogs worked inside. "I swear," she said, "you've got more balls than a three-peckered bull," but she was no longer angry. It was almost a compliment.

"Will you take me?"

"I don't know why I should, but all right. Ten minutes maximum at the mine, then I'm coming back down whether you're ready to leave or not."

"Fair enough."

He went around to the passenger side of the Jeep. The wind kicked up again, so violently that his hat was nearly snatched away. Grit stung his eyes again, got into his mouth and nostrils, and made him cough. When his vision cleared he saw that Dacy had tucked her head down and lowered the brim of her Stetson; she sat waiting patiently until the wind subsided. Then she started the Jeep and bounced them upward along the track.

He said, "Is it like that often around here?"

"Like what?"

"The wind. Blow hard and stop, blow hard and stop."

"Oh, that. Sometimes. You get used to it."

"Makes me a little edgy."

"You should be here when it goes on that way for days on end. Your nerves feel like they're baking inside your skin, like a potato inside its jacket."

"I hope I'm not here when that happens."

"Chances are," she said dryly, "you won't be."

The road twisted and turned into the naked hills, rising for the most part, dipping now and then. A hawk wheeling lazily in thermal updrafts was the only sign of life. Nothing grew up here but sparse clumps of sage; the rest of the landscape was gray broken rock, whitish dust, brown crumbling earth. For the last half mile to the mine, all that remained of the road was a pair of rock-studded ruts so deeply eroded in places that even the Jeep had to strain through them. Dacy was a good driver; she managed to miss most of the deeper pits and larger juts of rock. But it was a bone-jarring ride nonetheless.

The track hooked along the shoulder of one of the taller hills, with a steep fall-away on one side. From there Messenger could see a long way out across the desert plain. The southern reaches of Beulah were visible; and a cluster of ranch buildings that he thought must be John T.'s place. Dacy confirmed it.

When they dropped down on the far side of the hill he had his first look at the abandoned mine. There was not much left of it. Once there had been three good-sized buildings; two were now nothing more than jumbles of collapsed boards and sections of rust-eaten sheet metal. The one still standing, about the size of a two-car garage, listed a few degrees off-center and looked as though it would soon suffer the fate of its neighbors. Above the buildings, on another ash-colored hillside, was a long, flat-topped pile of ore tailings and the mouth of the mine tunnel.

Dacy parked near the one upright structure. Nearby a metal sign, bullet-riddled like every other sign in this country, hung from a pair of tall wooden posts: BOOTSTRAP MINE. Below it a newer and equally abused sign, probably put up by the BLM, read: BUILDINGS AND MINE UNSAFE. ENTER AT YOUR OWN RISK.

"Well, there it is," Dacy said. "Not much, is it."

"No, not much."

Desolate, he thought. A hermit's aerie in the middle of nowhere. The wind, much more constant up here, was the only sound. No—sounds, plural. Flutters and whistles, little moans and long, rattling sighs. Whimpers, too, clear and mournful. Wind music, almost jazzlike: a kind of natural blues melody, dirty-sweet and atonal, full of all sorts of keening improvisation and so emotionally charged it was as if he were hearing an outrush of suffering that verged on the human.

"Did Anna come here often?" he asked.

"Often enough."

"I'm not surprised. It's a kind of place I associate with her."

"Cradle of loneliness," Dacy said.

He looked at her; she was staring straight ahead, thinking about something that didn't include him. He swung free of the Jeep, picked his way uphill through fractured rock to the mine entrance. Before he reached it he heard Dacy following. The opening was covered with a narrow shedlike structure, to protect it against slides from above; the shed and the mouth's sagging support timbers were silvery with age. What he could see of the floor inside was clear except for wind sweepings of dust and dead matter. The smell that came out of the earth's bowels was one of warm must.

"Better not go in there," Dacy said as she came up beside him.

"I wasn't planning to."

"Main tunnel was blasted out of solid rock and most of it's safe, but the stopes are bad. A couple have caved in already. You know what stopes are?"

"Step layers where the ore was mined."

"Right. Mining one of your interests?"

"I read a lot. Lonnie said Anna didn't find much gold in there. She didn't really come up here to prospect, did she."

"No. She came here to hide."

"From what? Her husband?"

"Whenever they had a fight, which was pretty damn often in the last year, she'd head straight here. But he was only part of what she was trying to hide from."

"Herself, you mean," Messenger said.

"Only she couldn't. Hell, nobody can. That's why she ran off to San Francisco. That's why she killed herself."

"Did she always come here alone?"

"Brought Tess along once in a while. Not very often."

"What made her come the day of the murders?"

"If she was here at all."

"Why did she say she came?"

"Another screamer with Dave."

"Screaming fight? Over what?"

"Same old crap. His women, his good-for-nothingness."

"Something must have started it."

"He'd been out all night," Dacy said, "didn't come home until around eleven o'clock. He'd been drinking—was still about half drunk she said."

"Where did he spend the night?"

"He wouldn't tell her. One of his women, though, where else?"

"You used the word 'screamer.' Was that all it was? Just a lot of yelling back and forth—verbal abuse? Or did their fights get physical?"

"He wasn't above slapping her around."

"Nothing more serious than that?"

"No busted bones, if that's what you mean."

"Did he hit her that day?"

"Well, she didn't have any marks on her that you could see."

"If he was half drunk, maybe violent, why did she leave Tess there alone with him?"

"He never took his meanness out on Tess. Besides, I told you, that's what Anna always did when things got bad. Ran up here, ran off by herself."

"Nobody else was at the ranch when she left, nobody expected?"

"No."

"Lonnie told me you and he were away that day."

"That's right. I had to drive up to Tonopah and he was in school."

"He wouldn't have any reason to go over to Anna's ranch, would he? When he got home from school, I mean."

"No, no reason. Why?"

"Just wondering. How did he get along with his uncle?"

"Not any better than I did. What're you getting at?"

"I'm only asking questions."

"Well, you ask too damn many," Dacy said. "Lonnie wasn't at Anna's and he doesn't know anything about what happened that day. If he did he'd have said so."

"Dacy, I'm not trying to—"

"Your ten minutes are up. I'm leaving."

He trailed her downhill, hurrying to match her quick stride. She had the Jeep's engine revving before he finished buckling his seat belt.

"I guess I owe you another apology," he said.

"You don't owe me anything." She popped the clutch, slid the Jeep around in a dust-swirling arc.

"I just don't want you angry at me."

"Why should you care how I feel toward you?"

"I don't know," he said, "but I do."

Her glance still had heat in it. She said nothing, then or on the ten-minute jounce down to where his car was parked. But by then she was no longer miffed; her expression had smoothed and the look she gave him when he got out was neutral.

"What're you up to next?" she asked.

"Nothing definite. Back to town and kill some time until four o'clock."

"What happens at four o'clock?"

"I have a date with Lynette Carey."

Dacy raised an eyebrow. "Lucky you."

"Not that kind of date."

"With Lynette, it's almost always that kind of date." She studied him. "You want a piece of advice, Jim?"

"People have been giving me advice ever since I arrived in Beulah."

"Not like this piece."

"Go ahead."

She said, "Get yourself a different belt."

" . . . What?"

"The one you're wearing doesn't go with those Levi's. You need a good wide one, with a big buckle. Not too big, though, and not too fancy." Her smile was lopsided and faintly mocking. "If you're going to dress Western, man, do it right."

THE FORD RANGER pickup, its dirty green paint gleaming dully under the brassy sun, was angled across the road, blocking it, just west of John T. Roebuck's ranch gate. Two men had been sitting inside; they got out, almost leisurely, as Messenger approached. Waiting for me, he thought. That damn telltale dust.

There was no way around the pickup, even if he'd had the inclination to try; the earth on both sides of the road was crumbling soft, as ensnaring as beach sand. He slowed, watching the men stand together at the driver's door, arms folded, one booted foot each flattened back against the hot metal. Two peas in a pod: lean, weathered, wearing side-slanted cowboy hats, faded jeans, scuffed and manure-stained boots. The only difference between them, at a distance, was that one stood a few inches taller, wore a bandit's droopy mustache the same tawny color as the desert landscape. Inside the truck, a long-barreled rifle with a telescopic sight was conspicuously visible.

He knew he ought to feel at least some anxiety, but he was perfectly calm. Funny. If this were the city a week ago, and he was about to be braced by a couple of tough-looking types, he would probably have peed in his pants. Today, here, even though it was their turf, he felt equal to the confrontation. Maybe the sense of courage had to do with his early-morning thoughts about risks and edges. Well, one thing for sure: Just how sharp this edge turned out to be depended as much on him as it did on the two cowboys.

He drew a couple of deep, slow breaths. Then he set the parking brake, shut off the engine, and eased himself free of the sticky leather seat—keeping his movements deliberate, the way the men had. He stood for a few seconds, measuring them, before he closed the door and walked forward.

The mustached one said, "Mr. Jim Messenger," and spat into the grit a few inches from Messenger's right foot. "He don't look like much, does he, Tom?"

"Sure don't," the other one agreed. He was a few years older, around forty. The stubble on his cheeks was flecked with gray. "Hardly seems worth all the fuss."

"Reckon he'd break easy?"

"Oh, sure. Neither of us'd even work up a sweat."

"How about that, boy?" the mustached one said to Messenger. "You figure you'd be easy to break?"

"Not as easy as you think."

"By God, Tom, he's got sand in him after all."

"Might be we let some of it out."

Messenger said, "Tom Spears, right? And you'd be Joe Hanratty."

That stirred them a little. They exchanged a quick look. "How in hell'd you know that?" the mustached one, Hanratty, demanded.

"Lucky guess."

Spears did the spitting this time. The gob spattered against the toe of Messenger's hiking boot; he didn't move his foot.

"It's too hot to play games," he said evenly. "Why don't you just say what you're here to say and get it over with?"

Another shared glance. They didn't like the way he was behaving. They'd thought they could intimidate him, and now that he'd refused to let it happen they weren't sure what to do next.

Hanratty was the leader; he made up his mind first. He shoved off the Ford, crowded up close with his face a few inches from Messenger's, and poked him in the chest with a callused forefinger. Messenger didn't move, didn't react except to start breathing through his mouth. Hanratty's breath smelled sourly of cigarettes and beer.

"I don't like you messing around my sister, you hear?"

"I'm not messing with her. I talked to her while she served me breakfast this morning."

"That ain't all you did. Made a date with her for four o'clock this afternoon."

"She tell you that?"

"She didn't have to tell me. Ain't nothing you do in Beulah, city boy, that's a secret more than five minutes."

"I know it. But I'm not looking to keep secrets. Not from anybody, including you and your friend here."

"I don't want you messing with Lynette."

"I offered to buy her a beer, that's all."

"Yeah. What do you get in return?"

"Not what you're thinking. I don't have any romantic interest in your sister."

"Why not?" Spears said. "Ain't she good enough for you?"

Messenger said, "Talk, that's all I want with her."

"Talk about Dave Roebuck," Hanratty said harshly. "She don't have anything to say about that pile of shit."

"She was seeing him. She broke up with him not long before he was killed."

"So what?"

"I'd like to know why."

"None of your goddamn business."

"Something must have happened between them. You had a fight with Roebuck about it."

"Fuckin' outsider—it's none of your business! He's dead and damn straight good riddance. Anna did us all a favor, blowing his head off."

"Did he hurt Lynette in some way, Joe?"

The question earned him another poke in the chest, hard enough this time to make him wince. "Joe to my friends. Mr. Hanratty to you. Ask about Roebuck one more time, I'll knock you on your ass. Bother Lynette and I'll kick your ass until it's purple. Keep poking your nose in where it ain't wanted and I'll rip it off your face. You hear what I'm saying?"

"I hear."

"You believe it?"

I believe you're another one who's hiding something.

"Well? You want that kind of trouble, city boy?"

"Not particularly."

"Not particularly, he says. Not particularly."

"Ain't got so much sand at that," Spears said. "Good thing for him he don't."

"Damn good thing," Hanratty said. His eyes raked Messenger's face; then he snapped, "Just remember what you been told," and turned on his heel and stalked around to the pickup's passenger side.

Spears grinned, aimed another gob of spit onto Messenger's boot. When Messenger didn't move Spears lost the grin, slid in under the wheel, and slammed the door. The starter ground, gears clashed; the Ford bucked away, spewing dust, and then turned in through John T.'s gate.

Messenger had been holding his hands tight against his sides; he lifted them, extended them palms down. Steady. Not even the hint of a tremor.

Test passed. The first edge hadn't been very sharp at all.

13

H E   H A D   J U S T come out of the Western apparel shop on Main, wearing his new wide belt with its oblong Nevada buckle—not too big, not too fancy—when he spotted Maria Hoxie. She was maneuvering the Jeep wagon he'd seen at the parsonage into a space across the street. When she got out and headed west in no hurry, he jaywalked across at an intercepting angle. Before he reached her she entered one of the storefronts: All-Rite Pharmacy.

He followed her inside. It was an old-fashioned drugstore, the kind with a soda fountain along one wall—among the last of an endangered species, doomed to eventual extinction as surely as the great auk and the Great American Dream. Maria was the only customer; she had gone into the cosmetics section and was examining a bottle of something the color of mud. She looked flushed, a little wilted, her black hair windblown and sweat-damp at the temples. Preoccupied, too. She kept nibbling at her lower lip.

"Hello, Maria. Remember me?"

He hadn't meant to startle her, any more today than in the church cemetery on Tuesday; but she reacted in the same sort of defensive fashion—wheeling, tensing, raising the bottle as if to throw it. Even when she recognized him it took her a few seconds to relax. "Oh, it's you," she said, "the Messenger." She bit her lip again; her black-eyed gaze was almost accusing. "What do you want?"

"Nothing much. I just thought I'd say hello."

"You know, you could've confided in *me*."

"Confided? I don't . . ."

"The other day. I'd have told you everything my father did."

"Well, you seemed busy and I—"

"That poor woman. Don't you think I care about what she did to herself?"

"Anna Roebuck?"

"Suicide. God have mercy."

"Most everyone I've talked to thinks her death is a cause for rejoicing," Messenger said. "You don't feel that way?"

"No. No one's death is a cause for rejoicing."

"But you do think she was guilty, even if you didn't hate her?"

"God knows who's guilty and who's not," Maria said. "I don't hate anyone. I was taught to love, not hate."

"Did you love Dave Roebuck?"

She chewed her lip, ran a hand through her tousled hair. "No. I didn't love him."

"You and he were close once, though?"

"Close? No. He was—"

"What, Maria? What was he?"

"Wicked," she said. "Satan made him, not God."

"Why do you say that?"

"He hurt people. Everyone he touched."

"Did he hurt you?"

"Everyone he touched," she said. Then she said, "I have to go now," and backed away from him. She was at the door before she realized she still held the cosmetics bottle. She hesitated, flustered; started to turn back, changed her mind, put the bottle down on a display of plastic kitchenware, and then hurried out, half running, as if she were afraid Messenger might decide to chase her.

Strange one, he thought. Strange, confused mixture of child and woman, earthiness and piety. Seduced by Dave Roebuck, probably, and when he dumped her she was caught like the rope in a tug-of-war between opposing feelings: *I was taught to love, not hate.* If her rage at Roebuck had been strong enough, and her elemental side had won the inner struggle, she might have been capable of ignoring the biblical edict, Thou Shalt Not Kill. But the little girl, Tess? He didn't see how Maria could have committed an atrocity like that.

All his speculations kept coming back to the death of Tess Roebuck.

It was the central enigma and the key to the truth. How could anyone shatter an eight-year-old's skull with a rock? Why would anyone change a dead girl's clothing and then put the body down a well?

THE SADDLE BAR was just what he'd expected. Western decor dominated by saddles, bridles, and other tack room paraphernalia. Pool and snooker tables. Video poker and slot machines. Country music pounding from a jukebox. All that was missing was an electronic bucking bull. But then, that was the plaything of urban cowboys; real cowboys rode real bulls if they felt the need to prove their manhood.

He sat in a booth near the door, nursing a glass of beer and ignoring the glances and murmured comments of the bartender and the half dozen other customers. Whoever was playing the jukebox liked Reba McIntyre; her voice and her music beat at him in shrill, atonal waves. It made him yearn for Miles Davis. There were plenty of things he liked about this desert country, but its typical watering hole wasn't among them.

He'd been there fifteen minutes when Lynette Carey walked in alone. Her arrival was a small surprise. He hadn't really expected her to keep their date, particularly not after the in-your-face tactics of her brother and Tom Spears. But she was her own woman; she honestly didn't give a damn what anybody else in Beulah thought she should or shouldn't do.

She slid into the booth across from him, looking as flushed and wilted as Maria Hoxie had. "Whew," she said, "what a day. My legs feel like my ass weighs three hundred pounds. Where's that Heineken draft you were gonna have waiting?"

"I'll get it. I wasn't sure you'd come."

"Told you I would."

He went to the bar for her draft. The fat bartender and the customers were staring openly now, the bartender with thin-lipped hostility; he slammed the full glass down hard enough to slop foam out over the rim. Messenger smiled at him, thinking: To hell with you too, buddy.

Lynette drank thirstily, said "Ah!" and wiped her mouth with the back of her hand. Then she said, "Why did you think I wouldn't come?"

"In case you haven't noticed, I'm something of a pariah in this town. Just like Anna Roebuck was."

"What's that? Pariah?"

"Outcast. Somebody no one likes."

"You're not so bad," she said. "I like guys who do things, even if they're not popular things. Most guys I know just sit around on their hams like vegetables."

He smiled. "Hams like vegetables."

"Huh?"

"Your brother doesn't like me or anything I do."

"Joe? What's he got to do with you?"

"You haven't talked to him today?"

"No. Why?"

"He found out you made this date with me," Messenger said. "From someone who was in the café this morning, I suppose. He warned me to stay away from you."

"Oh, he did, huh. Where'd you see him?"

He explained, briefly.

She drank more of her beer. Wire-thin anger lines bracketed her mouth now. "I've told him and told him," she said. "Mind his business, not mine. But he doesn't listen. Mule-stubborn, that's Joe. And Skinny-Shanks Spears is worse. What'd they do, gang up on you?"

"They tried. Joe said if I bothered you he'd kick my ass purple."

"Big tough guy. Scare you?"

"Some," Messenger admitted. "From what I hear Joe's a fighter. And he's got a quick temper where you're concerned."

"Yeah, he's been known to go off half-cocked."

"Like he did with Dave Roebuck?"

Small silence. She broke it by saying, "Like that, yeah," in wary tones.

"What set him at Roebuck's throat the week before the murders—the fight in the Hardrock Tavern? You'd already broken off with Roebuck by then."

"What if I had?"

"Why would Joe jump him to protect you? Why not before, while you were still seeing him?"

Lynette didn't say anything.

Messenger asked, "Or *did* they have a fight before?"

"No."

"Then why the one at the Hardrock?"

"Why ask me? Why didn't you ask Joe?"

"I did ask him. He wouldn't tell me."

"Well, I'm not gonna tell you, either."

"Why the big secret, Lynette?"

"Some things you don't talk about, that's all. Not even to friends, let alone strangers."

"What could be that bad?"

"Plenty of things. They happen in Beulah, same as big cities like San Francisco. You like to think they don't but they do."

"Is it the reason you broke off with Roebuck?"

"Damn straight."

"Something he did to you?"

"I told you, I'm not gonna say. Don't ask me again."

"But it made you hate him. You and your brother both."

"I didn't shed any tears when I heard he was dead, that's for sure. If Anna hadn't blown his head off—"

"What, Lynette? Would you have killed him?"

"No. I couldn't kill anybody."

"How about Joe? He could, couldn't he?"

"What're you getting at? You think *Joe* killed him and that poor kid?"

"I didn't say that."

"Sounded like you're thinking it."

"No. Just tossing out possibilities."

"Well, toss that one in the garbage. He could've used a shotgun on that asshole, Dave, sure, but he'd never hurt a kid. He loves kids."

"Anna loved kids, too."

"Sure she did. She loved her daughter enough to bust her head with a rock and throw her into the well." Lynette finished her draft, slammed the glass down the way the bartender had. "You know something? I see why people don't like you, Jim. You're like a burr under a saddle with your goddamn questions."

"Mule-stubborn, same as your brother."

"Keep it up," she said, "and he really will kick your ass purple. You're no match for him. Or Skinny-Shanks Spears."

"I know it."

"So why keep banging your head against a wall? You one of those freaks who likes pain?"

"What I like is having something to believe in. All I'm after is the truth."

"The truth," she said. "Shit, the truth."

"What does that mean?"

"It means you and me could've been good friends, Jim. Real good friends. But you just blew it. A guy with crazy ideas is a guy with a busted head, likely. And a guy with a busted head is no damn good to me."

"I'm sorry you feel that way. I can use a friend right now."

Lynette shrugged, started to slide out of the booth. Messenger put a hand on her arm.

"At least stay long enough to have another beer with me."

"One's my limit." She shrugged off his hand. "Besides, I got to pick up my kid at the baby-sitter's. So long, Jim, I wish I could say it's been nice," and she slid free of the booth.

"We'll see each other again."

"From a distance, if you know what's good for you."

She tugged her uniform skirt down and walked to the door. One of the men at the bar said something; the others laughed raucously. Lynette turned long enough to say, "Up yours, boys," in a voice full of bitter dignity. Then she was gone.

THE TELEPHONE RANG five minutes after he let himself into his room at the High Desert Lodge. He was in the bathroom, splashing cold water on his heat-sticky face. He caught up a towel before he went out to answer.

A man's scratchy voice asked, "This Jim Messenger?"

"Yes. Who's this?"

"My name's Mackey, Herb Mackey. You heard of me?"

"No. Should I have?"

"Well, I don't know. I run a place down south of town a few miles. Mackey's Rocks and Minerals."

"What can I do for you, Mr. Mackey?"

"More like what I can do for you."

"How do you mean?"

"Asking around about the Roebuck murders, ain't you? Don't think that Anna Roebuck did it."

"Yes?"

"Well, I got something you ought to see. Something you ought to hear about, too."

Messenger sat on the edge of the bed. "Evidence that might prove Anna Roebuck innocent?"

"Better come out and see for yourself."

"If you have evidence of some kind, you should take it to the sheriff—"

"No. You or nobody."

"Give me an idea of what it is you have."

"You got to see it. Unless you ain't interested."

"I didn't say that."

"I shouldn't even be talking to you," Mackey said. "I ain't said a word to anybody else about this and I ain't going to."

"But if you think—"

"I don't think, mister. Thinking ain't what I do best. You coming out here or not?"

"I'm coming. Where are you, exactly?"

"About six miles south, off the main highway. Side road to the west. You'll see a sign at the junction—Mackey's Rocks and Minerals. Make it about forty-five minutes. I got to go and get what I want you to see."

"Forty-five minutes," Messenger said. "I'll be there. And thanks, Mr. Mackey. Thanks very much."

HUNGER DROVE HIM out of the room almost immediately. He hadn't had any appetite until Mackey's call; now he was ravenous. Sudden excitement had that effect on him, made him hungry for food along with whatever else he was anticipating. There wasn't enough time for a sit-down meal, but he'd noticed a Jack-in-the-Box in a little shopping center near the high school; he could eat a burger and fries in the car.

But he didn't get to the Jack-in-the-Box and he didn't get to feed his hunger. He was opening the Subaru's door when a familiar dust-caked station wagon turned off the highway into the motel lot, rattled to a stop nearby. The pint-sized stick figure of Reverend Hoxie popped into view.

"Going out, Mr. Messenger? I'm glad I caught you. Can you spare me a few minutes?"

Messenger said reluctantly, "Well, if it's no more than fifteen."

"Fifteen will be plenty." Hoxie's smile this evening seemed small and pasted on. Behind it was the kind of nervousness a person feels when he's on a difficult or unpleasant errand. "In your room, where it's more private?"

Messenger nodded and led the way inside. Hoxie glanced around, then sat gingerly on the edge of the room's only chair. The bed or an upright lean against the dresser were Messenger's only options; he chose the latter.

"What can I do for you, Reverend?"

"Well . . ." Hoxie cleared his throat. "I understand you had words with my daughter this afternoon."

"We spoke briefly, yes."

"Long enough for you to ask her embarrassing questions."

"Embarrassing?"

"You intimated that she . . . that there was something between her and Dave Roebuck."

"Did she tell you that?"

"She was upset and I made her tell me why. We both thought those vile rumors had been laid to rest, and now you've dredged them up again."

"So you did know about the alleged relationship."

"Oh, yes," Hoxie said with bitterness, "from the first. More than one member of my congregation saw fit to repeat the rumors to me. There's not a shred of truth to them." Absently he smoothed the crosshatched gray hair on his skull. "Maria is a good girl in the purest sense of that term. As close to an angel as any God ever made. She would never allow a man like Dave Roebuck to soil her."

"Then how did the rumors get started?"

"I have no idea. How does any false rumor find voice? This is a small town, Mr. Messenger, a closed community. People see and hear all sorts of things that are open to misinterpretation. And not everyone gets along with his neighbors. Not even a man of the cloth is exempt from pettiness."

"Enemies, Reverend?"

"I've made a few in my life, God knows."

"Who in Beulah, for instance?"

"I won't provide fodder for any more rumors."

"I don't start rumors," Messenger said. "Or repeat them. I asked your daughter some questions, nothing more. I didn't accuse her of anything."

"What right do you have to ask questions? You're not a member of this community. You have no purpose here except as a catalyst, an opener of old wounds."

"That's your opinion. I won't argue it with you."

"How long do you intend to stay?"

"Until I'm ready to leave."

Hoxie stood. "Then I'll ask—no, I'll demand—that you not bother Maria again. Not speak to her at all."

"All right. But with a proviso."

"And that is?"

"The rumors about her and Dave Roebuck really are false—"

"They are."

"—and she had nothing to do with the murders."

Hoxie flushed; his prominent Adam's apple slid up and down the column of his neck like a ball in a pneumatic tube. "Are you suggesting she was involved somehow?"

"I'm not suggesting anything."

"God help you if you are," Hoxie said. "God help you if you do anything, anything at all, to harm or shame my daughter."

It was not an idle threat. The little man's face was implacable; he meant every word.

14

THE SUBARU'S ODOMETER had clicked off 5.9 miles from the southern outskirts of town when he saw the sign:

MACKEY'S
ROCKS AND MINERALS

There was a third line of black lettering, but a strip of burlap sacking had been nailed over it. Some other attraction or service that Mackey no longer offered tourists and passing motorists.

Messenger turned on to another of the unpaved tracks that passed for roads out here. Ahead, a hundred yards or so from the highway, a cluster of weathered wooden structures squatted along the edge of a shallow cut-bank gully. A line of stunted, withered tamarisk trees grew in the gully, their branches turned a shiny liquid amber by the westering sun. The same hue softened the scrub-spotted plain beyond, except where rocky hillocks and yucca trees threw long, distorted shadows; the shadows were a deep indigo-black. The sky in that direction was just beginning to take on sunset colors above the distant mountains: burnt orange and cayenne red.

As he neared the buildings they separated into three: a mobile home with drawn muslin curtains, a twenty-foot-square box with what appeared to be a series of wooden trays built across the front, and an odd high-fenced enclosure, open to the sky, that had a low, roofed shed tacked on to the near wall. The box probably housed Mackey's collection of rocks and minerals. Messenger had no idea what the fenced enclosure was.

He parked near the trailer. Utter silence greeted him as he left the car; the freaky wind of earlier in the day had died completely. He went up and knocked on the door. There was no response, no sound from within. He called out, "Mr. Mackey?" and knocked again. Same results.

The dirty white nose of a pickup poked out from behind the trailer. He walked around to it. The body and bed were even dirtier, and half of its radio antenna had been snapped off. The cab was empty, but engine heat radiated through the hood. Mackey must be around here somewhere.

He circled the trailer to the wooden box. The trays across its front were all empty. On the door was a pair of homemade signs, not as artfully lettered as the big one at the highway junction. One was a price list of the rocks and minerals Mackey had for sale: coarse gold, fool's gold, garnets, agates, mica quartz. The other sign said CLOSED.

Messenger moved over to the fenced enclosure. It looked to be larger than the box, about thirty feet square; the walls rose ten feet high all the way around, the boards tightly fitted, without openings of any kind. But the shed was open, at least; as he neared it he saw that its door stood partially ajar. That must be where Herb Mackey was.

The shed door also bore a sign . . . no, half a sign. The upper section had been torn away. The remaining half read:

ADULTS — $2.00
CHILDREN — $1.00
KIDS UNDER 6 — FREE

He peered through the doorway into a dust-hung gloom. "Mr. Mackey?" The sound of his voice echoed emptily back to him. He pushed the door all the way open and stepped inside.

On his left was a short, bare counter; the shed was otherwise empty. Two doors had been cut into the rear wall, one behind the counter and the other ten feet away on the right. The door in back of the counter, like the outer door, stood ajar. The other was shut tight. Frowning, Messenger circled the counter. That door's hinges made a creaking sound as he nudged it wide. Beyond he saw that there were actually two fences: a short, tunnel-like passageway separated them. Yet another half-open door let him glimpse what lay past the inner wall—some kind of open space strewn with rocks. Fading sunlight stained the rocks, gave them an odd glowing quality as if they were radioactive.

"Mr. Mackey?"

And this time there was a response, words that seemed to come from a distance above his head. "In here. Come on through."

Three strides brought him to the inside door. This one opened inward; he dragged it back past his body and then stopped short, staring. What the hell was this? He was standing on the edge of a shallow pit, the rocky ground sloping down from the base of the inner fence on all four sides to a huge heap of rocks at the bottom. The fall-aways were steep, but the angle wasn't sharp enough to prevent anyone from walking up or down in an upright position. Above, the inner fence ended a few feet below the outer one, and between the two a narrow catwalk with a waist-high railing ran all the way around the enclosure. He noticed one other thing in that first sweeping glance—a woven quarter-inch wire mesh had been fastened to the board along the bottom of the inner fence, from ground level to a height of about two feet.

Movement distracted him then, on the catwalk directly over his head. Mackey. He leaned out, craning to look upward.

Sliding sound behind him in the passage. Instinctively he drew back, started to turn his head the other way. A man-shape appeared at the far corner of his eye—and then something struck him across the right temple, hard and vicious, like a hammer blow. Pain erupted; his vision slid out of focus. He felt his legs giving way, tried to grab the door or the wall. A second blow jolted him, this one a thrusting force just above his kidneys, and in the next instant he was off his feet and falling.

Impact with the ground, belly down and hard on the left side, drove all the air out of his lungs. He skidded downward, skin scraping from palms and forearms. A rock smacked his shoulder, changed and slowed the direction of his slide. When he finally came to rest amid a small avalanche of pebbles and dirt he lay there panting, disoriented, his thoughts mired in confusion. The only one of his senses that seemed to work was the aural. Clear and sharp he heard a door slam shut, steps running on wood. A voice shouted something, but the words ran together unintelligibly. More sounds followed, less distinct, jumbled. After that there was nothing but his own rasping breath.

He lay there for a little time and then he was up on his knees, with no sense of having risen. He opened his eyes, but his vision was still cockeyed; everything was shadows and wavery images, like objects viewed through murky water. He blinked and blinked, and the shadows merged and formed a wall of darkness. Panic gripped him. But the blindness lasted for only a few seconds. There was a kind of flash behind his eyes and suddenly he could see again, although now rocks and fence and catwalk seemed to have vague, fuzzy halos.

He lowered his gaze to the loose earth in which he knelt, trying to focus on small objects—pebbles, a piece of wood. They began to blur, and the panic nipped at him again until he realized that his eyes were tearing. He cleared the wetness away with the back of his hand. The pebbles and the wood still had their fuzzy halos, but the aureoles were dimmer now, fading.

All at once he was aware of pain. Pulsing on the right side of his head, above the ear. Stinging along his arms and palms. He held the hands out in front of him and focused on them. Abrasions, blood. He reached up to probe the pulpy spot over his ear, recoiled from his own touch, then looked at his fingers. More blood.

Hit and shoved from behind. Two men, one on the gallery and the other hiding outside. Trap.

Why?

Dry hissing sound.

His ears picked it up, faintly at first, then more clearly. It was alien to him. He peered around for the source, but he couldn't seem to locate it. Close . . . why couldn't he find it?

Something moved—a feathery slithering.

Something rattled.

As soon as he heard the rattle he knew what it was. The panic surged; he struggled to drag one foot under him, but then he didn't have enough strength to lift himself. Sluggish, movements and thoughts both, like reaction to terror in a nightmare. He knelt there struggling for control of his motor responses, panting again, and all that would move was his head, his still-fuzzy gaze swiveling left, right, up, down. Where was it? Where —?

There. Close. On one of the rocks no more than three feet away.

Huge.

Jesus!

Thick body coiled, tail vibrating, head poised forward, blood-red tongue flicking the air. And the eyes . . .

He fought to get up, couldn't get up. Paralyzed! The snake's eyes were black evil, mesmerizing. The mottled hexagonal pattern on its body rippled and gleamed—death shining in the dying sun. He couldn't look at the eyes any longer; he watched the scaly body moving sinuously, changing the shape of its coil, the neck twisting into a long S-wave, the head lifting higher, the lower sections forming a wide circle. Coiling to strike, it was going to strike!

Adrenaline rush. And a jarring sensation in his head; his vision came into sudden sharp focus. A second later, the paralysis left him. It was as if his body were like the snake's: tight coiled and then releasing all at once. He lunged to his feet, staggering, flailing for balance.

His foot slipped and slid in the loose earth. Instead of twisting back away from the snake, he stumbled closer to it.

And it, too, released.

The lancelike drive of the head was a blur; he had no time even to brace himself. It was like being struck in the ankle with a thrown rock. The leg went out from under him; he sat down hard, staring in terror at the diamondback's fangs embedded in the high top of his hiking boot, its thick coils writhing as it struggled to free itself.

A noise came out of his throat. He kicked wildly at the ugly flattened head, the wide-open mouth, again and again until the rattler pulled free or he drove it free. It flopped and slithered backward, already starting to squirm into a new series of tight loops. On all fours he scuttled frantically away from it along the slope, his feet kicking up a shower of rocks and dirt, images in his mind of the snake coming after him, chasing him with bared fangs dripping venom. He didn't stop moving or expecting a second strike until he realized he was all the way over on the far side of the pit. And only then did he look back to see how close the snake was.

It wasn't close. It was still down where he'd last seen it, coiled, hissing, rattling again.

Relief flooded him, but it lasted no more than two or three heartbeats. His ankle! He twisted over onto his left hip, dragged the right foot up so he could peer at the boot. Fang holes in the leather, a thick whitish dribble of venom. Penetrated deep enough to break the skin? He felt no pain . . . there'd be pain if he was bitten, wouldn't there? The impulse was strong to tear off the boot and sock under it, examine the skin with eyes and fingers to make sure. Another fear and an even stronger desire kept him from doing it.

How many more snakes hidden in those rocks?

Get out of here!

He managed to stand upright. His head ached where he'd been clubbed, but he had his equilibrium again and all his senses seemed to be working more or less normally. Only his breathing was erratic, wheezy. He scanned the ground around him, the rocks, the rest of the enclosure, and the catwalk above. As far as he could tell he was alone except for the diamondback. A closed door—stairway up from the shed, he thought—gave access to the gallery. The only opening in the inner fence, down here, was the now closed door to the passageway, directly across from where he stood.

He knew what this place was, now. What it was and why he'd been lured out here and then thrust down into the pit. And under the layer of fear a thin, bitter rage began to simmer.

He looked again at the diamondback. It was still coiled, still hissing faintly and tasting the air with its black-tipped tongue, but it no longer seemed to be rattling. His chest felt hot, constricted; he drew several deep, shallow breaths to stave off hyperventilation. Then he climbed higher on the slope, almost to the wire mesh at the fence's base, and began to make his way around toward the lower door.

The rocks littering the slope were smaller than those in the nest below. A few were clustered together; he avoided these. Something else lay on the earth twenty feet from the door, half hidden by dust and dirt—a long, light-metal rod, about the size and length of a fishing pole, with a wire slip noose at one end and a cord running from the wire loop to the butt. Snake catcher. He stepped over it, took two more strides before movement caught and held his eye, at the base of the fence just ahead.

He froze. Another snake lay in shadow between the mesh and a chunk of limestone that was the same blotched brown as its body—the reason he hadn't seen it before. Different species: shorter, the body thinner and less clearly patterned, a projection above each eye like a budding horn. Sidewinder? Whatever kind it was, it looked just as deadly as the diamondback.

It was already moving, swelling and coiling. He heard the dry sound like escaping steam, then the buzz from its tail. His first thought was to detour downslope and then over and back up to the door. But to do that he would have to venture close to the diamondback again. Fear made him indecisive, held him rooted until he remembered the snake catcher.

He backed up a slow, careful step. The sidewinder was coiled now, its tongue licking out; its eyes had vertical pupils, malevolent black slits. He kept retreating until his heel struck the metal pole, rattled it. The dark jutting head shifted that way. Messenger bent, not taking his eyes off the snake, and caught up the pole and brought it around in front of him as he straightened.

The cord leading from the loop to the butt was frayed through. Didn't matter; he had too little knowledge to try snaring a poisonous sidewinder. Fend it off—that was his idea. Try to ease around it, and if it struck make it strike at the wire slip noose instead of him.

He moved forward again with the pole out at arm's length, the blood-pound in his ears so loud he could no longer hear the rasp of his breathing. Sidesteps, baby steps. The snake watched him or the loop, he couldn't tell which. Sweat hazed his eyes; he blinked rapidly, keeping both hands on the rod so it would remain steady. Just a little farther—

His sliding foot dislodged a rock, sent it clattering downslope. His nerves were as frayed as the cord on the snake catcher; his hands jerked involuntarily, thrusting the wire loop six inches closer to the side-winder—close enough to provoke it into action.

The ugly horned head glanced off the loop and off the metal end, almost ripping the rod from Messenger's grasp. The snake flopped down, squirmed, started to recoil. Frantically he jabbed at it with the pole, missed, jabbed again, and succeeded in snagging the lower section of the body and flipping it a short distance downhill. The sidewinder re-covered, hissing, and seemed in Messenger's overwrought state to turn toward him as if it were about to launch an attack. He threw the rod at it, lurched around and uphill for the door.

There was no knob or latch on this side. He flung himself against the heavy wood, felt the shock all the way through his upper body when the door failed to yield. He lunged at it again. It wouldn't give an inch. Bastards had barred it somehow on the inside. . . .

He twisted his head. The sidewinder appeared to be closer than it had been, tight-coiled now, head lifted high; in the fading sunlight the knobby horns gave it a Satanic look. He backed away from it in the shadows along the fence.

The gallery, he thought, the other door up there.

He pushed away from the fence, back into pale sunlight. The upper door was directly above where the sidewinder waited, but in line with where he stood was one of the vertical supports for the catwalk railing. It and the board floor were no more than a foot above his head. He shifted his gaze to the mesh at the base of the wall, shifted it upward again; then he stepped back into shadow, set himself, and made his jump.

He managed to lock both hands around the support. It gave a little—old, dry wood, rusty nails—but held his weight as his boots scrabbled against the mesh for a toehold. He found one, started to pull himself up . . . and his foot slipped and he lost his grip at the same time and dropped, skidding to one knee in the loose earth. He was up instantly, not looking anywhere but at the support, focused only on escape.

Again he jumped, again he locked hands around the beam. His toehold this time was firmer; he dug his boot hard into the mesh, lifting with arms and shoulders, pain in the straining muscles, pain a roaring stroke in his head. He got one knee over the lip, slipped, held on, and heaved upward—and he was onto the gallery, crawling under the railing and then lying flat on the rough boards.

He lay there for seconds or minutes, until his pulse rate slowed. The fear-drain left him with leaden limbs and dulled thoughts. He shoved onto all fours, got to his feet with the aid of the railing. Standing, he could see over the top of the outer wall. On the highway a tractor-trailer rig rumbled by, heading toward Beulah. Beyond the highway, dusk crawled in plum-colored shadows across the desert flats, lay ink-black in the creases and notches of the hills. Time distortion: It seemed that he must have been in the pit for an hour or more, when in fact it hadn't been much more than ten minutes.

He moved closer to the fence, to look down into Herb Mackey's yard. His Subaru was parked where he'd left it; from here it appeared untouched. The dirty white pickup was long gone from behind the house trailer.

Wobbly-legged, using the railing, he made his way to the gallery door. It was neither locked nor barred. A short flight of steps took him down into the shed. When he reached the car he opened the driver's door and sat on the edge of the seat without getting in. His fingers were clumsy as he unlaced his right boot, took it off. Small spot of sticky venom on his sock; he dragged the sock off. Just below his ankle bone were a pair of faint reddish marks that were tender to the touch. He held his breath while he probed them, then let it out in a thin sigh. The skin was unbroken.

He leaned in to adjust the mirror so he could examine the right side of his head. The skin had been broken there, but the gash was neither long nor deep. The blood on the wound and on the hair around it was dirt-flecked and coagulating. Not much physical damage, really. Most of his anguish had been mental.

Another test passed, barely. The edge this time had been needle-sharp, as sharp as the diamondback's fangs.

The sun was gone now, darkness closing in. He sat slumped, elbows resting on his thighs—waiting until he felt strong enough to put his sock and boot back on and then to drive.

15

SHERIFF ESPINOSA LOOKED at him as if he were either drunk or demented. "That's the goddamnedest story I've heard in years," he said.

"Every word is true."

"Herb Mackey died four weeks ago. Heart attack. First thing we did was destroy his snakes, and his place has been closed up ever since."

"I had no way of knowing that," Messenger said. "I believed the man on the phone; why wouldn't I? And I told you, they covered the lower half of the highway sign—the words *Rattlesnake Farm* and the *Closed* sticker over them. I tore the burlap off before I left."

"Still doesn't make much sense."

"Look at me. You think I hit myself on the head? Scratched my hands and arms, ripped and dirtied my clothes? All just to come in here and file a false report?"

"For all I know," Espinosa said, "you were in a brawl. Put your nose in somewhere it wasn't wanted."

His head still ached and the anger in him had risen close to the surface. He bit back a sharp reply and replaced it with, "Go out to Mackey's then. Look around. Those two snakes are still in the pit, along with God knows how many more."

"Proving what? They could've crawled in there on their own. Diamondbacks and sidewinders grow like weeds in this country."

"So you're not going to do anything."

Espinosa leaned back in his chair, making the swivel mechanism creak. The only other sound in the Sheriff's Department at City Hall was static from the dispatcher's radio. Messenger had caught the baked apple just as he was about to leave for the day; now he was beginning to think he shouldn't have bothered coming here at all.

"What would you have me do?" Espinosa asked at length. He had his pipe out and was loading it methodically with black shag-cut tobacco. "Two men, you said, but you didn't get a look at either of them and you didn't recognize the voice on the phone or the voice of the one who spoke to you at Mackey's. I don't suppose you noticed the license plate on the pickup?"

"No. I didn't pay much attention to the truck. I thought it was Mackey's, that it belonged there."

"What make and model?"

"I'm not sure. American-made, I think."

"What color? What year?"

"White. Not old but not new either. It had a broken radio antenna, I remember that much."

"American-made, white, not old and not new. You know how many pickups in this county fit that description, even with the busted antenna?"

"All right," Messenger said.

"And there's still the point of the whole thing. Why would these two men go to all the trouble of trapping or buying two or more rattlers, luring you out there, and then blindsiding you and locking you in with the snakes? There're easier ways to warn a man to mind his own business."

"It was more than a warning. They didn't care if I was bitten and died in that pit."

"You weren't bitten and the odds were that you wouldn't be, unless you landed on top of one of the critters." Espinosa paused to light his pipe. He liked the taste of the smoke; a small smile appeared around the teeth-clamped bit. "Besides, if you had been bitten, you'd likely have survived. Not many people die of rattlesnake bites, Mr. Messenger. It's a myth that they do."

"Maybe so, but some people *do* die. And the ones that don't get deathly sick. I tell you, it was more than a warning. It was attempted murder."

"Why would anybody around here want you dead?"

"You know why, Sheriff."

"Stirring up a matter better left alone is hardly cause for attempted murder."

"It is if I'm right and somebody other than Anna Roebuck is responsible for those two killings. That person is afraid I might get at the truth."

"Who? Got any ideas about that?"

"All I know is, I've had warnings from John T. Roebuck and from Joe Hanratty and Tom Spears."

Espinosa's eyes took on a glass-hard shine. "You saying it could be John T. wants you dead?"

"I'm not saying anything. I'm giving you information so you can do your job."

"John T.'s great-grandfather was one of Beulah's first settlers. Him and his family are the best friends this town has ever had. I know John T.; known him all my life. He's never harmed a single person, not one."

Then why do his sister-in-law and Jaime Orozco dislike him so much? Why is his wife a drunk? Why did he come on to me like Brando playing the Godfather?

Messenger said, "And I suppose Hanratty and Spears are Godfearing pillars of the community, too."

"They're not killers."

"Neither was Anna Roebuck."

Espinosa stared at him, hard, for a clutch of seconds. Messenger matched the stare with an unblinking intensity of his own. "You know what I think, Mr. Messenger?"

"I've got a pretty good idea. Quit my crusade and get out of town while I'm still alive."

"That isn't what I was going to say."

"Different words, maybe, but the same message. Another warning. Well, I'm sick of warnings and I'm damned if I'll stand still for an attempt on my life."

Espinosa asked tightly, "What're you planning to do about it?"

"I don't know yet. But I'll tell you what I'm *not* going to do. I'm not leaving Beulah with my tail tucked between my legs, the way I'm supposed to."

"That mean you're looking to cause more trouble?"

"What it means, Sheriff, is that I'm staying until one of us finds out who tried to kill me tonight. And who really murdered Dave and Tess Roebuck."

IN HIS CAR in the City Hall parking lot he slid a random jazz tape into the cassette player, turned the volume up loud. Louis Armstrong and his Hot Five, a short-lived combo but still among the best ever. Opening press roll by Zutty Singleton on the drums that ended in a series of hard, fast rim shots to set the tempo. Straight, simple pattern woven by Louis's magical trumpet and Fred Robinson's trombone, Fatha Hines on the keyboard creating contrapuntal harmonics and then an amazing run of rich chord progressions. Jimmy Strong's clarinet developing a wail that matched the piano note for note, chord for chord, then fading to let Fatha carry the sweet, hot harmony. New Orleans–style twenties jazz that soothed him, kept his rage from boiling over the edge of control.

He had never been this angry in his life. And why the hell shouldn't he be: Nobody had ever tried to kill mild-mannered Jim Messenger before. But it was a blind anger, without direction or focus. The baked apple would do nothing to track down the men who had lured him to Mackey's; he would have to do it himself if it was to be done at all. But how? Not a detective, not a hero, just an out-of-his-element CPA with a midlife compulsion and a frustrated mad-on. *How*, for Christ's sake?

Louis's trumpet was dominant now, one of his celebrated solos: hard, powerful, and so dirty-sweet and low-moaning it made you ache to hear it. Brilliant departure on . . . was that "Wild Man Blues"? No horn man had never blown as hot as Armstrong. No horn man had ever been able to improvise like Armstrong—

Improvise, he thought. Improvisation.

The soul of jazz. "One person's mad concept balanced against the correct counterbalance of restraint and understatement"— he'd read that somewhere once. Three kinds of melodic improvisation: soloist respects the melody, with the only changes the lengthening or shortening of some notes, repetition of others, use of atonal variations and dynamics; the melody is recognizable in the soloist's rendition but its phrases are subject to slight additions and alterations; soloist departs entirely from the melody, uses the chord pattern of the tune rather than the melody as a point of departure. Broad musical definitions for what was really undefinable. Still, if you were trying to explain the concept to someone who knew nothing about music, you could simplify it into a more or less apt capsule definition: Improvisation is that which is bold and unpredictable.

Soloist respects the melody; soloist departs from the melody. Bold and unpredictable, either way. But no soloist can work completely alone. He has to have rhythm and harmony and syncopation—backup help, input from sidemen that may also be bold and unpredictable.

When you looked at it that way—didn't the same thing apply to him, his life? For all of his adulthood hadn't he been a frustrated soloist playing the same written chords over and over again without departure or assistance, straight through toward the end? The only "mad concept" he'd ever had was the one that had led him here to Beulah.

And didn't the same apply to the situation he was facing now? Hadn't he been approaching it in the same linear, uninspired fashion that he'd approached his life? Yes, and it would be useless to go on that way; he'd never get anywhere without help and a change in method.

He'd given his life edges. Time now, by God, to give it a little bold unpredictability.

HE PROMISED HIMSELF that if he slept badly, or awakened with a severe headache, he would go to the hospital for X rays first thing in the morning. Head injuries were nothing to fool with; they could be serious, no matter how minor they seemed at first. But he slept all right, and felt reasonably well when he awoke—just a dull throbbing in his temples and some tenderness to the touch. No concussion, then. It had been shock as much as the blow itself that made him fuzzy-headed and cockeyed those first few minutes in the pit.

He drove rather than walked to the Goldtown Café for breakfast. His appetite was good; another positive sign. He caught Lynette Carey's eye when he walked in; she acknowledged him with a brief nod, but she didn't smile and she didn't look his way again. Nor did she serve him, despite the fact that he made a point of sitting in her section. No help there. Not that he'd expected any, as poorly as he'd handled the meeting with her in the Saddle Bar.

Two possible allies, then. One was Jaime Orozco. Messenger felt certain Orozco would do whatever he could to help clear Anna's name, but his resources were limited. The other possible ally and best hope was Dacy Burgess.

He would go talk to Dacy first, as soon as he finished breakfast. Try to convince her that the plan he'd developed last night was worth risking. She had more to gain than he did if she agreed. The trouble was, she also had more to lose if the scheme backfired.

16

WHEN HE DROVE down into the Burgess ranch yard, Lonnie and the yammering and snarling Buster were there to greet him. Dacy was in the stable, the boy told him; he didn't have much else to say. And if he noticed the bandage above Messenger's ear, the iodine-stained abrasions on his hands and forearms, he didn't ask about them.

The interior of the stable smelled of manure and trapped heat. Dacy was bent over next to the hindquarters of a copper-red horse, applying some sort of sticky brown substance to the animal's right leg just above the hoof. When she heard his footfalls on the rough floor she glanced around briefly, then resumed her work on the sorrel's leg. She didn't seem any more surprised to see him than Lonnie had been.

He watched her, not speaking. She had a sure, gentle touch, and when she murmured soothingly to the horse, it pricked up its ears and tossed its head as if it understood the words. Maybe it did, he thought. Some people had that kind of rapport with animals.

Dacy straightened finally, put the cap back on the bottle of brown gum, and then pretended to notice him for the first time. "Well, well, look who's here," she said. The sarcasm was mild and without rancor. "How long has it been, Jim? A whole twenty-four hours?"

"I have a good reason for coming back."

"Don't you always? Keep this up and folks'll think you're looking to move in permanently."

"I am," he said, "but not permanently."

"Now what does that—" She broke off, her eyes narrowing into a squint. The light in the stable was thin and dusty; she'd only just noticed the bandage. "What happened to you?"

"Some trouble last night."

"What kind of trouble?"

He told her about it, tersely. She didn't interrupt and she showed no reaction. When he was done she shook her head, but not as if she disbelieved him; it was more an expression of disgust and anger.

"That's a hell of a thing to do to somebody," she said. "Diamond-backs and sidewinders are damned poisonous critters."

"Not as poisonous as some people."

"You got that right. Who you think was behind it?"

"I don't know. Is John T. capable of a trick like that?"

"With the right reason."

"The right reason in this case is guilt. I'm sure of it, Dacy. The only person with a reason to want me hurt or dead is the real murderer of Anna's family."

Her mouth quirked sardonically, but she didn't argue with him. She said, "Two men out there at Mackey's. Hirelings, you reckon?"

"Either that, or the guilty man and a friend. Joe Hanratty and Tom Spears, for instance."

"Why them?"

He told her about his run-in with the two cowhands. "The pickup they were using was a green Ford. Spears's truck? He was driving."

"Yeah. But Joe drives a Blazer, not a white pickup with a busted antenna. I wish I could tell you who belongs to that truck but I can't. Lot of white pickups in this county." She paused. "John T., Hanratty, Spears—they can all be hardasses. But cold-blooded killers? I don't see it."

"You saw it in Anna. You still do."

No response. Dacy withdrew a cigarette from the pack in her shirt pocket, put it between her lips. Almost immediately she yanked it away and crumbled paper and tobacco between her fingers. "Fucking cancer sticks," she said.

Messenger said, "People snap sometimes—we both know that. You can't tell what somebody might do if he's pushed far enough."

"That goes for my sister, too."

"Yes, but the point is, it goes for everybody. I don't even know my own limits. Do you know yours?"

"Up to a point. After that . . . maybe not."

"Dacy, isn't there *any* doubt in your mind about Anna's guilt? Even a shred?"

"Sure, a shred. You think I *want* to believe she killed my niece? But I tore myself up denying it at first, and I'm not going through all that again without proof. Show me some proof, Jim, any kind. Then I'll fight like hell to clear her name."

"I can't find proof without help, your help. Give it to me and in exchange I'll help you, if you're willing to take a chance."

"What're you talking about? Chance on what?"

"Having me around for a while. Giving me a job."

Dacy stared at him the way Espinosa had last night. "A *job*? Doing what?"

"Whatever Jaime Orozco used to do here. Whatever you want me to do—chores, scut work, anything."

"I can't afford a hired hand—"

"You don't have to pay me," Messenger said. "I'll work for room and board. Sleep in the trailer outside; I've had enough of that motel in town."

"You're serious," she said, as if she still couldn't quite believe it.

"I've never been more serious."

"And just how am I supposed to help you?"

"Not only me—you and Lonnie, too, if I'm right about Anna. You know the people involved, things about them I couldn't find out on my own. If we put our heads together, there's a chance we could come up with some fact or angle that's been overlooked. That's one possibility. Another is that my moving in here might force the real murderer's hand."

"Force it how?"

"It's bound to shake him up, because it says I can't be frightened off, I'm determined to settle in and keep digging for the truth. If he's worried enough he might just make a mistake, do something desperate."

"Like trying to kill you, is that it? You want to set yourself up as a target."

"Not exactly. I'm not going to fall for any more tricks and I won't get into a position where I can be caught unawares."

"Famous last words." Then she said, "But you'd be all right as long as you were on my land. Nobody'd dare come after you here."

"Are you sure? The one reservation I have is that my moving in might put you and Lonnie in danger."

"Shit, that's not a worry. I know how to take care of myself and my son. You've seen what I can do with a rifle, Jim. Lonnie's an even better shot than I am." Her gaze now was speculative. "You really think this could lead where you want it to—prove somebody else killed Dave and Tess? I mean *prove* it."

"I think it's the only way either of us is likely to have a chance of proving it. All I'm asking for is ten days. What's left of my vacation. If something hasn't broken by then, I'll go back to San Francisco and you'll never see or hear from me again."

"Ten days, huh? You ever work on a ranch?"

"No, but I take orders and I'm a fast learner."

"Know anything about cattle? Horses?"

"A little about horses. I used to ride when I was a kid."

"When you walked in here, what was I doing to Red?"

"I don't know. What were you doing?"

"Putting on Cut-Heal medicine. He's got a cut on his right fetlock." She sighed, reached out distractedly to stroke the sorrel's flank. "God knows," she said at length, "there's plenty of work that needs doing around this place, and most of it doesn't require an expert hand. Hard work, dirty work. That kind bother you?"

"It never has."

"You'd do as you're told, no backsass?"

"No backsass."

"I'll have to talk to Lonnie. He's got as much say as I have."

"Of course."

"Okay. While I'm doing that, you lead Red here outside and turn him loose in the corral. You can do that, can't you? And take off his halter first?"

"Consider it done. And Dacy—thanks."

"Don't thank me yet," she said. "When you're finished wait by the corral gate."

He had no trouble with the sorrel. It plodded along docilely enough after him, stood still while he opened the corral gate and again while he unhooked the halter, and then trotted off to join the other two horses. He took the halter into the stable and hung it up. Then he went back out to wait.

Dacy was gone ten minutes. When she reappeared she had Lonnie with her. Without preamble she asked, "How soon would you want to start?"

"Any time," Messenger said. "Right now."

"Nothing you want to go and do first?"

"No. Am I hired?"

"You're hired. Temporarily, anyhow. Lonnie, take him into the barn and show him where we keep the shovels and brooms."

HE SPENT THE rest of the morning and half the noon hour cleaning the barn and the stable. It was hot, dirty work—shoveling manure, sweeping out stalls and floors, forking hay so dry the air swam with its chaff. At first the heat and exertion made his head pound furiously, built a thin churn of nausea under his breastbone. But hurt and discomfort were old acquaintances from his time as an endurance runner; he'd learned how to use them back then, how to channel negative feelings into positive energy—an old trick that every long-distance runner picks up and adapts. Once he applied it to his clean-up work, he began to feel better, to gain stamina. By the time Lonnie came to call him to lunch, he was nearly finished and even feeling a little of the exercise high you get from marathon running.

Lunch was tacos and a bowl of thick bean soup; he wolfed down his portion. Dacy said approvingly, "Looks like hard work may just agree with you, Jim."

"Well, I've never shied away from it."

"See if you feel the same in two or three days."

"Planning to work me like a mule?"

Her grin had a wry bend in it. "Why not? You're strong enough and sure as hell stubborn enough."

After he was done at the stable, she set him to digging a new irrigation ditch for the vegetable garden. And when he'd taken care of that she told him to give Lonnie a hand repairing the broken blade on the windmill. He thought that might present an opportunity to draw the boy out a little, see if he could get an idea of what Lonnie knew and was hiding—another reason he'd wanted the job here. But the opportunity wasn't there. The platform was too narrow for more than one of them at a time; his job was to stay below, fetch materials as they were needed, and send items up to Lonnie by rope.

The workday ended at five o'clock. He was stiff and sore, and there were blisters on his hands along with last night's abrasions, but his headache was gone and he wasn't as tired as he'd expected to be. Internally he felt fine—buoyed by a sense of having accomplished something worthwhile, of finally making progress. He washed up at the pump near the well, was drying his hands on a rough towel when Lonnie joined him.

"Ma says to tell you she put sheets and a blanket and some other stuff in the trailer. And to leave the door and windows open so it can air out."

He nodded. "Lonnie, before you go—thanks for agreeing to let me stay on here."

"No big deal to me. You're working free and we need the help."

"You still think I'm wrong, though. About your aunt."

"Damn right you are. She did it. Nothing you do or say's gonna change that."

"If there's a reason you're so sure, tell me what it is. Convince me."

"There's no reason. I just know it, that's all."

Messenger said, "Your ma tell you what happened to me last night?"

"She told me. Whoever those two guys are, they were just trying to scare you."

"Pretty dangerous way to scare somebody. I could've been bitten and I could've died."

"Yeah, well, you weren't and you didn't."

"A white pickup with a busted antenna, Lonnie. Ever see one like that in town?"

"Might have, once or twice."

"Any idea who owns it?"

"Nobody we know, that's for sure."

Messenger went to have a look at the trailer. Single room inside, with a hanging drape to separate a sleeping area (rollaway bed with a lumpy mattress) from a sitting area (one ancient armchair, one straight-backed chair). The "kitchen" was a two-burner propane stove and a tiny countertop refrigerator. A sink, a shower stall so narrow you wouldn't be able to turn around in it, and a chemical toilet set tight between metal partitions completed the facilities. Crude quarters, really—and a sweatbox by day and on hot nights. But he'd never been a slave to creature comforts. It would do well enough for however long he was here.

He took a quick shower, put on a shirt and a pair of slacks that he'd brought from the motel, and then went to the house. Dacy was in the living room, working at her computer terminal. She'd changed clothes too—a blouse and white slacks—and tied up her hair with a ribbon, dabbed on a little lipstick. He wondered if she'd done it for him, as he had showered and changed for her. Probably not. Just conceit to believe she had.

He leaned over her shoulder to peer at the screen. "Looks like some kind of chart," he said.

"Ear-tag records. Fall roundup's due soon. Every cow, steer, and calf we own carries color-coded and numbered ear tags. Gives us an accurate head count according to age and sex and lets us keep track of genealogy lines and production from different matings."

"So that's what you use the computer for."

"That and a lot of other things, like keeping tabs on supplies and running models to see what kind of feed conversion we can expect if we bring in different stock. What'd you think I used it for? Playing video games?"

"No. Don't get your dander up."

"It's not up. I just want you to understand, since you're working for us now, that Lonnie and me don't run some half-assed Western movie ranch. We may be small and hardscrabble but we're as modern as we can get. We have to be to survive."

"I didn't think any differently. Okay?"

"Okay." A small smile let him know she wasn't really angry. "I'll put supper on soon. Be ready in a couple of hours, maybe less."

"That'll give me enough time to take care of a few things in town. How late does that Western shop on Main stay open?"

"Seven."

"Good." He started out.

"Jim?"

"Yes, Dacy?"

She looked at him steadily for a little time; but whatever it was she meant to say remained unspoken. "Never mind. Just be back by seven-thirty if you want your supper hot. We don't wait meals for anybody on this ranch."

HIS FIRST STOP in town was the Ramirez mobile home. Jaime Orozco showed no surprise when Messenger told him he'd hired on temporarily at the Burgess ranch, and his reasons for doing so. Orozco seemed to approve, despite saying, "I hope you know what you're doing, my friend."

"So do I. I'm willing to take the risk as long as Dacy and Lonnie are." He paused. "You knew about what happened at Mackey's before I got here, didn't you."

Orozco nodded. "Ben Espinosa enjoys the sound of his own voice. Sometimes what he says is worth listening to."

"He's doing nothing about finding those two men. And won't unless they're identified by somebody else and I file charges against them."

"I know."

"I don't suppose you have any idea who drives a white pickup with a broken antenna?"

"No. But if the owner lives in this county, someone will know him. Or soon find out who he is."

"Will you ask your friends? Pass the word?"

"It has already been done."

"Thank you, Señor Orozco."

"*De nada*. If it wasn't for this leg . . ." Orozco thumped it with his knuckles, then shrugged and said solemnly, "A man does what he can in the cause of justice."

"If he's a good man."

"Yes, *amigo*. If he is a good man."

I N   T H E   W E S T E R N apparel shop he bought two more pairs of jeans and two khaki shirts. Dacy had said she would take care of his laundry, but he couldn't expect her to wash and rewash the same sweaty change of work clothes. Then he drove to the High Desert Lodge.

Mrs. Padgett had pale, shiny eyes that made him think of fat cells floating in blobs of cream. They turned avid as soon as he told her he was checking out. "Of course, Mr. Messenger," she said. "I'll have your bill ready in a jiffy."

"Fine."

"Going down to Vegas, are you?"

"No."

"Back home then. You *are* leaving Beulah?"

"Not exactly."

"Not exactly? I'm afraid I don't—"

"I've taken a job at the Burgess ranch. Hired hand."

"You . . . Dacy Burgess hired you?" Her mouth hung open as if it were hinged. The avid eyes crawled over his face like insects. "You're going to *live* out there at her place?"

"That's right. For the next ten days, at least," Messenger said. There was a small, malicious pleasure in telling her, watching her reaction, knowing what she'd do as soon as he walked out the door.

"But . . . why? Why would a man like you, a city man, want to work as a ranch hand?"

"Why do you think, Mrs. Padgett?"

"I can't imagine . . ."

"Sure you can. I'll bet you have a very good imagination."

Her trap was open again; she snapped it closed. Quickly, without looking at him again, she punched up his bill on her computer and ran his American Express card through the machine. She was eager to be rid of him now. But no more eager than he was to be rid of her.

He drove straight back to the ranch. It took him less than thirty minutes, but when he passed through the gate his headlights picked out an unfamiliar station wagon already parked at an angle near the house. Mrs. Padgett hadn't let him down. She'd been on the phone the instant he left her.

Messenger pulled up next to the wagon. He was just opening his door when John T. Roebuck, with Dacy and Lonnie following, stormed out of the house to confront him.

17

THE INTENSITY OF John T.'s emotions surprised him; he'd expected anger but not raw, seething fury. Roebuck got right up in his face, stretching on the balls of his feet so that his nose was an inch or so below Messenger's. His breath, hot and moist, stank of sour-mash bourbon and Mexican cheroots. The black eyes under their craggy brows caught the outspill of light from the house; it made them look as if fires burned in their depths. They reminded Messenger of the eyes of the diamondback rattler in the pit at Mackey's. But he stood his ground, met them with a lidless stare of his own.

"What the fuck do you think you're doing, Messenger?"

"Standing here smelling your bad breath."

"You son of a bitch, I warned you not to hang around and make any more trouble. And now I find out you've moved in. Talked Dacy into giving you a job and moved the hell in."

Behind him Dacy said, "I told you, John T., he didn't talk me into anything." She was angry too, standing with arms folded tight across her breasts. But from her tone and the crooked set of her mouth Messenger sensed that satisfaction and a hint of amusement lay under the anger. "I make my own decisions."

"You goddamn well made the wrong one this time," John T. said without taking his hot eyes off Messenger.

"None of your business if I did."

"Yours and his, that it?"

"That's it."

"What other kind of business you and him got, Dacy?"

"What'd you just say?"

"You heard me. Been a long time since you had a man around to tend to your needs. Pick up a better man than this one at any bar on Saturday night, good-looking woman like you. Or maybe you just like short-peckers from the big city."

Dacy's amusement was gone. She came forward in a jerky rush and caught Roebuck's arm and pulled him around to face her. "Get off my property. Now."

"When I'm good and ready."

"Now. I mean it."

"Or what? You figure to put me off? Or you gonna ask this sorry hunk of horse turd to do it for you?"

Messenger said thinly, "It won't work, Roebuck."

"What won't work, asshole?"

"Trying to provoke me into a fight so you can call the sheriff and file an assault charge. I won't fight you, not that way. And you won't get rid of me that way, either."

"You son of a bitch—"

"You used that name already. Try a new one."

Dacy laughed. She'd relaxed again. "When it comes to cussing," she said to Messenger, "he's about as original as a kid in a schoolyard."

Roebuck's fury was on the edge of explosion; you could see him struggling to maintain his control. He tried to reestablish an aggressive position by getting back up in Messenger's face. Messenger stood with his arms flat against his sides, his expression neutral—giving John T. nothing to blow up on.

They maintained their positions for what must have been a minute or more. Messenger knew the game; it was called staredown. The first one to blink or look away was the loser. He'd never played it before, would have considered himself a poor prospect if he'd thought about his chances. Old Jim was too passive for a game like that. But this wasn't Old Jim; this was New Jim. And New Jim played John T. Roebuck to a draw.

Dacy broke it up. She said, "Lonnie, if John T. isn't off our property in three minutes, you go get your Ruger carbine and shoot out two tires on that station wagon of his. It'll be a freak accident. You and me and Jim'll swear to that."

John T. backed up a step—a slow, sinuous movement like a snake uncoiling. He had his anger in check now. "We both know that's an idle threat," he said.

"You think so? Lonnie, you timing what I said?"

"Two and a half minutes left, Ma."

"What'll you do when the time's up?"

"Go get my Ruger and shoot out two tires on his wagon."

"Bullshit," Roebuck said, but he no longer sounded convinced. He said to Messenger, "I'm not through with you, boy, not by a long shot. I'm just getting started."

"Is that so? How do you plan to get shut of me?"

"There are ways, by God."

"Sure there are," Dacy said. "Night riders with buckets of tar and sacks of chicken feathers, that's one. Or maybe you could hire a couple of men to lure him out to Mackey's and shove him down into the snakepit."

"What the hell?" John T. said, and for the first time since Messenger's arrival he put his gaze on her. "I didn't have anything to do with that. If it even happened."

"It happened," Messenger said.

"Well, I didn't make it happen. I don't do things that way."

"Too violent for you? Or not violent enough?"

"Could be you'll find out."

Dacy said, "How much time's he have left, Lonnie?"

"Less than a minute."

"Just won't learn, none of you. Just won't learn to leave well enough alone. Well, all right. It's on your head too now, Dacy. His and yours."

Roebuck walked to his station wagon, back and shoulders rigid. Messenger expected him to drive off with another little show of aggression—fast and reckless, fouling the night air with dust. But he didn't. His departure was slow, measured, as if he were afraid to slacken the tight rein he'd put on his control.

When the wagon's lights reached the gate, Dacy said, "Well, you wanted to shake things up, Jim."

"Yeah."

"Having second thoughts?"

"No." He was wondering why John T. had come flying over here in such a high state of rage. He was no real threat to the man, unless John

T. was involved in his brother's death. Or unless some other kind of guilty knowledge was driving him. He was hiding something: Messenger felt as certain of it as he did that Lonnie was hiding something. The same thing, maybe? Even if John T. wasn't behind the snake trap at Mackey's, it had upset him in some way that wasn't quite clear. The fact that the target had survived unharmed? The fact that the trap had been set in the first place?

Dacy said, "Well, I'm not either, so you don't need to worry on that score. I like seeing that strutty rooster with his feathers ruffled and his pecker down."

"Just as long as he doesn't . . . what's the phrase? Do you a meanness?"

"He won't. But we better watch out he doesn't try to do you one."

"I'm not afraid of him."

"That the truth, or just bravado?"

"I don't know," he said. "Maybe a little of both."

After supper he and Dacy spent an hour on the porch, talking. Her opinion on the intensity of John T.'s reaction was that it didn't necessarily mean anything. "That's the kind of man he is. Something upsets him, he goes off like a damn firecracker." In addition to John T. they discussed his brother, his wife, Joe Hanratty, Lynette Carey, Maria Hoxie, and others who in one way or another had been involved with Dave Roebuck—Messenger probing for specific background information, some factor in personalities and relationships that might be worth exploring. Neither he nor Dacy found one. But he did come away from the talk with a definite conviction.

Beulah's closets were full of secrets. More, it seemed, than in most small towns; uglier ones, too. And the more you shook the closet doors, the louder the skeletons would rattle.

IN THE MORNING he and Lonnie finished work on the windmill and then went to the holding pens to repair a loose panel on a large cagelike device called a squeeze chute. Made of welded bars, its two main panels were used to immobilize steers during spring and fall roundups for branding, castration, and inoculation against disease.

Just before lunch they began replacing broken rails in the corral fence and loose and warped boards in the stable and barn. Next week,

Lonnie said, if the wind cooperated and the weather remained dry, they would weather-seal the wood and then spray paint both buildings. They were running low on lumber and ten-penny nails by midafternoon, and Messenger volunteered to drive into town to the building outfitters. Dacy gave him a list of supplies to pick up that included paint and turpentine and a new pane of glass for the kitchen window. She also gave him the keys to their pickup.

The truck was a GMC product, fifteen years old. Lonnie was a good enough mechanic to get it running again whenever it quit (which was too damn often lately, Dacy said), but not quite good enough to keep the engine from idling high and rough and funneling hot-oil fumes into the cab. The suspension was shot too; every time a tire thudded through a chuckhole, the pickup jolted and shuddered and threatened to come apart like one of those comic cars in a Mack Sennett two-reeler. By the time he reached town he felt as shaken as a marble in a box.

The clerk at the building supply knew who he was. He wasn't refused service, but he was subjected to obvious and sullen slow down tactics that kept him there nearly an hour. He endured it without comment. A pointless confrontation with one of Beulah's citizens was the last thing he needed right now.

A thought occurred to him while he waited—something he should have done by now but hadn't. When the pickup was finally loaded he drove over to the library. Thin and juiceless Ada Kendall was alone inside the stifling trailer. She drew back in her chair when he entered, as if she fancied he might leap over the desk and attack her. Then she sat spine-locked and fixed him with a sour look of disapproval.

"You're not welcome here, you know," she said.

"I know. But it's a public place and you're not going to ask me to leave, are you, Miss Kendall?"

"It's Mrs. Kendall. I'm a widow." She spoke the last sentence proudly, as if it were a badge of honor. "What is it you want?"

"Your file of the Tonopah newspaper, if you have one."

"The past twelve months only."

"That's all I'm interested in."

"Going to read about the murders, I suppose."

"No. The real estate ads."

"Real estate?"

"Didn't you know? I'm thinking of settling in this area."

Her mouth opened and she blinked at him behind her glasses.

"In your neighborhood, maybe. One of the places next door to you wouldn't be up for sale or rent, would it?"

"Why, you . . . you . . ."

"Easy, Mrs. Kendall. This is a library—no obscenities permitted."

He found the newspaper file on his own, in an airless alcove at the far end. Sweat ran freely on his face, dripped from his nose and chin, as he culled the issues containing stories about the killings. There were several, despite the fact that the Tonopah paper was a weekly: a bizarre, double homicide was big news in a small county like this one.

The initial account was prominent on the front page, and was accompanied by photographs of both Anna and Dave Roebuck. The one of Anna was a smiley wedding photo a dozen years old; the likeness between the woman and the one Messenger had observed in San Francisco was so slender they might have been two separate people. The photo of her husband was more recent but the reproduction was grainily poor; it conveyed no clear impression of the man.

He didn't expect to learn much from the lead story and follow-ups that he didn't already know. But he did find out one detail that neither Dacy nor Reverend Hoxie had mentioned—a detail that made Tess Roebuck's death even more of a puzzle.

The child had been found not only wearing a white Sunday dress, but with a sprig of something called desert verbena tightly clenched in one hand. The fact appeared in two of the news stories, each time without either explanation or speculation.

Messenger left Ada Kendall glowering behind her desk and drove the rattling pickup back out to the ranch. Lonnie helped him unload the supplies, and when they were put away he went to talk to Dacy.

"Verbena?" she said in response to his question. "It's a flowering desert plant. Common enough around here."

"Why would Tess have had a sprig of it clutched in her hand?"

"Don't go trying to make anything out of that, Jim. It's not important."

"The white dress is important—it has to be. Why not the verbena too?"

"Anna had bushes growing in the yard, along with some other plants. County cops found where the branch'd been broken off one of the bushes near where she was hit with the rock, and they figured when she fell she clutched at the bush and the branch snapped off in her hand."

"Makes sense, I guess," Messenger admitted. "Still, what if they were wrong? What if the murderer broke it off and put it in her hand, for the same reason he changed her clothes and put her in the well?"

"Jim, nobody could figure an explanation for the dress or the well. Maybe there isn't any that makes much sense. You'll only make yourself crazy trying to come up with one that includes the verbena, too."

"Crazier than I already am, you mean."

"You said it, I didn't. Why don't you go on back to work and let me do the same?"

He went back to work. But he couldn't get the Sunday dress, the well, the verbena out of his mind. Or the feeling, groundless or not, that the three were connected somehow, and that if he knew their purpose he would know who was guilty and why.

18

ONCE THE USUAL morning chores were done, Sunday was a day of rest on the Burgess ranch. This suited Messenger. He'd had a good eight hours of sleep, but he was still tired—and sunburnt and saddle sore—from Saturday's truck-and-horseback ride across their grazing land.

He and Lonnie had set out early, with a loaded two-horse trailer hooked onto the back of the GMC pickup and the pickup's bed stacked with fresh salt blocks. With water at a premium out here, salt blocks were essential to the survival of sagebrush cattle. They'd spent all morning jouncing over rough, arid terrain along the eastern foothills where the Bootstrap Mine was located. Most of the small herd were loosely scattered there, on land that belonged to the BLM. In another six weeks or so, Lonnie told him, the beeves would be bunched and driven back onto Burgess ground. That was when however many head they needed to sell would be culled and put into the holding pens, and any necessary doctoring taken care of; it was also when a BLM agent would come down from the regional office in Tonopah and take an inventory, one of the steps in setting next year's quota. All the late calves would be on the ground then, too, and would have to be branded, earmarked, and inoculated. It was too much work for two people, so they'd scrape together enough money to hire a seasonal hand for a few weeks. A part-time buckaroo (yes, that was a word they still used out here) would also be short-hired for the spring roundup.

Cattle and the land were the only subjects Lonnie would discuss.

Messenger tried twice to turn their desultory conversation to the murders; each time Lonnie withdrew into a moody silence. He had a feeling that whatever the boy was concealing, it was like a wad of bitter phlegm caught far back in his throat: He needed to spit it out, but he couldn't do it even though it was choking him.

In the afternoon they'd saddled the horses and ridden along the southwest boundary line, over even rougher terrain, to check fences and look for far-straying cattle. It had been after three, Messenger feeling butt-sprung and as if he were cooking in his own juices, when they found the injured and dying steer. The animal had wandered too close to the edge of a shallow wash, and the powdery earth had given way and pitched it down into the cut. One of its hind legs had been broken in the fall. The accident must have happened within the past twelve hours, Lonnie said grimly; otherwise the steer, weak and bleating with pain, would already be dead. He'd wasted no more time with words, just gone and gotten his carbine and put the animal out of his misery, while Messenger waited with the horses. Afterward the boy grew moodily silent again. When Messenger asked him if he was upset over losing a steer from an already thin herd, Lonnie shook his head. "It's not that," he said. "I just don't like to see anything suffer."

At the time the statement had impressed Messenger as deep-felt; he was even more convinced of it this morning. Lonnie's secret might be significant in some way, but it wasn't murderer's guilt that he had locked away inside. Lonnie Burgess was not capable of killing a family member in cold blood. Messenger was as sure of that as he'd been of anything, including Anna Roebuck's innocence, in the past week.

The rest of Sunday stretched out ahead of him: free time to pursue his quest. But he couldn't think of anything productive to do with it. He considered a trip to the Hardrock Tavern, a talk with the bartender and any customers he could locate who had witnessed the fight between Joe Hanratty and Dave Roebuck. It seemed futile, maybe even dangerous: asking prying questions in a bar was a good way of provoking trouble. Even if anybody knew what lay behind the fight, which was unlikely, the chances were slim to none that they would tell him. He'd have as much luck canvassing the town, ringing doorbells and trying to interrogate whoever answered.

He wasted the better part of an hour lying on the Airstream's rollaway bed, brooding over what he knew, the bits and pieces of information Dacy had confided. All that came of it was frustration. It was like blundering around in darkness and finally locating a wall, on the other side of which was light: You were close to the light, you knew it was there, but you couldn't get to it because you couldn't find a way to scale the wall.

What nagged at him, too, was the fact that nothing more had come of his move to the Burgess ranch than John T.'s angry outburst on Thursday evening. He'd expected other visitors, protests, or actions of some kind. Lull before the storm? The real murderer *had* to be wondering what he and Dacy were up to, and worried that whatever it was might lead to the truth. He wouldn't just sit back and wait and do nothing, would he? After the scheme with the snakes at Mackey's, it didn't seem likely. Cat-and-mouse game? That didn't seem likely either. Something was going to happen. And the sooner the better, whatever it was.

Past noon he took himself to the house, detouring around where Buster squatted at the end of the short chain. The rottweiler had come to a grudging acceptance of him, to the point where there were no more barks or snarls when he was near, but the dog's fur still bristled and the bright watchful eyes held no hint of friendliness. Dacy and Lonnie were both in the kitchen, companionably preparing what she called "Sunday dinner" even though it would be served at one o'clock. He hadn't had much appetite at breakfast, but the aroma of pot roast was seductive.

"Decide yet if you're joining us for dinner, Jim?"

"I'd like to, thanks."

"We'll set another place."

"Anything I can do to help?"

"Nope. Beer in the icebox, if you want one."

He helped himself to a bottle of Bud. "Dacy," he asked then, "would you have any family photos?"

Her glance was wry, Lonnie's unreadable. "Of Anna, you mean," she said. "Anna's family."

"Yes."

"A few. Why you want to look at them? They won't tell you anything."

"It's not that."

Lonnie said, "People who died the way they did—it's not right to look at pictures of them."

Anna's real to me, but her husband and daughter . . . not enough. I don't know their faces—just names, statistics. I want to see them as individuals. But he didn't put the thoughts into words; they would have sounded harsh, even cruel. Instead he said, "If you'd rather I didn't . . ."

"Oh, hell," Dacy said, "take your beer out to the porch. I'll bring the album."

He sat in a canvas sling chair, looking out over the broken, empty land. Heat pulsed on the flats; the effect was miragelike, interestingly so. He felt comfortable with the heat, the silence, the stark desolation. Comfortable with the ranch too, and the kind of work he'd done here the past few days. Quantum leaps from city apartment to sagebrush cattle ranch, from white-collar CPA to blue-collar ranch hand; yet he seemed to have made the transition with almost no effort. Funny. It was as if this place and this lifestyle, not San Francisco and the life he'd built there, were his natural ones. As if this was where he belonged.

Dacy appeared shortly, carrying a small photo album. She let him have it without speaking, then went to sit in another of the canvas chairs. She didn't watch him as he opened and began to page through the album; her gaze held on the heat shimmers in the distance.

Less than fifty photographs, most in color, most poorly framed and focused—snapshots taken at a birthday party, different Christmas gatherings, a barbecue at Anna's ranch. The ones of Tess covered a span of years from toddler to seven or eight. She'd been slender, dark blond, gray-eyed—unmistakably Anna's child. Active and animated too, with a smile that created cleftlike dimples. Dave Roebuck had been predictably handsome in a sharp-featured, unkempt, don't-give-a-damn way; his smile contained a smirk and his eyes a smoky sexuality that was evident even in these pictures.

Messenger didn't linger over any of them; it was less than five minutes from opening to closing the album. He knew their faces now: they were as real to him as Ms. Lonesome had been. Too real, in Tess's case.

Dacy said, "Satisfied?"

"Satisfied isn't the right word."

"What is the right word?"

"I don't know. Sad, maybe."

"Sad over a man and a kid you didn't know existed until a few days ago?"

"Is it so hard to believe?"

"For people like you and me, I guess not."

"Lonely people? Or just sad ourselves?"

"Both. Combination gives you empathy, right?"

"Right," he said. What he didn't say was that too often, at least in his case, the empathy got turned inward and became self-pity.

N O N E   O F   T H E M had much to say at dinner. But there was no strain in the silence, no lack of appetite: a quiet meal, period. Lonnie left as soon as they were finished, to spend the rest of the day with a friend in town. Messenger, without being asked, helped with the cleanup. Dacy's approval was evident; for all her independence and hard-shelled exterior, there was a part of her—just as there was a part of him—that responded to a measure of old-fashioned domesticity.

Today she seemed to want to prolong it, too. When they were done in the kitchen she asked, "You play chess, Jim?"

"I used to." With Doris, constantly during the time they'd been together; she was a big Bobby Fisher fan back then. "It's been years, though."

"How good were you?"

"Fair."

"I'm a little better than fair. My daddy taught me and I taught Lonnie. But he doesn't have enough patience to play well."

"I'm not sure I do either, these days. But if you'd like to play a game or two, I can probably provide some competition."

"I'll get the set."

"Question for you, first. How do you feel about music?"

"Some I like, some I don't."

"Jazz?"

"Not bad, what little I've heard."

"Well, I'm a jazz buff," he said, "have been for years. One of my passions." *One of the few.* "I own a fairly large collection of tapes and old records, and I brought a few cassettes with me. If you have a cassette player and wouldn't mind some background while we play, I could bring them in. . . ."

"Fine by me. Tape deck in the stereo unit over by the fireplace."

They played on the porch, where it was cooler, with the windows and front door open so they could better hear the music. He'd taken a little time in selecting tapes, because he wanted to give her an idea of the broad range of jazz, old and new. The three he'd settled on were a hot-jazz medley of artists and arrangements from the forties, a late-seventies Miles Davis album, and a mixed bag from improvisational swing to electric funk by such contemporaries as Joe Henderson, Charlie Hunter, Ornette Coleman, and Sonny Rollins. Dacy seemed to like them all. It pleased him that her strongest response was to the forties tape. She particularly favored Louis Armstrong's "Potato Head Blues," Sidney Bechet's "Polka Dot Rag," Bunk Johnson's "St. Louis Blues," and Billie Holiday's "Keep Me in Your Dreams"—all favorites of his.

Her enthusiasm led him, without realizing it until he was already launched, into a fervent discourse on jazz. He told her about its central laments of wasted youth and lost loves and bittersweet dreams, its shrieks and whispers of melancholy and pain, its mournful expressions of that all-gone feeling on the morning after a long, troubled night. He told her the old folk theory that the true originator of the blues was the mighty Mississippi; that W. C. Handy had stood on an old wooden bridge in Memphis, listened hard and close to Old Man River singing its lonesome songs, and lifted out "Memphis Blues," "St. Louis Blues," and others whole, words and all. He told her about the mechanics of improvisation, how each instrument worked to complement the others and what each brought in terms of harmony, melody, rhythm, and syncopation: the hard-driving moan of the trumpet, the hoarse bray of the alto sax, the insistent, sometimes raucous tones of the clarinet, the burry cry of the trombone, the steady throbbing four-four beat of the piano and the drums. And in the vocals, the glides and skidding elisions, the lyrical invention, the husky and tender tones that only good hot singers like Billie Holiday and Mildred Bailey and Bessie Smith could achieve.

Dacy didn't interrupt. Unlike too many people these days, she listened to and absorbed what she was hearing; and her interest seemed genuine. When he finally ran out of steam she gave him another of her long, speculative looks before she spoke.

"You really love that music, don't you, Jim."

"I do. Yes. It's . . . another world to me."

"Better than the one we live in?"

"Reflective of it. And a lot more honest."

"No argument there. You play an instrument yourself?"

"God, no. I was born with plenty of musical appreciation but not a scrap of musical talent. I tried trumpet, clarinet, and guitar when I first developed an interest in jazz in college. Hopeless in each case."

"So now you just listen and yearn."

He liked that; it made him smile. "Now I just listen and yearn."

He was no match for her on the chessboard. She played a calculated, determined game, and made no move without carefully considering it first; and like all good chess players, she was capable of thinking and planning several moves ahead. She checkmated him in twenty-two moves the first game, in nineteen the second.

Jazz and chess on an isolated desert ranch, he thought as he set up the board—an old one made in Mexico, its alabaster pieces chipped and worn smooth from long use—for a third game. Incongruous to some; perfectly natural to the two of them. Shared enjoyments between two people who at first meeting had seemed to have little or nothing in common. Easy and relaxed with each other. Kindred spirits: partners in loneliness. Maybe . . .

No, he warned himself, don't go jumping the gun. Some connection here, yes, but she's still the boss and you're still the hired hand and there's been nothing to suggest any change in that relationship. Jazz and chess on a Sunday afternoon—that's all this is. If it's enough for her, it ought to be enough for you, too.

She broke into his thoughts by saying, "We're about to have company."

Messenger glanced up from the board. Dacy was looking toward the valley road, at what he saw then were chutes of dust above and behind a fast-moving car or truck. The vehicle had passed the gate to John T.'s ranch; there was little doubt that it was headed here.

"Lonnie?" he said.

"No. He won't be back until late."

They waited without speaking. In half the time it took Coleman Hawkins to blow "Body and Soul" on his sweet tenor sax, the vehicle reached the Burgess gate and turned in—a high-riding Ford Bronco with a rack of spotlights atop the cab.

Dacy said, "That's Henry Ramirez's Bronco."

"Ramirez?"

"Jaime Orozco's son-in-law. You didn't meet him when you talked to Jaime?"

"No."

Messenger went ahead to meet the Bronco as it slid up. Buster had begun his usual furious barking and lunging; Dacy yelled at the dog to shut up and for once it obeyed. The man who swung down from the high cab was in his thirties, dark-mustached, and building a beer belly; he and Dacy exchanged greetings. The nod he offered Messenger was brief but not unfriendly.

"What brings you out, Henry?"

"Favor to Jaime."

Messenger asked eagerly, "He found out who owns the pickup with the broken antenna?"

"Little while ago," Ramirez said, nodding. "Man named Draper, Billy Draper."

"You know him?"

"No. Miner, works at the King Gypsum Mine. The other one's probably Pete Teal, another miner out there—word is the two of 'em are always together."

"Are they close to anyone in Beulah?"

Ramirez shrugged. "Not that Charley Wovoka knows about. You know Charley," he said to Dacy. "Bartender at the Wild Horse."

"Sure, I know him."

"Well, he's the one who tied them to the pickup. They come in once or twice a week to gamble. Sports book, mostly. Big sports fans. He saw Draper parking the truck once."

Messenger said, "If they're in the casino that often, there's a good chance John T. knows them, too."

"Wouldn't be surprised."

"Where's the King Gypsum Mine located?"

"Montezuma Range," Dacy said, "northwest of here. But you don't want to go out there, Jim, if that's what you're thinking."

"Why don't I?"

"Those gypsum miners are pretty rough boys," Ramirez said.

"That's one reason," Dacy said. "Another is that the King is privately owned and the land is posted and patrolled. It isn't likely you'd get past the front gate."

"So what do I do then? Espinosa won't do anything without the kind of proof he can't ignore—we all know that."

Ramirez said, "They'll be in the casino bar at six tomorrow night."

"Draper and Teal? How do you know?"

"Charley Wovoka says so. He says they come in every Monday night during football season. Watch the Monday night game on the Wild Horse's big-screen TV."

"That's it, then. Thanks, Henry. Tell Jaime I'm in his debt."

"Tell him yourself. He likes company." Ramirez paused. "Watch yourself, man. I wasn't kidding when I said those gypsum miners are rough trade."

When he and his Bronco were headed back to the valley road, Dacy said, "Henry's right. You'd be a fool to try bracing Draper and Teal by yourself."

The prospect should have worried him, maybe, but it didn't. He relished it the way he relished the imminent arrival of a vital piece of information in a complicated tax case: It would put him that much closer to a solution. "The casino bar's a public place," he said. "Besides, what other choice is there?"

"I can think of a couple."

"Such as?"

"We'll talk about it tomorrow."

"Why not now?"

"Tomorrow," Dacy said. "What we both need right now is the rest of Sunday."

19

HE COULDN'T SLEEP.

He was tired enough and his still-sore body needed the rest. But unlike the other nights he'd been here, there was a restlessness in him tonight that kept his eyes wide open. The prospect of confronting Billy Draper and Pete Teal tomorrow evening, probably. That, and the fact that the solution to the murders might be just that close.

After an hour or so he switched on the lamp beside the rollaway and got up to hunt for something to read. No books in the trailer; he hadn't thought to buy a paperback or two in Beulah, and neither Jaime Orozco nor any of the trailer's part-time occupants had left reading matter behind. There wasn't even a mail-order catalog or phone book to page through. Books in the house, but he couldn't go wandering in there without permission. Not at this hour, almost midnight by his watch. Unless Dacy was still up . . .

But she wasn't. The house, he saw when he opened the trailer door, was completely dark. He stood for a time, looking out and around. Warm, windless night, bright with more stars than he'd ever seen before, so many and so small-seeming they were like scatters of iridescent dust. No moon yet. Nothing stirring anywhere that he could see. Another hologram: Desert Night with Ranch Buildings.

On impulse he turned back inside, pulled on jeans and a shirt, leaving the shirt unbuttoned, and went outside. The air had a subtle fragrance compounded of earth, rock, sage, greasewood, horses, traces of woodsmoke. He sniffed it slowly several times, savoring it, thinking how much better the air quality was out here than in the city. Thinking how quiet it was.

Thinking, then, how lonesome it was.

Lonesome in the city, lonesome in the wide-open spaces. You couldn't get away from it no matter where you went, not the old Jim Messenger and not the new one. A more tolerable form of loneliness here, but loneliness just the same. He felt it like a dull ache deep inside him, a bruise on the skin of his soul.

The ache, or his awareness of the ache, intensified the restlessness, drove him away from the trailer, over past the stable and holding pens into open desert along one of the low hills. Above him the sky was immense. He walked at a retarded pace, peering up, occupying his mind by trying to pick out star clusters and individual stars. Milky Way, Orion's Belt, Big Dipper, Little Dipper. Rigel, Betegeuse, Arcturus. Sirius, the dog star—

A distant ululating howl broke the silence. Coyote's hunting song. The coincidence of the coyote starting up just as he located the dog star made him smile. But the smile didn't linger. The predator's song only added to the night's loneliness and deepened his own.

He walked on a short way. Other coyotes joined the first one in a yapping, trilling chorus that woke Buster and started him barking inside the house. Dacy had taken to keeping the rottweiler inside at night—not for protection, she'd told Messenger, smiling, but because he tended to go off into barking and chain-rattling fits when he was left out at night.

The coyote chorus tapered off and finally ceased; so did Buster's responses. The new quiet had an oppressive edge. Messenger turned and started back in longer strides. He'd sit in the car for a while, listen to one of the tapes with the volume turned down low. Jazz, the soft, soothing variety—Teagarden, maybe, or the King Cole Trio—sometimes helped him get to sleep at home.

As he passed the stable he could hear the horses stirring around. Coyotes must have woken them, too. He wondered if Buster had disturbed Dacy's sleep; if so, she hadn't put on a light. He went around the side of the trailer, over toward where the Subaru was parked.

He smelled cigarette smoke just before Dacy's voice said his name.

He swung around. She was sitting on the trailer's steps, a blob of white in the silvery darkness. The glowing end of her Marlboro made a red slash pattern as she moved it down from her mouth.

"How long have you been sitting there?"

"Few minutes. Saw you out prowling."

"I couldn't sleep. Restless for some reason."

"It's that kind of night."

He didn't have to ask her what she meant. "Feel like talking a while? Or do you just want to sit?"

"Both."

He sat down next to her. His hip touched hers; she didn't move away, and he was conscious of the taut warmth of her body under the cotton nightdress and loose wrapper she wore. She smelt of soap and toothpaste, bed and cigarette smoke. He felt a stirring in his loins, the first since the episode with Molene in San Francisco. *Don't get ideas. Boss and hired hand, remember?* But he didn't shift his leg. And she didn't move hers, either.

When she finished her cigarette and dropped the butt into the dirt, he said, "Dacy, I'd like to know something. But if it's too personal, just say so."

"Go ahead."

"What happened with your husband?"

She didn't answer. She sat hunched forward, forearms on her drawn-up knees.

"None of my business, right?"

"Probably not. But what the hell, it's all water under the bridge anyhow. I don't know where Howard is these days or what he's doing. Don't much care. Last I heard he was working on a ranch over near Ely, but that was four years ago."

"I meant what happened to the marriage. What broke the two of you up."

"I did. Like Popeye says, you can stands so much and you can't stands no more."

"No more of what?"

Dacy lit another cigarette. "Howard's a good old cowboy. You know what that means?"

"Not exactly."

"Two things he likes to do best is drink and fight. Work his ass off all week, ten-, twelve-hour days, and come the weekend—off to the nearest bar to get shitfaced with his buddies and raise some hell. At least once a month I'd get a call from the sheriff's office to come bail him out of the drunk tank."

"And you got tired of it."

"I got real tired of it after nine years. Tired of bailing him out, tired of nursing his hangovers and his cuts and bruises. Tired of being left alone with Lonnie. Tired of sleeping with a man who had nothing much to say to me except, 'Well, how about a little tonight, woman?'"

Messenger said, "That's a pretty sad story."

"Living it was a lot sadder than telling it."

"Was he always like that? Even in the beginning?"

"Not so bad at first. Just kept getting worse until it killed all the love either of us ever had."

"What did he say when you asked him for a divorce?"

"Didn't ask him, I told him."

"And?"

"Hardly a word. Drove off to town and got drunk and got in a fight that busted three of his ribs and ended up in jail. I bailed him out for the last time. Next day he loaded all his belongings into his pickup and left without saying good-bye to me or Lonnie. He stopped in town long enough to clean out our bank account—eight hundred dollars. I never saw or heard from him again."

"He didn't contest the divorce?"

"Didn't contest it, didn't hire a lawyer—nothing. I guess he figured the eight hundred was enough of a buyout. Judge gave Lonnie and me the ranch free and clear."

"When did all of that happen?"

"Seven years ago."

"There must've been someone else for you since then."

Dacy made a sound that might have been a chuckle. "You trying to find out if I've been celibate for seven years, Jim?"

"I didn't mean it that way—"

"Oh, hell, I know you didn't." She drew deeply on her cigarette; in the glow of the burning tobacco, her face had a masklike allure. The unruly topknot that always seemed to spring up when her hair was tousled made her even more attractive. "I've had relationships. One was with a doctor in Tonopah—the one who told me about catathymic crisis—that lasted a year and could've been permanent. He offered me a ring; I turned him down. That ended it between us."

"Why did you turn him down?"

"He wanted me to sell this place and move to Tonopah and live in his house in town. Be a mother to his two kids. I wouldn't have lasted six months in that kind of arrangement. I like running my own life, not three other people's. And I like living right here where I am."

"Alone."

"I'm not alone. I've got Lonnie."

"You know what I mean, Dacy. What happens when Lonnie gets older, moves out on his own?"

"Cross that bridge when we come to it."

"Do you miss being married? Want that kind of relationship again some day?"

"Sometimes. Most days, no."

"Because you're afraid of another failure? Or just of being hurt again?"

No response for five or six beats. Then, "Back off, Jim."

"If I touched a nerve, I'm sorry."

"Maybe you missed your calling," she said sardonically. "Kind of questions you ask, you'd've made a good head doctor."

He laughed, even though what she'd said wasn't funny. "Head doctor, heal thyself."

"Uh-huh. So what about you? You ever been married?"

"Once. A long time ago, in college."

"Divorced?"

"Yes."

"What busted yours up?"

He told her. All about Doris and their time together, Doris and the prelaw track star. He even found himself telling her an edited version of the incident at Candlestick Park, of what Doris had said to him on the ride home and how he'd only recently come to realize how right she'd been.

Dacy said, "That's a sad story, too. Almost as sad as mine."

"I know it."

"Well, we're a pair, aren't we? Birds of a feather."

"Ostriches. But I don't want to be that way anymore," Messenger said. "That's part of the reason I came here to Beulah, why I'm still here."

"Trying to find yourself?"

"No, a new self. The old one . . . well, Popeye applies there, too. You can stands so much, you can't stands no more."

"What's this new self gonna do when you get home?"

"I don't know yet. Cross that bridge when I come to it."

"You're a funny one, Jim. You really are."

"Sure. *Loco la cabeza.*"

"Not hardly. Just a guy having himself a midlife crisis. You think?"

"I think," he said, "I don't want to think anymore right now."

Again she was silent. A breeze had begun to blow, warmish at first, now suddenly cool. Carried by it, the pungent creosote odor of grease-wood overpowered the night's subtler scents.

Dacy moved beside him. She said, "Chill coming on. We'd better get to bed."

"All right."

They stood up together, and when she turned toward him she was still close—close enough for him to feel the full warmth of her body and the softness of her breath against his chin. The loin stir began again, more urgent than before. His mouth was dry.

"Dacy . . ."

"I know," she said.

"If you don't leave right now . . ."

"Who said anything about leaving? I didn't mean we should go to bed separately." She took his hand. "It's that kind of night, too," she said.

SHE MADE LOVE with more intensity than any woman he'd been with, Doris included. She held him fiercely with arms and legs and body, straining, pulling, clutching, as if she sought a fusion greater and more complete than the sexual. And she talked nonstop the whole time, urgings and entreaties, the words and her breath hot in his ear, now and then making little moaning sounds deep in her throat—all in a kind of desperate frenzy. It was over for both of them too quickly, even though he struggled to make it last. When her climax came it was in a series of shuddering spasms, as if she were being electrically shocked; and she pressed her mouth tight against his throat to muffle sounds that were almost like cries of pain.

It took a minute or so for her body to grow still afterward, her hands on him to relax. Panting, she whispered, "Oh Lord! Been so long I'd about forgotten how good it can feel."

"Best, the best . . ."

"Now don't pat yourself on the back, Jim."

"I wasn't. Other way around."

"Look at us, half off this damn bed. Wonder we didn't end up on the floor."

"Wouldn't have noticed if we had."

They disentangled and lay close, letting their breathing settle. Then Dacy laughed softly and said, "Funny."

"What is?"

"A week ago I didn't even know you existed. Then here you come out of nowhere and half turn my life upside down. Next thing I know I've got you working and living here. And now I've let you screw me. Maybe I'm the crazy one. You think?"

"Is that all it was for you?"

"All what was?"

"Just screwing."

"What was it for you?"

"Making love."

"Come on, Jim, you don't love me."

"How do you know I don't?"

"I don't love you."

"All right," he said.

"Two lonely people with itches to scratch, that's all."

"I don't think that's all. I don't think you do, either."

"Well, you're wrong. Isn't this enough for you? Being together like this?"

"For now."

"Now's all there is," Dacy said. "Now's all there ever is."

Outside the wind rattled something. A coyote yipped querulously in the far distance and then was still. Messenger shifted position, half turning so he could take one of her breasts in his hand.

Dacy said, "You like that saggy old tit?"

"It's not saggy. Not old, either."

"Maybe not quite. Pretty soon though."

"How old are you, Dacy?"

"Not supposed to ask a woman that question."

"I don't really care. I'm just curious."

"Well, it's no secret. Thirty-four, next birthday."

"Thirty-four's young."

"Not when you live in this desert, it isn't."

"Young," he insisted. "Young and beautiful."

"Shit."

"Don't say that word when you're in bed with me."

"Why not? It's just a word."

"I want to keep things clean between us."

"Clean," she said. "Whoo. No man's ever said *that* to me before."

"I'm serious, Dacy."

"All right." She yawned, stretched. "You should've seen them when I was eighteen. My boobs. So firm they hardly even bounced when I walked around naked. Skin so soft it was like satin."

"Still like satin."

She heard or sensed the change in his voice, the faint catch in the breath he took. "All this talk making you horny again?"

"Yes."

"No surprise. Men are easy."

"We don't have to make love again. . . ."

"Did I say I didn't want to?" She turned on her side, felt for him, and took hold of him gently. "So damn easy," she said.

SOMEONE WAS SHAKING him, roughly and urgently. Saying his name and telling him to wake up. "Wake up, Jim! Wake up!"

He struggled through sticky layers of sleep. The tugging hands lifted him; he sat up groggily. His eyelids felt glued together from sleep-grit. He couldn't seem to blink them open, had to use his fingers to get them unstuck.

The bedside lamp was on. He squinted against its glare.

Dacy.

She was fully dressed, her hair a wild tangle, her face dark with controlled fury. One clear look at her and he was completely awake.

"What is it?" he said. "What's wrong?"

"Anna's ranch," she said. "It's burning. Some son of a bitch set the whole damn place on fire."

20

DACY DROVE THE Jeep at better than sixty over the washboard road, its front end bobbing, hurling darts of yellow-white through the darkness with each bone rattling bump. Messenger sprawled next to her, his feet braced, holding on to both seat support and dash. In the rear, Lonnie sat hunched and jut-necked like a pointing hound. The boy hadn't said a word before they left the ranch, had barely acknowledged Messenger's presence. He wondered again now, as he had when they piled into the Jeep, if Lonnie knew or suspected his mother had spent part of the night in the trailer with the new hired hand. And if he did know or suspect, what he thought about it.

Ahead and to the north, the sky above the low hills radiated a smoky orange glow. The smoke rose in thickening billows; he could smell it, harsh and wood-flavored, on the fitful night breeze. The whole damn place, Dacy had said, and that was how it looked from down here. No way a blaze of that size could have kindled and spread naturally on a clear night like this. (It had been after 1:00 A.M. when she woke him; he'd checked the time as he pulled on his clothing.) Deliberately set . . . but who would torch a ghost ranch in the middle of the night? For what reason?

They were nearing the intersection with the rutted track that led to Anna's property. Above both the track and the valley road ahead, clear in the light from moon and stars, was a hanging residue of fine, talcum-pale dust. One or more cars had come down the track not long ago, going fast enough to raise dust clouds as high and thick as the ones in the

Jeep's wake, and then headed off toward town. Or to John T.'s ranch? Across the desert flats he could see the Roebuck property's night-lights—half a dozen spread out on tall poles. But just those lights, no others. Everybody there must still be asleep and unaware of the fire. Or pretending to be unaware of it.

Dacy braked to make the turn in front of the storage shed. The Jeep skidded, yawed, and for a sickening instant Messenger thought they would slide over into a roll. But she knew what she was doing; she spun the wheel to control the skid, and the tires caught, churning, and the Jeep's nose wobbled and then straightened out. The engine whined as she geared down for the climb to higher ground. The track's stone-studded and cratered surface forced her to hold their speed down; even so, she drove fast enough for juts of rock to scrape the undercarriage, dislodged fragments to explode against metal with pops like gunshots. Fast enough, too, to lift him up off the seat and whiplash his neck, even braced as he was, when a front tire slammed through a deep pothole.

The fireglow and the roiling smoke grew and spread in front of them. The wind carried the faint crackle of flames to his ears; and when the Jeep surged bouncing through the shallow canyon, started up the curving rise beyond, the wind laid the fire's heat across his skin. They were sixty or seventy yards from the closed gate before the high-licking flames appeared. In their reflection he saw the vehicle drawn off onto the hard-pan to one side.

Station wagon. Newish and light-colored.

John T.'s wagon?

Dacy brought them to a slewing stop. Messenger stumbled getting out; Lonnie caught his arm, kept him from falling, but the look the boy threw his way was unreadable. He leaned both hands against the gate, staring down into the hollow below.

Everything made of wood was sheeted with fire—ranch house, barn, chicken coop, pump shed, remains of corral and windmill. Burning tumbleweeds rolled crazily across the yard, as if the wind were playing some kind of fiery game of bowls. Clumps of sage and greasewood burned here and there on the flats, ignited by sparks and cinders. The heat beat against Messenger's face in pulsing waves.

He said to Darcy, "Nothing we can do."

"Didn't figure there would be."

"Okay by me," Lonnie said. It was the first he'd spoken and his voice held an odd, flat inflection. "Let it all burn to the ground."

"Why?" Messenger asked him. "It won't make the past any easier to forget."

"Might. What my uncle did—"

"Your uncle? What did he do?"

Lonnie shook his head.

Dacy said, "Never mind that," and Messenger saw that her gaze had shifted to the station wagon. "By God, if *he's* the firebug he'll pay for it one way or another."

"John T.?"

"That's his wagon."

"Why would he want to do this? And in the middle of the night?"

"Who the hell knows? He doesn't need a good reason for half of what he does."

She stalked angrily to the station wagon, Messenger and Lonnie following. She yanked the driver's door open, bent to look inside—and then jerked as if she'd been struck and froze in place. In the firelight the sudden play of emotions across her face was plainly visible. The one that alarmed him was a wincing revulsion.

"Sweet Jesus," she said softly. Then, louder, "Lonnie, you stay where you are. Stay there—I mean it!"

Tensely Messenger moved up beside her. One clear look into the wagon and his stomach kicked, his gorge rose; he gagged, locked throat and jaw muscles as he backed away. His eyes were on Dacy, but the image of the wagon's interior remained in sharper focus, as if it had been burned against the backs of his retinas.

Dead man lying in a twisted sprawl across the front seat. Black blood glistening where his face had been. Spatters of blood and brain matter and bone fragments gleaming on cushions, dashboard, window glass . . .

"What's the matter?" Lonnie's voice, raised above the roar of the fire. But he'd obeyed Dacy; he was poised ten paces shy of the station wagon. "He in there?"

"Dead. Shot."

"Shot? Somebody shot John T.?"

Blew his face away, the same as his brother. I wanted to make something happen but not this. Christ, not this!

"Get the flashlight out of the Jeep. Hurry."

Again Lonnie did as he was told. When he came back she went to meet him, and said something Messenger couldn't make out, then returned to the wagon and shone the light inside. Not long, just a few seconds. Then she switched it off and retreated to where Messenger stood and said in a thin, strained voice, "Well, he didn't shoot himself. No sign of the gun."

"Shotgun?"

"No. Large-caliber handgun, close range. One round, I think, but I couldn't tell for sure."

"Whoever did it was up here in another car. We didn't miss it by more than a few minutes."

"I know, I saw the dust, too."

Lonnie said sharply, "Somebody's coming."

Messenger hadn't heard anything, and still didn't for another few seconds. Then he picked up the faint race-and-whine of a car or truck engine laboring along the track.

Dacy was already moving at a half-run to the Jeep. By the time he joined her she had her rifle—a .25 bold-action Weatherby magnum, he'd been told—free of the clamps that held it behind the front seats. She jacked a cartridge into the chamber and stood with the weapon at port arms, watching downhill. None of them said anything as they waited. The silence had a charged quality made more acute by the thrumming crackle of the fire at their backs.

It was three or four minutes before headlights flicked erratically over the bare canyon walls below. The beams steadied; the vehicle took shape behind them. Pickup. It rattled uphill, and when it slid to a stop behind the Jeep, Messenger recognized it: Tom Spears's dirty green Ford. Spears was driving, and Joe Hanratty was with him.

The two men came out running, but they pulled up short when Dacy lifted the Weatherby. Their attention swung confusedly from her to the burning ranch buildings to John T.'s station wagon. Both had the look of men dragged out of sleep: uncombed hair, pouched eyes, wearing nightshirts tucked haphazardly into their jeans.

Hanratty said, "What's going on here, Dacy?"

"What does it look like?"

"You set that fire?"

"No. You?"

"Hell no. What's the idea throwing down on us?"

"Somebody set it. That's the idea."

"If we'd wanted to burn this fucking place, we'd've done it long ago. We don't know any more'n you do. I got up to take a leak, spotted the fireglow, and rousted Tom."

"Just Tom?"

"Wasn't any sense trying to wake up Mrs. Roebuck."

Spears said, "How long's John T. been here?"

"Long before we came."

"Chrissake, *he* didn't torch the place, did he?"

"We don't know who did it."

"Well, where's he at? John T.?"

From down in the hollow there was a thunderous rumble that turned their heads: The barn's roof had collapsed in a fountain of sparks and embers. Waves of heat rolled over them, driven by wind gusts. Sweat prickled Messenger's neck, flowed down from his armpits. The smoke-heavy air was raw in his lungs.

He said, "John T.'s in his car. He came up here to meet somebody, the way it looks."

"Meet who, this time of night?"

Hanratty said, "Why don't somebody ask him? Why ain't he over here by now?"

"Go take a look."

The cowhands exchanged a glance. Messenger watched them approach the station wagon; Hanratty opened the door. Their shocked reactions seemed genuine; Spears's "Shit!" was explosive. When they came back to the Jeep Hanratty looked shaken and angry, Spears stunned.

"We found him like that," Dacy told them, "five minutes before you got here."

Spears said, "Who'd do that to John T.?" in a sick voice.

"This bugger, for one." Hanratty had stepped close to Messenger, "By Christ, if you had anything to do with it—!"

"He didn't," Dacy said. "Jim was at my place all day and all evening."

"You with him the whole time?"

"Most of it."

"He could've snuck out after you went to bed—"

"No. We were together until after midnight."

"Yeah? Doing what, so late?"

"Talking, not that it's any of your business."

"Talking. Bet you were."

Messenger glanced at Lonnie. The boy didn't seem to be listening; he stood jut-necked again, either lost inside himself or fixated on the blazing skeletons below.

"You go to sleep easy every night, Joe?" Dacy asked coldly. "Sleep like a baby every night?"

Spears said, "What's the matter with you two? Jesus Christ, John T.'s lying over there dead with his face blowed off. Ain't anybody gonna *do* something?"

"He's right," Messenger said, "the sheriff has to be notified. Mrs. Roebuck, too."

"I don't want no part of that job."

"We'll go down and do it," Dacy said. "You and Joe stay here and keep watch until Ben Espinosa comes. All right?"

"No, it ain't all right," Hanratty said. "But I guess we got no choice." He moved even closer to Messenger and did his chest-poking number again. "John T. was a good man, twice the man you are, city boy. Maybe you didn't shoot him, but I'll tell you one thing, sure. He's dead on account of you. One way or another, no matter who done it, he's dead because you brought your sorry ass to Beulah."

Messenger kept silent. There was no point in arguing: Hanratty was right.

THE ROEBUCK RANCH seemed smaller up close than it did from a distance. Even so, there were twice as many buildings as Dacy managed—two barns, two trailers, a long structure that was probably a bunkhouse, several sheds, an old soddy that might have been the original home of John T.'s father and preserved for that reason. Plus a number of tumbledown ricks and a maze of corrals and cattle-loading chutes. The main ranch house was of native stone and shaded by geometric rows of cottonwoods, but it wasn't much larger than Dacy's.

The house remained dark as she piloted the Jeep across the floodlit yard. In front she switched off engine and lights, told Lonnie to stay put, and she and Messenger went to the door. He banged an old-fashioned horseshoe knocker; the thudding noise it made echoed like a thunderclap. But it produced no response. He had to use the knocker half a dozen times, with increasing force, before a light finally went on inside.

When Lizbeth Roebuck opened the door, Messenger thought immediately that she'd been hard to wake because she was passed out drunk. Bleary-eyed, puffy-cheeked, the smell of stale bourbon on her breath and leaking from her pores; sexless and sagging inside a blue chenille bathrobe. Steady enough on her feet, though—the carefully cultivated balance of the habitual alcoholic.

She focused on Dacy and said, "So it's you. What's the idea making so much noise?" Her husky voice was almost a growl, but you had to listen close to hear the slur in it.

"Something's happened, Liz. We need to come in."

"You know what time it is?"

"It's important. Talk to you and use your phone."

"Phone? What for?"

"Call the sheriff."

"Sheriff," she said. She backed up, slowly, to let them enter. "What happened?"

"It's bad, Liz. You'd better sit down."

"Hell with that. Tell me."

"No way to say it except straight out. John T.'s dead."

No reaction, not even the flicker of an eyelid.

"Lizbeth? I said John T.'s dead."

"I heard you. How?"

"Somebody set fire to Anna's ranch. Burned everything that was left. Maybe John T., maybe not—but he was there. Still is. Whoever else was there shot him inside his station wagon."

Still no reaction. Messenger remembered Dacy telling him Lizbeth Roebuck was a cold fish. Could be that was the reason, or it could be shock. The other possibility was that the news of her husband's death *wasn't* news to her.

A stretch of silence; then she said, "Phone's in the kitchen," and went slowly to a red leather wet bar that dominated one wall. Neither Dacy nor Messenger moved. Lizbeth poured a tumbler three-quarters full of sour-mash bourbon and drank it slowly, steadily, pausing for air only once, until the glass was empty. She set it down and then stood as she had before, rigid, expressionless. "Well?" she said to Dacy. "I told you where the phone is. Go make your call."

"I will."

"But first, get him out of here." She wasn't looking at Messenger; she hadn't looked at him the entire time. "I don't want that bastard in my house."

"Jim didn't have anything to do with—"

"Get him out. Tell him get the fuck out right now."

Dacy said, "Jim . . ."

He nodded. "I'll be with Lonnie."

Lizbeth Roebuck was still talking to Dacy, saying, "Out, out, get him the fuck out of my house," when he opened the door and went outside.

The wind had died again; the hush over the ranch yard and buildings had a layered quality, like the hushes he was used to on foggy nights in San Francisco. The sky above the hills to the north was still flushed and smoke-stained, but the red glow was fading and the smoke columns had thinned and shortened. By the time Ben Espinosa arrived, the fire would be mostly spent and there'd be nothing left of Anna's ranch except charred wooden bones.

Lonnie was sitting quietly in the Jeep, head tipped back, a lighted cigarette in one corner of his mouth. It was the first time Messenger had seen him using tobacco of any kind.

"She didn't want me in her house," he said as he climbed in on the passenger side. "Mrs. Roebuck."

"That surprise you?"

"No."

"What'd she say about John T.?"

"Nothing. Whatever she feels, she didn't say or show it."

"Yeah, well, that's the way she is. Nobody knows what goes on inside her head."

"How about you, Lonnie? What's going on inside your head right now?"

"About John T.?" He drew on the cigarette without taking it from his mouth. "I didn't much like him, you know that. But I hate it when anybody suffers or dies sudden—anybody or anything. I guess mostly how I feel is bad."

"That's how I feel, too."

"Yeah? I figured you'd be happy."

"Why would you figure that?"

"You think whoever shot John T. killed my uncle and Tess, that it's all part of the same thing. Don't you?"

"Don't *you*, now?"

"No. Two separate things that don't have anything to do with each other."

"Lonnie . . . when we first got to the fire you started to say something about your uncle. 'What my uncle did—' You remember that?"

"I remember."

"Finish the sentence. What did he do that makes you hate him so much?"

Messenger thought he wasn't going to get an answer. But then, as Lonnie flicked away what remained of his cigarette, "You know what he did."

"No, I don't."

"All the women he cheated with."

"That isn't it."

"How do you know it isn't? You don't know anything."

"What did he do, Lonnie?"

"No, goddamn it. I don't want to talk about it."

"You do want to talk about it. It's half choking you, and if you don't spit it out pretty soon you'll strangle on it. I know; I keep things locked up inside me, too."

Another silence, shorter this time. "I can't tell you," Lonnie said. "I couldn't even tell Ma."

"Sometimes it's easier for a man to talk to another man. Even one he hasn't known for long."

"I can't. I just . . . can't."

"All right. But if you change your mind . . ."

They sat in the quiet dark, Messenger unmoving, Lonnie restlessly shifting position, lighting another cigarette and then discarding it after two drags. A voice rose from inside the house—Lizbeth Roebuck's, making some kind of drunken protest that didn't last long. The smoky fireglow died away behind the hills, leaving the sky clean again. The immense canopy of stars seemed even brighter, not quite real, like a heavenly map in a planetarium.

And Lonnie said suddenly, as if the words were being torn out of him, "He messed with her."

" . . . Say that again?"

"My uncle. Tess. He messed with her."

"Sexually abused her?"

"I don't know if he . . . you know. But he touched her, played around with her. More than once."

Jesus. "How do you know, Lonnie? Did you see him touch her?"

"No. She told me."

"When?"

"Not long before she was killed. A few days." The words came spilling out of him now, a purge like the emptying of a pus pocket. His voice was heavy with anguish. "She used to like to be tickled, it was a game we all played with her. I was in the barn at our place forking hay and she came in—they were down visiting that day—she came in and I started tickling her. She said, 'Stop it, stop it!' and then she started to bawl. She didn't want to tell me but I got it out of her. I didn't want to believe it but it was the truth, she wasn't making it up."

"What did you do then?"

"I didn't know what to do. I wanted to break his fucking head—that's what I *should* have done. Instead I told Tess . . . I said she . . ."

"You told her to tell her mother."

"Yeah. Tell her mother. Because I didn't want to do it myself."

"You did the right thing. Better for it to come from her."

"That's what I thought. I thought my aunt'd believe her easier than she would me. I made Tess promise she'd tell. I made her promise. . . ."

"You think she did tell," Messenger said. "You think that's the reason your aunt went crazy and killed them both."

"She must've blamed Tess as much as him. But it wasn't Tess's fault. Him, it was his fault. And mine."

"No, Lonnie—"

"Mine. That's why I couldn't tell Ma or anyone afterward. It's *my* fault Tess is dead!"

21

IT WAS THE heat that finally woke him. The interior of the Airstream trailer was like a sauna: He lay marinating in his own sweat, the sheets sodden and tangled around him. What time was it? The sun must be high already for it to be so hot in here. . . .

He rolled over, fumbling for his wristwatch. Almost eleven. That late? Dacy must have gotten up by now; why hadn't she called him? Get moving, he thought, there's work to do. But he couldn't seem to make his body respond. He felt logy, desensitized: not enough sleep, and the few hours he'd had had been too shallow and exhausted to be restful. Almost dawn before Sheriff Espinosa had allowed them to leave the Roebuck ranch, and another hour after that before he'd been able to drift deeper than a fitful doze.

He lay listening to the hot silence. As sweat-soaked as the bedclothes were, he could still smell Dacy's scent on the sheets and pillowcase. That part of last night was clear in his memory: their lovemaking, everything they'd said to each other. But most of the rest had a blurred quality, like a poor black-and-white film print. In particular the scenes involving Espinosa's endless questions, and the long, pointless drive back to Anna's ranch that he'd made them take with him. The baked apple had been antagonistic enough toward him, though he'd seemed more bemused than anything by John T.'s death: a man who had suddenly lost his leader and didn't quite know how to handle the situation. If it hadn't been for the presence of Dacy and Lonnie, Espinosa's hostility would have had a sharper focus and Jim Messenger might well have spent a rough night in a jail cell. He was the only person the sheriff could conceive of who had a motive for murdering another Roebuck.

The only other parts of the night that were clear to him were the image of John T.'s bloodied corpse, and Lonnie's revelation. There'd been no time at John T.'s ranch to think about what Lonnie had told him, to sort out its implications and possibilities; Dacy had come out of the house right afterward, and not long after that Espinosa and his two deputies arrived. No time to work on it now, either. He was too dull-witted from sleep and the trapped heat.

He rested another couple of minutes, then dragged himself off the rollaway and into the tiny shower stall. The tepid water woke him up a little more. By the time he'd brushed his teeth, run a comb through his hair, and dressed, he was in a functioning state again.

As soon as he stepped out of the trailer he saw Dacy. She was standing in the yard, facing out toward the valley road; and she clutched her rifle by its barrel, the butt down in the dirt at her side. What had her attention was a small, loose bunching of half a dozen vehicles and twice that many men and women on the road just beyond her gate. Like a ragtag encampment, he thought, that had sprung up overnight.

She heard him approaching and swiveled her head. "There you are. I was fixing to go pound on the door."

"You should have. I didn't mean to sleep so long."

"Well, it was a long damn night."

"What's going on out there?"

"Vultures," she said bitterly. "Goddamn bone pickers."

"Media?"

"Mostly. Some longnecker from town, too. One of those TV trucks drove in a while ago and I ran the bastards off. I put up with that trespass shit when Tess and Dave were killed, but not this time. Not *this* time."

She hadn't slept much either; that was plain. Lines of fatigue were shaped out around her eyes, and bloody-looking veins mottled the pupils. Her hair was uncombed: the topknot had a curl in it like Woody Woodpecker's. The fact that she looked vulnerable this morning made her even more desirable. Male ego: man the protector, the comforter. Right. Put that thought into words, and she'd probably laugh in his face.

He wondered if, after all, he was in love with her.

He had no reliable measuring stick for his feelings. The only other woman he'd thought he loved was Doris, but with her it had been little more than body heat; they'd been at each other like rabbits before and for a while after their marriage. He'd been hurt when she divorced him, but it hadn't been the kind of wrenching, lingering pain of something ripped loose from deep inside. No, he hadn't really loved Doris; time had taught him that. His feelings for Dacy were stronger, more emotional. A sense of kinship and the sort of bond that could lead to oneness. But there was no use in kidding himself—the potential oneness might be all one-sided. And transitory and delusional on his part, an outgrowth of the passion they'd shared last night. Middle-aged body heat could fool a lonely man just as easily as teenage body heat could fool an immature one.

Take it slow, he thought. Don't push it. There's too much else going on right now.

"Where's Lonnie?" he asked.

"Gone. He got up before I did, saddled his horse, and rode off. Christ knows where."

Messenger closed fingers lightly around her arm. She didn't draw away from his touch, but she didn't respond to it, either. "Dacy, let's go inside. We need to talk."

"If it's about you and me—"

"It isn't."

"Good, because this isn't the time."

"I know it."

They went into the kitchen, Dacy leaving her Weatherby propped against the wall near the front door. She said, "Coffee's on the stove. You look like you could use some."

"The biggest mug you've got."

"Cupboard above the sink."

He found the mug, poured coffee. Thick and bitter—just what he needed.

Dacy said, "Something's eating on Lonnie. And I don't think it's what happened to John T."

"It isn't. Not directly."

"That mean you know what it is?"

"Yes. That's what we need to talk about. He knows something that's been cutting him up inside ever since Tess and his uncle were murdered. He spit it out to me last night, while you were in with Liz Roebuck."

"Spit what out? What could he know?"

"He believes he's responsible for Tess's death."

"He . . . *what*?"

"He's not, I tried to convince him of that, but he's too guilt-ridden to listen to the truth."

"For God's sake, Jim, don't dance with me. Just say it."

He told her. Exactly what Lonnie had told him.

She took it stoically. But when he was done she sank onto one of the dinette chairs and slapped the table, hard, with the palm of her hand—a gesture of angry frustration. "That poor kid. Both those poor kids. If he'd just told me . . ."

"He couldn't," Messenger said. "You're too close; he was afraid you'd hate him."

"As if I could. All my hate's for the lowlife son of a bitch Anna married. If she did blow his head off she had every right. I'd've done it myself if I'd known."

"She didn't kill anybody. You don't believe that anymore, after what happened to John T.?"

"No, not anymore."

"Lonnie does. He'll go right on believing it until the real murderer is exposed."

"Maybe if I talked to him . . ."

"It'd do more harm than good. He can't face you as long as he feels responsible."

"He ask you not to tell me?"

"Yes."

"Then why did you?"

"You have a right to know," Messenger said. "Too many secrets in Beulah as it is."

"And it may have something to do with the killings and two heads are better than one. All right. But I don't see how it could."

"Neither do I, right now. One thing I'm fairly sure of: Tess didn't tell her mother, in spite of what Lonnie believes."

"What makes you so sure?"

"Anna kept a pocket watch that Dave's father gave him when he was a boy; it's among her effects in San Francisco. She wouldn't have held on to a memento like that if she'd known he was molesting her daughter."

"Hell, no, she wouldn't. Child abuse sickened her as much as it does me."

"Would she've let on to you if she'd known or suspected?"

"Not right away, maybe. But sooner or later."

Messenger said, "I wonder—" but he didn't finish the thought or the sentence. Outside Buster began a new round of barking; and a few seconds later Messenger heard the rattle and growl of an incoming car.

Dacy was on her feet. She said, "If that's another goddamn TV truck . . ." and hurried to the front door, scooping up her rifle as she opened it. He followed her onto the porch.

Not the media this time; the car that pulled up in front was a state police cruiser with two occupants. The driver was a beefy individual dressed in a Western-style suit, Stetson hat, and string tie. His passenger was Ben Espinosa.

Dacy leaned the Weatherby against the porch railing as the two men climbed out. "More bullshit," she said to Messenger in an undertone. But her expression, now, was one of weary resignation.

The beefy man was a state police investigator named Loes. Despite his outfit, he was strictly professional: direct, businesslike manner and the diction of a college graduate. Espinosa was deferential to him. As he would be to anyone in a position of authority, Messenger thought. The sheriff looked haggard, and relieved to have the investigation out of his hands. But his gaze, whenever it cut to Messenger, showed an antipathy that bordered on hatred.

He blames me. The whole town does by now. Hypocrites. If I'm responsible for John T., they're responsible for Anna. Blood on their hands long before there was any on mine.

Loes questioned Dacy and him in greater detail than Espinosa had. His attitude was noncommittal: just a good, thorough cop doing his job without any bias. From the questions, Messenger determined that the authorities still had no idea why John T. had gone to his brother's ranch at such a late hour, or whom he had met there. He put this into words, and Loes confirmed it.

"Mr. Roebuck was last seen at the casino around ten o'clock," he said. "He didn't go home from there. No one seems to know where he went."

"Did his wife expect him?"

"She says she didn't. He kept irregular hours."

Dacy said, "It could've been a woman he met."

178 / BILL PRONZINI

"What makes you say that, Mrs. Burgess?"

"Nothing. It was just a suggestion."

"Was he involved with a woman, to your knowledge?"

"Not to my knowledge, no. But it's two miles from the valley road up there—two miles of bad road, especially at night. Why go all that way unless you wanted to make sure you were alone with whoever you were meeting?"

"A good point," Loes said. "But I can make another just as good: There are hundreds of places around Beulah where a man and a woman could meet in complete privacy. Why would Mr. Roebuck pick his brother's ranch, where his brother was murdered?"

"I can't answer that. Maybe on account of it's close to his own property."

"An even better reason to pick a spot farther away."

"Yeah. See what you mean."

Messenger said, "You must've searched the area up there pretty thoroughly. Find anything at all?"

"Nothing conclusive."

"Well, we did find the gun," Espinosa said.

Loes slanted a look at him. Then he shrugged and said, "Yes, we found the murder weapon. Thirty-eight-caliber Ruger Magnum loaded with hollow-points. Evidently it was thrown away into the scrub after the shooting."

"Hollow-point bullets? Any significance in that?"

"Hell," Espinosa said, "everybody out here uses 'em."

"Including you, Sheriff?"

"Watch what you say to me, man. I got no patience left with you."

Loes said, "Hang on to your temper, Ben." Then, to Messenger, "No significance. Not under the circumstances."

"How many times was he shot?"

"Just once. A thirty-eight hollow-point fired at point-blank range does considerable damage."

"What about fingerprints on the gun?"

"Smudged."

"I don't suppose it was registered?"

"Yes. To Mr. Roebuck. According to his wife he kept it in the glove compartment of his car."

"Then whoever shot him knew him well enough to know that."

"Or someone he didn't know found the gun by accident," Loes said. "Or took it away from him during an argument."

A few more questions, a tight-lipped warning from Espinosa—"I'll be seeing you again, Messenger, so you stay where you can be found"—and the two men folded themselves back into the cruiser. Dacy watched it all the way to the gate, shading her eyes against splinters of sunlight that came off the rear window. When Loes made the turn onto the valley road, she turned to Messenger.

"We may've just made a mistake, you know."

"Mistake?"

"Not telling Loes about Billy Draper and Pete Teal."

"I thought about it," he said. "But I didn't want to say anything in front of Espinosa. He thinks I exaggerated what happened at Mackey's and he'd claim I was trying to shift suspicion. Besides, we don't have anything definite against them yet."

"Could be one of them shot John T."

"Possible, if he was the one who hired them. A falling-out over money or something like that. But I still think the same person killed both Roebucks, and maybe that person is the one who paid Draper and Teal. If I can get a name out of them, then I'll have something definite to take to Loes."

"Still fixing to brace those two tonight?"

"I have to, Dacy."

"Even if it turns out to be a bigger mistake."

"It won't."

"Man's gotta do what a man's gotta do, right?"

"Sometimes. If it means enough to him."

"Well, it's your ass," she said, thin-lipped. "If you wind up in the hospital or in jail, don't call me. I had all I can stand of that crap with my ex."

"I can take care of myself. Don't worry."

"I won't," she said, and brushed past him and walked away to the stable.

22

DACY SAID FLATLY, "I'm going with you. No arguments."

"I don't think that's a good idea. . . ."

"I do. I'm tired of macho bullshit."

"Macho? That has nothing to do with—"

"Doesn't it? Male ego, pure and simple. You figure you're man enough to handle any kind of trouble. Well, you're dead wrong."

He said, "I thought you weren't going to worry about me."

"Yeah, well, I changed my mind. I'd feel the same about a poor dumb animal that was about to blunder into a nest of scorpions."

She'd been waiting when he emerged from the trailer at a few minutes past five. Like him, she had spent the afternoon doing chores, though not as compulsively: He'd gone on a nonstop four-hour binge of sawing boards and hammering nails and putting the new pane in the kitchen window, killing time with physical labor. And like him, she'd washed up and changed clothes. She wore an old chambray shirt, one that had probably belonged to her ex-husband, its tails hanging loose over faded jeans. Her hair had been wet-combed and the stubborn curl plastered down. There was little of the strain and fatigue in her eyes that dulled his own, but he sensed the tension in her just the same. He wore his like a badge; hers was all hidden inside.

He said, "There won't be any trouble. Draper and Teal won't make a scene in a public place like the casino."

She laughed, a sound like a coyote bark. "You really are a babe in the desert, you know that? As much shit happens in public places as in private ones in this county. You come on tough to those two boys, you're liable to wind up a big stain on the floor. And they'd make it look like you're the one at fault."

"I wasn't planning to get tough with them."

"Sweet-talk 'em into telling you the truth? Appeal to their reasonable sides, man to man?"

"Don't talk down to me, Dacy."

"I'm not. Just trying to make you understand that this is my turf and I know it a hell of a lot better than you ever could. I know how to handle men like Draper and Teal. You don't."

"Handle them how?"

"That's my lookout."

"You want to do all the talking, is that it?"

"What I want," she said slowly and distinctly, as if she were talking to a younger version of her son, "is for you to let me call the shots. And to keep quiet except to follow my lead. Think you can do that?"

"If it means getting answers."

"It does. Okay, then? Settled?"

"What about Lonnie? Don't you want to be here when he decides to come home?"

"What for? We can't talk about what's bothering him—you made that clear enough. You're the one who needs me tonight, not Lonnie."

Not just tonight and in more ways than one.

"Well?" she said.

He'd already given in. He wouldn't be much good at this sort of tricky improvisation and she would; wiser for him to play sideman and let her handle the solo. He said, "All right. We'll do it your way."

They took the Jeep and rode most of the distance across the valley in silence. Messenger broke it as they neared the Y fork by asking, "Dacy, does it surprise you that Dave Roebuck was the kind of man who'd molest his own daughter?"

Quick sidelong glance. "Back to that subject, are we?"

"Not talking about it won't make it any less painful."

"I haven't been avoiding it. Just brooding on it."

"And?"

"It surprises me some, yeah. No woman was safe around that bastard, but I never knew him to go after one that wasn't of legal age."

"A recent aberration, then. Degenerates can always find a new low to sink to."

"I reckon. Lonnie was sure it hadn't gone as far as actual sex? Just fondling?"

"That's what Tess told him."

"At least she didn't have to endure rape before she died. Damn little consolation, but at least that."

"Did she have any adult friends?"

"You mean somebody she'd confide in?"

"Besides you and Lonnie."

"No, I don't think so. Not many people went out there to visit. If she couldn't bring herself to tell Anna or me, and Lonnie had to practically drag it out of her . . . no, she didn't tell anybody else."

"Roebuck liked to brag. Maybe he told someone."

"About a thing like that? He'd have been lynched."

"Let something slip, then. When he was drunk."

"Not likely. Not in the bars he drank in. One thing that boy didn't have was a death wish, drunk or sober."

Drunk or sober. The bars he drank in . . .

"The Hardrock Tavern," he said. He sat up straighter. "The fight at the Hardrock Tavern!"

"Fight he had with Joe Hanratty? What about it?"

"We're not going straight to the casino. I want to make another stop first."

"Where?"

"Lynette Carey's house."

"What for? What've you got in your head now?"

"She has a child a year older than Tess was," Messenger said. "I can't recall her or anybody else saying if it's a boy or girl. Girl?"

"That's right. Karen."

"Lynette broke up with Roebuck suddenly, remember? For no clear reason. And just as suddenly her brother attacked him at the Hardrock. And neither Lynette nor Hanratty will talk about why." *Some things you don't talk about. Not even to friends, let alone strangers.* Lynette's words to him in the Saddle Bar.

"My God, you don't think—"

"I do think," he said. "Roebuck had been molesting Tess; isn't it just as likely he'd try to molest somebody else's daughter, too?"

Small, built of cinder blocks overlain with cheap, sand-scoured aluminum siding, Lynette Carey's house squatted on a hillside south of City Hall. A scraggly cactus garden composed the front yard. Half a dozen child's toys and a forgotten sweater strewn among the plants gave the yard an afflicted look, like the aftermath of a windstorm or flash flood on a small section of desert topography.

Dacy said as they pulled up in front, "You'd better let me do most of the talking here, too."

"Do you and Lynette get along?"

"Well as any two people in this town."

Lynette opened the door to Messenger's knock. She had exchanged her uniform for a pair of crotch-tight shorts and a halter top that revealed swelling white flesh spattered with freckles. Cool air from a noisy air conditioner flowed out around her. The other loud noise from within was the blather of a television cartoon show.

A scowl pulled Lynette's round face out of shape. "Well, well, look who's here. Bonnie and Clyde."

Dacy said, "Now what does that mean?"

"Half the town thinks you two murdered John T. last night. They don't see how it could've been anybody else. You should hear some of the reasons they're throwing around."

"That half include you?"

"Nope. I think he got what he deserved, whoever shot his face off. So what brings you around? Looking for a hideout?"

"Some things that need talking about."

"Such as?"

"In private, Lynette. All right if we come in?"

The big woman hesitated, then shrugged and stood aside for them. The interior was cool from the rattling air conditioner and as chaotic as the front yard. Through a doorway off the hall, Messenger could see the Roadrunner and Wile E. Coyote assaulting each other on a snow-flecked TV screen. Lying on the carpet in front of the set, chin in cupped hands, was a plump, dark-haired girl of nine or ten, dressed in T-shirt and shorts. She might have been in a hypnotic trance for all she moved; as far as she was concerned, she was alone in the house with the beep-beeping bird and the witless predator.

"That's Karen," Lynette said to him, "my daughter. She's a TV junkie—likely to grow up deaf and blind. Come on in the kitchen where it's quiet." And when she'd shut the three of them inside the cramped, yellow-walled kitchen, "How about a beer? Some cold Bud in the fridge."

Dacy said, "No, nothing," and Messenger shook his head.

Lynette opened a bottle for herself, sat with it at a Formica-topped table. But when neither of them moved to join her, she sighed and stood up again.

Messenger asked her, "Why do you think John T. got what he deserved?"

"Why? He was an arrogant bastard, that's why. All the Roebucks were and good riddance to the last of the breed."

"That sounds as though you knew him as well as you knew his brother."

"What do you mean by that?"

"Just what I said."

"Me and John T.? You're nuts, if that's what you think. He never interested me. I wouldn't've spread my legs for that *chingado* if he'd had the last dick in Nevada."

"But another woman besides his wife might have."

"You saying some woman he was laying killed him?"

"It's one possible explanation."

"That why you came? You got an idea *I* blew John T. away?"

Dacy said, "No, that's not why we're here."

"Well, I didn't. I wouldn't've met him in the middle of town at high noon to spit in his face. I don't have any damn reason to want him dead or to burn up what was left of Anna's ranch."

"But you did have a reason to want Dave dead."

"Dave? Why bring him up?"

"He's what brought us here, Lynette."

"Oh, so that's it. Well, you're dead wrong there, too. I never had a reason to want him dead."

"We figure you did. Same one that made you bust up with him. Same one that set Joe on him at the Hardrock."

"I don't know what you're talking about. . . ."

"Karen, he was messing with Karen. That's it, isn't it?"

She reacted as if Dacy had slapped her. "No," she said. Then, more forcefully, "No!"

"Lynette, I'm about to tell you something we found out last night, something nobody knows except Jim and me and Lonnie."

"Found out—?"

"Dave was molesting Tess."

"Oh Jesus!"

"It's true. For a month or more before he died."

"You mean he—"

"No, he didn't rape her. Touched her, that was as far as it went."

"Touched her." Lynette slumped onto one of the chairs. Anger puckered her mouth, drew the skin tight over her cheekbones. "I should've known," she said.

"He did the same with Karen, didn't he."

"Yeah."

"How many times?"

"Just once. She told me right afterward; I taught her right."

"What'd you do?"

"Went after him with a butcher knife. He took it away from me before I could cut him. Then he tried to laugh the whole thing off. Said I was making a mountain out of a molehill." She took a long, nervous swallow from her beer. Foam dribbled from a corner of her mouth; she didn't bother to wipe it away. "I'd been out at the store and Karen was in the tub. He walked in on her . . . just wanted to help her wash, he said . . . fuckin' pervert. Bad enough with her, but his own little girl . . ."

"Why didn't you report him to the sheriff?" Messenger asked.

"What good would it've done?" she said bitterly. "That kind of charge against a Roebuck in this town? Besides, I couldn't put her through a thing like that, all the damn questions. If he'd actually raped her . . . but just messing around, her word against his . . . I couldn't do it. Best thing for us was to get shut of that pig and just forget it ever happened."

"You told Joe about it."

"No. Karen told him. Blurted it out. If I hadn't been there to calm him down, he'd have been the one to blow Dave's head off. I should've let him get his gun, even if he is my brother. Then Tess might still be alive."

"Maybe you only stopped him temporarily."

"No. I told you before, it wasn't Joe. He brooded about it, sure, who wouldn't? And when he saw Dave at the Hardrock he lost it and started beating on him. But that's all he did. He'd never hurt a kid, not in a million years."

"Neither would Anna," Dacy said. "She didn't kill either of them. I'm as sure of that now as you are about Joe."

Lynette blinked up at her. "Dave," she said. "He would."

"Would what?"

"Hurt a kid. Molesting his own flesh and blood is hurting her, isn't it? Not much of a step from that to worse. What if he tried to . . . you know, with Tess, and she got free and ran off to tell on him? What if *he* busted her skull with that rock to keep her quiet? And Anna came home and saw it or saw him putting her in the well?"

"My God."

"It could've happened that way, couldn't it? He's the one who killed Tess and that's why Anna killed him?"

23

THE WILD HORSE Casino was closed. Parking lot empty, windows dark, the high bucking stallion frozen and lightless.

"Damn!" Messenger said. "They must've shut down because of John T. Now we'll have to go out to the gypsum mine to talk to Draper and Teal."

"Don't jump the gun, Jim. Casino bar's not the only place in town with a big-screen TV."

"How many others?"

"Two. Murphy's and the Hardrock Tavern."

"Will either of them be open?"

"Both. They're shitkicker bars; they wouldn't have shut down the day after Christ died."

"Which one's closer?"

Dacy said, "Murphy's," and swung the Jeep into an illegal U-turn across the highway.

Except for sporadic traffic passing through, the town had an empty look and feel. No pedestrians, not many parked cars, most of the businesses along Main—even the ones that normally stayed open late—closed and dark. Town in mourning for its boss hog, he thought. That was part of it, anyway; the other part was fear. Three brutal murders in less than a year, including the last two surviving members of one of Beulah's pioneer families. People had closed ranks, locked windows and doors, dusted off pistols and rifles and shotguns. Their fear made them angry and skittish, and the combination of all three made them dangerous. It was a bad time for him to be roaming around here with night coming on, even in Dacy's company. They'd turned on Anna, one of their own, and hounded her out of Beulah and eventually into oblivion in a tubful of bloody water. It wouldn't take much for them to turn on the man they blamed for John T.'s murder, an outsider, a pariah. And if that happened, they wouldn't settle for just driving him away.

The wind was hot and abrasive against his face as they dipped downhill past the new high school. He tasted the dryness, felt the tension in his body. But he wasn't afraid. Fear all around him, hidden and gathering, but none in him. It occurred to him that he was no longer in a state of crisis or flux; no longer the same person he'd been a week ago, and not even a shadow of the one he'd been before Ms. Lonesome came into his life. The internal forces had finished their work and the changeling process was complete. Thirty-seven years old, and he'd finally gone through the chrysalis stage—his own personal rite of passage.

Dacy's voice dragged him out of himself. " . . . Lynette said before we left?"

"What?"

"Before we left her. What she said about Dave killing Tess and Anna shooting him because of it. You think it could've happened that way?"

"No," he said. *And yet . . .* "And you don't either."

"Tell me why I don't. Ease my mind."

"If it'd happened that way, why wouldn't she have admitted it? The only reason to keep quiet would be to hide the abuse, and at that point it didn't matter. She wasn't that much of a martyr, was she?"

"Wasn't a martyr at all," Dacy said. "She'd have admitted it, all right. She never wanted pity, but it's a hell of a lot easier to deal with than hatred and suspicion."

Not that way, no. But suppose . . .

Draper and Teal weren't at Murphy's, a roadhouse on the flats below the shopping center: None of the half dozen pickups parked on its front lot was white. Both Messenger and Dacy were silent as she wheeled the Jeep back onto the highway heading north. The sky to the west, where the sun was sliding down toward the jagged crest of Montezuma Peak, was streaked with crimson and orange—fire colors, like the blaze that had consumed the skeletons of Anna's ranch. Cloud puffs in that direction had dark red underbellies, as if they had been used like cotton swabs to mop up blood.

Back through the empty town, past the High Desert Lodge. A sheriff's cruiser passed them there, but the driver wasn't Ben Espinosa and he paid them no attention. Downhill and onto the northern plain. Pale flickering neon—the outlines of a blue miner with a red pick and a yellow gold pan—jutted from the roof of the Hardrock Tavern, marking its location when they were still some distance away. A cavvy of motorcycles and a dozen pickups and four-by-fours jammed front and side lots. He began scanning for the white pickup even before Dacy turned in.

Two white trucks. And the second of the two, near the end of the side lot, had a broken radio antenna.

Dacy parked across from it, in the only available space. When she shut off the Jeep's engine, Messenger could hear the throb of country music and the muted jumble of voices from inside the low-slung building.

She caught hold of his arm, stopped him from getting out. "No, you wait here. I'll bring them."

"Bring them? Why not talk to them inside?"

"We're doing this my way, remember?"

"I'm not arguing, just wondering."

"It's crowded in there," she said. "The two of us walk in together and you're recognized, we might not get a chance at Draper and Teal. You understand what I mean?"

She'd been sensitive to it, too, driving through town—the fear and nervous anger, the potential danger. He nodded and said, "I understand."

"All right. Just stay put until you see the three of us by the pickup. Then walk on over."

She was inside the tavern less than five minutes. When she came out she had two men with her, both in their thirties and rough-dressed, one sporting a thick freebooter's beard. She spoke animatedly to them, gesturing with her hands, as she led the way to the white pickup. The bearded one bent to peer at the driver's side door, the side farthest away from the roadhouse. Messenger, out of the Jeep and approaching at a fast walk, heard him say, "What the hell? I don't see any dent. There ain't even a scratch." The voice was the same one he'd heard on the phone pretending to be Herb Mackey.

The other man, red-haired and wiry, saw him first. "Christ, Billy, look who's coming."

Billy Draper straightened; the two men stood staring at Messenger as he slid around the pickup and joined Dacy. She had positioned herself

190 / BILL PRONZINI

at the front of the truck, her back to the west; that put the glare of the setting sun in the eyes of the two miners. There was no room for them to sidestep in the narrow space between the pickup and the four-by-four next to it. All they could do was squint and raise shading hands.

"You're Dacy Burgess," Draper said to her. "Yeah, I thought you looked familiar. What's the idea, Dacy? You and this dickhead up to something?"

"We're after the answers to some questions."

"Yeah? Well, we're fresh out."

"You haven't heard the questions yet."

"Don't matter. We're still fresh out."

"Who paid you to set that snake trap at Mackey's?"

"Snake trap? What's she yammering about, Pete?"

"Beats me," Pete Teal said. "Drunk or stoned, maybe."

"Let's cut the bullshit, boys."

Almost casually Dacy slid a hand under the loose tails of her shirt, brought it out filled with a short-barreled revolver. Messenger was as taken aback as Draper and Teal. He might have expected that this was the sort of tactic she'd use, a pure Western improvisation, but he hadn't. Babe in the desert, she'd called him earlier. Right.

The gun made Teal twitchy; his gaze was fixed on it and his hands moved jerkily up and down the legs of his Wrangler jeans. Draper's reaction was one of angry bluster. He said, "Who're you kidding, honey? You ain't gonna shoot nobody with that thing."

"You think? Check out where it's aimed, Billy. Take one step this way, you'll spend the rest of your life half-cocked."

"Big talk."

"Take the step then."

Staredown.

Neither the revolver nor her hard-bright eyes wavered. Messenger had known there was a core of steel in her, but he hadn't realized just how deeply forged it was. He kept learning things about her, and one of them was that there was a lot she could teach him, a lot he wanted her to teach him. Listen and learn, listen and yearn.

Draper recognized the steel in her, too; he didn't move. Teal kept rubbing his pants legs, staring at the revolver. When Draper said, "Hell with you and your gun, mama," the words came out sounding more sullen than angry. "We don't have to tell you nothing."

"You do if you want to stay out of jail."

"Jail, shit. We never even been to Mackey's and you can't prove different."

"I'm not talking about Mackey's. I'm talking about John T. Roebuck's murder last night."

That jump-started Teal. He flapped an arm and said, "Hey! We didn't have nothing to do with that."

"Looks to me like maybe you did."

"No way. Listen—"

He broke off because a bright red four-by-four had come sliding into the parking lot and was swinging around toward where the four of them stood. Dacy lowered the revolver, hid it behind her leg, as the four-by-four—a Chevy Blazer—slewed into a space near the Jeep. Two men got out. Hanratty and Spears. Hanratty's wheels tonight, with him driving.

"What's goin' on over there?" Hanratty called. He sounded drunk and looked drunk: unsteady on his feet, red-faced, his shirt partly untucked.

Dacy called back, "Just a friendly conversation. Isn't that right, boys?"

"That's right," Teal said. "No problem here."

"Sure about that?"

"Like the lady said. Buy you and your buddy a beer when we're done, all right?"

"Whiskey tonight. Honor of John T. You hear about John T.?"

"We heard."

"Son of a bitch there, that city boy, it wasn't for him John T.'d still be alive."

Nobody said anything to that. Hanratty's red face took on a belligerent expression; he started in their direction. Messenger tensed. But Tom Spears wasn't as drunk as Hanratty, or as inclined to be vindictive. He said in lugubrious tones, "Unpin your ears and let your hackles smooth down, Joe. We come here for whiskey, not hassle."

Hanratty muttered something, glaring at Messenger. But he held on to his temper, and after a few seconds he let Spears prod him away to the tavern.

Teal said to Dacy, "I'll tell you again: We didn't have nothing to do with any killing. We was at the King mine last night and we can prove it."

"Maybe you can. But concealing evidence makes you accessories."

"Evidence? What evidence?"

"Name of the person who paid you to set that snake trap."

Draper said, "Back to that."

"That's right, back to that. Who was it? John T.?"

"Hillary Clinton."

"Jim," Dacy said, "you take the Jeep and go fetch the sheriff. I'll hold these boys here until you get back."

"Right." Messenger started away.

Teal flapped an arm again. "Wait a minute," he said, "wait a minute. Leave the goddamn sheriff out of this. All me and Billy did—"

"Shut up, Pete, for Chrissake."

"All we did was a favor for a friend, just a favor. Even if one of them snakes'd bit him, he wouldn't've died from it. Just scare him into leaving town, I swear that's all it was."

"What friend? Name him."

"John T.," Draper said. The sun had gone down and he was no longer squinting or shading his eyes; he seemed more sure of himself. "Yeah, it was Roebuck. He come out to the mine and give us two hundred bucks to set up the trap. You satisfied now?"

Dacy asked Teal, "That right, Pete? It was John T.?"

"Right. That's who it was."

For some time there had been a slow spread of realization and understanding in Messenger's mind, like oil being poured through a funnel. Now it was as complete as his rebirthing process. He said flatly, "No, it wasn't."

"You asked us, we told you," Draper said. "You don't believe it, that's your lookout."

"It wasn't John T. He went out to the mine to see you, all right, but not until afterward—yesterday or the day before. He knew who drove a white pickup with a broken antenna; he must've seen you around the casino. He asked the same question: Who put you up to the trap? And you told him. If he gave you money, that's what it was for."

"Man, you're full of crap."

Dacy said, "Jim?"

"That's exactly how it was," he said. "They're lying mostly to protect themselves and partly to protect their friend. They told John T. and it made him mad as hell. He got in touch with the friend and they arranged a meeting at Anna's ranch. And it wasn't the first time. Come on, Dacy, we're leaving."

"What about these two?"

"They won't follow us. Not if they want to stay out of jail."

"You hear that, Billy? Pete?"

Neither man answered. Neither moved as Messenger, with Dacy behind him, circled the pickup and went across to the Jeep. They were still standing there, growling at each other now, when she drove out to the highway entrance.

"All right," she said, "where to now?"

"Back into town." And when she'd made the turn: "The sprig of verbena that was found in Tess's hand—what color were the flowers?"

"What color . . . Jesus, Jim!"

"Tell me what color."

"White. White flowers."

"Her Sunday dress was white, too."

"What does that have to do with—?"

"How big is a verbena plant? What does it look like?"

"Not tall—foot high or so. Spiky branches with a lot of little flowers in clusters. Now for God's sake will you tell me what's in your head?"

"The truth," he said grimly. "I'm pretty sure I know who committed the murders. And I think I know why."

THE TROUBLE CAME while they were stopped at an intersection near the top of the hill, waiting for the red signal light to change.

He had just begun an explanation. As inwardly focused as he was, he wasn't aware of the vehicle roaring uphill behind them until Dacy said, "Shit!" and smacked the steering wheel with her fist. High-beam lights slashed through the rapidly settling dusk, filled the Jeep for a few seconds, then cut away as the oncoming car changed lanes. When it skidded up next to them in the inside lane he saw that it was the red Blazer with Joe Hanratty at the wheel and Tom Spears beside him.

Hanratty's belligerence had escalated into a rage, with or without the prod of more whiskey. He leaned across Spears and hurled spittle along with half-slurred words: "Not gonna get away so goddamn easy. Pull over, Dacy."

"No," she said. "We got nothing to say to each other."

"Pull over, I mean it."

"Don't make trouble, Joe. I mean that."

"Listen, you and that city bastard—"

The light flashed green. The highway ahead was empty; Dacy made the mistake of popping the clutch and accelerating, an action that served only to provoke Hanratty. Messenger, half turned in his seat, saw the Blazer's tires spin black smoke, heard and smelled rubber burning as they caught traction. The four-by-four rushed up on them, yawing so wildly that its front end scraped the Jeep's side before Hanratty was able to bring it under control. It shot ahead by twenty yards. Then its brake lights brightened and it swung toward them again, deliberately this time.

Dacy cut the wheel hard to the right to avoid a collision. The Jeep bounced up over a high curb, rattled down with a jolt that nearly caused her to lose control. Something bulked up large in front of them; he yelled a warning, but Dacy was already jamming on the brakes. If he hadn't had his seat belt fastened and his body braced, he would have gone through the windshield or right up over it when the Jeep shuddered to a dead-engine stop. Closed Chevron station, he realized then. They were on the apron, nose up to one of the pumps on an outer island.

Hanratty had gone on past but now he was reversing, fast off the highway and in onto the apron at a sliding angle twenty yards away. Dacy was out and running by then. She yanked the Blazer's door open, caught hold of Hanratty's shirt, and all but dragged him out.

"You crazy drunken fool!" she yelled with her face inches from his. "You could've killed us!"

He swatted her hand loose. Then, as Spears came around from the passenger side and Messenger ran up, Hanratty swatted her—a backhanded blow that knocked her off her feet and sent her sprawling.

Messenger hit him in retaliation. Didn't plan it, didn't have time to think about it, just swung in sudden fury as soon as he saw Dacy go down. His fist caught Hanratty on the side of the head; pain erupted in his knuckles as the big man stumbled back against the Blazer. But Hanratty wasn't hurt. He caromed off, bellowing, and bull-charged Messenger, wrapped powerful arms around him.

Their feet got tangled together and they collapsed in a clawing embrace, Hanratty on top when they landed; his weight and impact with the asphalt drove most of the air from Messenger's lungs. Gasping, he flailed with arms and legs, managed to free himself and pull away. He got his feet under him and lurched upright.

A flat banging noise penetrated the blood-pound in his ears.

Another.

His vision was clouded; he blinked his eyes clear, looking for Dacy. She was over behind the four-by-four, unhurt and wearing an expression of cold rage, the short-barreled revolver in her hand. Spears stood motionless a few feet from her, staring at the back end of the Blazer. Hanratty had gained his feet, too and was shaking his head in angry disbelief. It seemed to Messenger that enough noise had been made to bring the law and half the town; he was surprised to see that the highway was still empty, the four of them alone in what was left of the desert twilight.

A loud hissing reached his ears. And he saw then that the four-by-four's rear end was settling at a backward slant. Dacy had shot out both rear tires.

"What the hell'd you do that for?" Hanratty said to her. He took a step toward her.

"Stay put unless you want some of the same. I'm not kidding, Joe."

Hanratty stopped, glowering.

"How about you, Tom?"

"Not me," Spears said. "Wasn't my idea to chase after you."

"Goddamn it, Dacy, you're gonna pay for them tires."

"Sure I am. Just like you'll pay for the damage to my Jeep."

Blood dribbled down from a cut on Hanratty's temple; he swiped at it distractedly, as if it were a bothersome fly. "Second time in two nights you throwed a gun on me," he said. "I oughta take that one away from you."

"Go ahead and try. I'll send flowers."

"Huh?"

"To your hospital room. Takes a while to get over a gunshot wound, Joe. I hear they're real painful."

"Kind of talk don't scare me," Hanratty said, but at some level it must have. Like Billy Draper earlier, he held his ground.

"Jim," she said. "You all right?"

His knuckles throbbed, and his chest ached with the hiss and rattle of his breathing. But he said, "Not hurt."

"Go get in the Jeep."

He went immediately. Headlights had appeared on the highway: two cars, one passing in each direction at retarded speeds. But their gawking occupants wanted nothing to do with what was happening in the station. Both sets of lights had vanished when Dacy settled in beside him.

"Damn rednecks!" she said when they were back on the highway. She was still furious. "You sure you're okay?"

"Yes. You?"

"I've been hit harder. You handled yourself pretty well back there."

"Did I? I haven't been in a fight since grade school. Tell me something, Dacy. Would you have shot Hanratty if he'd come at you? Or Spears? Or Billy Draper earlier?"

"What do you think?"

"I think I'd like to know, one way or the other."

"My daddy taught me to always finish what I start. That answer your question?"

"Yes."

"Bother you?"

"No."

"Good. Now suppose you finish what you started to tell me back there at the stoplight."

24

I T W A S F U L L dark when they drove up onto the bluff top. This was
supposed to be a place of sanctuary, but to Messenger the buildings and
the blobs and spatters of light and color had a strangely uninviting
aspect. Imagination, perhaps, tainted by the knowledge that had brought
them here. Just the same it all seemed remote and empty, secretive, like
an island floating in the evening sky above Beulah.

On the grounds there were amber night lights; in the parsonage, a
white globe burned behind an unshaded kitchen window and a pale gold
rectangle marked a bedroom or study; in the Church of the Holy Name
low-wattage bulbs and possibly candlelight turned the stained-glass
windows into religious scenes like those in old illuminated manuscripts.
But all of the light was stationary, frozen in the windless, purple dark.
Cold light, where it should have been warm: as cold as the metallic silver
dusting of stars overhead. The splashes of white radiance from the Jeep's
headlamps was all that moved as they jounced across the parking area;
and when Dacy halted near the church entrance, the beams too became
solid and cold.

She switched off lights and engine. Silence folded around them, a
thick hush; but almost immediately sounds came out of the shadows that
stretched away behind the church. Messenger stiffened with one leg out
of the Jeep; Dacy reached over to grip his arm. The sounds continued
almost rhythmically: chunking thuds and hollow scrapings. Metal on
earth.

Somebody was digging in the cemetery.

He finished his exit and stood waiting, rubbing his still-sore knuckles. When Dacy joined him he saw by the starshine that she'd drawn her revolver. He said, "You won't need that."

"Probably not, but I'll feel better with it handy."

"Don't show it unless you have to. Keep it out of sight."

"Okay." She tucked the weapon back under her shirttails, but she kept her hand on the butt.

He led the way along the church's south wall. At the rear, near where the sand-pitted marble angel bulked grotesquely above the Roebuck plot, they paused to probe the shadows. Fifty yards distant, under one of the cottonwoods, a lone figure stood just below ground level, wielding what in drawn-back silhouette he recognized as a pick. Chunking thud as the tool smacked down, hollow scraping as its pronged head dragged through loose earth. Back up again, poised. And back down.

They approached slowly, not making noise to announce their presence but not being stealthy either. The digging went on unabated. They stopped once more, a few feet away. The hole under the tree was more than a foot deep and roughly rectangular in shape—obviously a grave. No surprise in that, and none in the identity of the person swinging the pick. From the moment he'd heard the digging sounds he'd known who was making them.

"Maria," he said.

No response, then or when he spoke her name a second time. It was as if she were working in a vacuum. Or a trance.

Dacy touched his arm again. "Let me try." She went closer, to within two paces of the grave's edge. Softly she said, "Hello, Maria."

The pitch of another woman's voice penetrated where his hadn't. It didn't startle Maria Hoxie or make her react with defensive fright; skittishness was not a part of her tonight. She merely paused with the pick's point at shoulder level and peered around, her head cocked to one side like a bird's.

"Who's that?" she said.

"Dacy Burgess."

"Oh." Then, "Somebody's with you."

"Jim Messenger."

His name didn't seem to bother her, either. She stood silently as he joined Dacy. Tree-shadow mottled her bent body and upturned face, but there was still enough light to show him the sweat-plastered black hair, the widened eyes with a little too much white visible. Working here a long time, he thought, since before nightfall. Calm enough outwardly, but on the inside? How close was she to the edge?

"I didn't want you to come," she said to him. She meant to Beulah in the first place, not here tonight. "I tried to make you go away, even though I knew down deep that I couldn't. The Lord sent you, didn't He? You're the Lord's Messenger."

When he didn't answer she said, "Yes, He sent you," and lifted the pick high again, swung it down again.

Dacy asked, "What're you digging there?"

"A grave. What else would I be digging?"

"For John T.?"

"No."

"For who, then?"

"For me," Maria said. "This is my grave."

The flesh between Messenger's shoulder blades bunched and rippled. Dacy edged closer to him; both hands were at her sides now. She said, "You're not going to die, Maria."

"Everyone dies. The Lord wants my soul too—I understand that now. That's why He sent His Messenger to bring out the truth."

"Suicide is a mortal sin. You know that."

"I know. Oh yes, I know. But there are worse sins."

"The taking of someone else's life."

"Even worse than that." A shudder passed through her, visible even in the half-light, and made her pause again in her digging. She tipped her head back to peer up at the velvety sky. "It's dark," she said, as if she had just realized the fact. "I'd better go get a lantern."

"Wait, Maria. Talk to us first."

"I am talking to you."

"About John T. About what happened last night."

Another tremor. She dropped the pick and hugged herself. "I don't like the dark," she said. "I have to sleep with a light on, did you know that?"

He said gently, "What happened with John T., Maria?"

"Oh, it was his fault. Really. He made me do it."

"He made you shoot him?"

"I thought he wanted to love me, like the other times we met up there. But he never loved me. He only wanted to hurt me."

"Hurt you how?"

"He yelled at me and called me names. Slut, whore—terrible names. Why did I let men like Billy and Pete have my body? Why did I tell them to turn serpents loose on the Messenger? Why couldn't I let him make the Messenger go away? Why, why, why, over and over. So I told him why. I told him everything."

"That you were the one who killed his brother."

She didn't seem to hear him. "He hit me. In the stomach, hard. I'll kill you for what you did, Maria, he said, and he hit me again. But I knew about the gun, I saw it once when I was looking for tissues. I took it and I . . . it made a terrible noise inside the car and he . . ." She hugged herself more tightly. "We punished him," she said, "God and I."

Dacy, in a voice with a rusty edge: "Why did you set fire to the ranch?"

"God told me to. It was an evil place. Satan made evil things happen there, he made me keep coming back and doing evil things with men like John T. The only way to save my soul was to drive Satan back to the Pit. Fire to fight fire."

"Did God tell you to shoot Dave Roebuck, too?"

"Yes."

"Because he was evil?"

"Yes. 'There shall not be found among you any one that maketh his son or his daughter to pass through the fire. For all that do these things are an abomination unto the Lord.' "

Messenger said, "He hurt his daughter, he made Tess pass through the fire."

"Yes."

"And you were a witness."

"Yes."

"Why did you go to his ranch that day? To see him?"

"No. To talk to his wife. To beg her forgiveness for my sin of lying with him. The night before . . . he was drunk and he laughed at me, he said all he ever cared about was fucking me. There was no love in him either. Only evil."

"But Anna wasn't there."

"Just him. And Tess. He was drunk again. Staggering out of the barn, chasing her—that poor little naked child."

"Tess had no clothes on?"

"Naked. Screaming 'Leave me alone, leave me alone, I'll tell Mommy what you did!' She kicked him when he caught her and he yelled and picked up the rock and he . . . I heard the sound it made, I saw the blood when she fell. From the top of the hill by the gate. But he didn't see me. He carried her back to the barn and I went down and the shotgun was there on the porch. God put it there for me to see, in plain sight. I took it to the barn and he was bending over the little girl, crying, saying he was sorry, he didn't mean to hurt her. But he wasn't sorry. He was drunk and evil and God told me to pull the trigger and I did. He was an abomination unto the Lord."

"Then what did you do?"

"I mustn't leave her there like that. I mustn't. I found her clothes and took them into the house and picked out a pretty dress and covered her nakedness."

"And after that you picked a sprig of flowers and put it in her hand. From a bush like the one you were planting here on Wednesday, on Tess's grave."

"Verbena. The first one I planted for her died." Maria sat down on the low mound of dirt, placed her hands together like a supplicant. "Everything dies," she said. "Sooner or later."

"White dress, white verbena. White for purity."

"Yes."

"And that's why you put her body in the well."

"Yes. Pure water to cleanse away the evil, to prepare her for her entry into the Kingdom. She suffered, but not for long. Then she was at peace in the arms of the Lord."

"But you're not at peace, Maria."

"I will be soon."

"You suffered too, didn't you? The same way Tess did, and for a much longer time. That's the real reason you're not at peace."

"Yes."

"That's why you did what you did at the ranch." *Has to be. It's the only way it all makes sense.* "And why you didn't tell anyone afterward. You couldn't talk about such things, not even to save Anna. Your father made you swear never to talk about such things, didn't he?"

"People wouldn't understand, he said. It wasn't wicked, what we did together, because we loved each other. I love you more than life itself, Maria, you're the closest to an angel God ever made. I need to show you how much I love you. I can't stop myself, Lord help me, I can't. That's what he said."

Dacy made an angry sound in her throat. Messenger said, "It wasn't love, Maria. You know that now."

"Yes. I know that now."

Reverend Walter Hoxie. He was responsible for everything that Maria had done, not she. He drove her to look for his kind of love with the Roebucks and Draper and Teal and God knew how many others. He gave her a warped view of religion and sowed the seeds of murder. And at some level she'd known all along what he was and what he'd done to her. It wasn't Dave Roebuck she'd killed in March, it was her adoptive father. It wasn't John T. she'd shot last night, it was the man who'd begun molesting her when she was no older than Tess.

"Where is he?" Messenger said thickly. "Where's the good reverend Hoxie?"

"In the church."

"Stay here with her," he said to Dacy. "I'm going to see Hoxie."

"Jim, don't do anything foolish—"

"I won't. I just want to confront him with it."

He hurried back around to the front of the church. The hinges squeaked when he pushed open one of the double doors. Electric light was all that burned inside; the votive candles on the altar were unlit. He noticed that first, before anything else registered. Then—

Light and shadow: one elongated shadow, half bulky and half finger-thin, stretched out over several of the empty pews. The Virgin Mary on one stained glass window, the twelve apostles on another, thorn-crowned Christ on the bronze cross behind the altar . . . all of them seemed to be staring, as he was staring, at the abomination in their midst.

Reverend Walter Hoxie hung stiff and straight from a length of rope looped around one of the rafter beams. The crude noose he'd fashioned hadn't fit tightly enough and his neck hadn't broken when he stepped off the top of one of the pews. He had died of strangulation: mottled red face, distended tongue a charred-looking black. Like a burnt offering, Messenger thought.

It was the second dead man he'd seen in less than twenty-four hours, but this time he felt nothing. His footfalls echoed hollowly as he walked closer. There was a piece of paper pinned to the front of Hoxie's coat;

by stretching upward on his toes he could just make out the words printed on it in a shaky hand.

May God forgive me for what I have done. Just that, nothing else.

The door hinges squeaked again behind him. He turned to see Maria come inside, then Dacy a few paces behind; heard the audible intake of Dacy's breath as she saw Hoxie. In the diffused light Maria's face was clear to him for the first time: without animation or color, eyes flat and empty like the eyes of someone close to death. Like Anna Roebuck's eyes in San Francisco. Until this moment he'd been certain that no one could possibly be sadder, lonelier than the woman he'd seen that first night in the Harmony Café. But he had been wrong.

The true essence of blue lonesome was the girl who stood facing him now.

"I confessed to him this morning," she said. "Everything, all my sins and all that God told me to do. He cried the way Dave Roebuck cried and told me how sorry he was. Then he came out here. I knew what he was going to do but I didn't try to stop him. I didn't want to stop him. I dug his grave first, on the other side of the cemetery from mine."

She advanced to Messenger's side, her empty gaze on what was left of Walter Hoxie. A vagrant air current stirred the body, made the rope creak faintly. In his ears the sound was like a whimper—a child's whimper in the night.

"'I am the rose of Sharon,'" she whispered, "'and the lily of the valleys. As the lily among thorns, so is my love among the daughters. I sat down under his shadow with great delight, and his fruit was sweet to my taste. He brought me to the banqueting house, and his banner over me was love. Stay me with flagons, comfort me with apples: for I am sick of love.'"

And she sank to her knees and bowed her head, and in a clear, steady voice she began to pray.

25

"I KEEP THINKING about her," Dacy said.

"I know. So do I."

"The things she said to us, the way she looked . . . I can't get it out of my mind."

"She's in good hands now," Messenger said. "Just keep telling yourself that."

"Doesn't do any good. I'll never forget that night. If I live to ninety it'll still be haunting my sleep."

"You think so now, but it's only been three days."

"Time heals, Jim?"

"Doesn't it?"

"Some things. Others . . . all you get is a scab that you can pick off without even half trying. Time won't heal Maria, no matter how many head doctors she has working on her. And it won't heal Beulah either. Towns are like people. Tear the guts out of one and even if it survives it'll never be the same again."

"Everybody blames me. You too, a little?"

"No," she said. "I blame the Roebucks. And Walter Hoxie. You did what you had to do. What nobody else would do. You gave Anna back her good name and took the hate and bitterness out of Lonnie and me. I'll always be grateful to you, Jim."

"I get the feeling there's a 'but' in there somewhere."

"Not where you're concerned. The only 'but' is that I may not be able to keep on living here. I always figured I'd stick on this ranch until the day I die, but now . . . I'm not thinking that way anymore."

"Would it be so bad to go somewhere else, make a fresh start?"

"I don't know. Maybe not. Tonopah, Beatty, up around Winnemucca—I wouldn't mind any of those. Main problem is, I couldn't get much for this place and decent cattle land's expensive."

"You could use some or all of the money Anna left. You and Lonnie really do deserve to have it."

"Maybe. I don't know about that yet, either."

"Have you said anything to him about moving?"

"No. He's got enough to deal with right now."

"He'll be all right, no matter what you decide to do. He's a strong kid. No, a strong man. He'd make a fine veterinarian."

"I know it. You reckon he'd put all this behind him quicker and easier somewhere else?"

"Yes. And I think you would, too."

She didn't reply. Instead she sat listening for a moment to the jazz tape playing softly inside; then she leaned forward to study—or pretend to study—the arrangement of the chess pieces. The westering sun slanted in under the porch overhang, put shimmery gold highlights in her hair. He restrained an impulse to touch the unruly topknot and shifted his gaze to the desert. For the first time in three days the valley road lay empty of official and unofficial cars and media vehicles; it and the sagebrush plain were bathed in a soft, buff-colored radiance. Peaceful, he thought. Finally, for all of us, a little peace.

With a knuckle Dacy moved one of her pawns, then leaned back and looked at him. And they both spoke at once.

He said, "I've been doing a lot of thinking—"

She said, "When're you leaving, Jim?"

"Saturday morning. That's part of what I was about to say."

"Been on both our minds, I guess."

"Dacy, why don't you come with me? We could go together to make the arrangements for Anna's burial—"

"No. I can't leave Lonnie here alone, not now."

"He could come, too."

"Abandon the ranch? No way. Besides . . ."

When she didn't continue he prompted, "Besides?"

"It'll be easier for you and me to say good-bye right here."

"Good-bye. You make it sound final."

"That's the way it has to be."

"No it doesn't."

"Jim, we aren't going to carry on a long-distance relationship. I go out to Frisco for a few days, you come visit next year on your vacation . . . it just wouldn't work. It's not what either of us wants or needs."

"I agree, but—"

"We had our time together, and the good parts . . . I won't forget them either. But it's over. We're different people, we live in different worlds. . . ."

"What if we lived in the same world?"

"Oh God, Jim, I'm not Anna. No way I could live in an apartment in a big city. I'd shrivel up and die inside a year."

"Dacy, listen—"

"Same goes for Lonnie. We're desert rats, plain and simple. Our roots go too deep in this piss-poor soil to ever yank 'em up completely."

"Dammit, *listen* to me. When I get back what I want to do, what I'm aching to do, is give my boss three weeks' notice, work out a settlement with my landlord to break my lease, pack up what I own that's worth keeping, and then drive straight back here. In plenty of time to help you and Lonnie with the roundup. If you do decide to move, you won't be able to manage it before then and I work cheaper and harder than any regular cowhand."

Dead silence. Then, slowly, "I don't believe what I just heard."

"Believe it. Believe this, too: I love you, Dacy."

"Oh, now . . ."

"And I think that if you don't love me, just a little, you at least care for me. Am I right?"

She was shaking her head, but it was a gesture of exasperation rather than negation. "I swear, I never knew a man like you. Just when I figure I've got you pegged, you go unpredictable on me."

"Good. That's good. I used to be as predictable as a morning sunrise. Now I'm mule stubborn, batshit crazy, improvisational, unpredictable, and never more sincere or sure of my own mind."

"You'd give up everything you have in Frisco and move out to some hardscrabble ranch in the middle of nowhere?"

"Everything I have? Dacy, what I've got back there is a dead-end job I've never much liked, a handful of acquaintances who won't miss me two weeks after I'm gone, and a lifestyle that has been slowly suffocating me most of my adult life. I don't have *anything* in San Francisco. I can shuck it all in three weeks, no regrets, no looking back. But I can't do it, I won't do it, unless I've got something worthwhile to exchange it for."

"Me."

"You, Lonnie, a hardscrabble ranch in the middle of this or some other nowhere—a fresh start for me, too. Absolute commitment on my part, but it doesn't have to be on yours. You set the terms and I'll abide by them. Trial period, if you like: three months, six months, a year. Hired man, part-time or full-time lover . . . whatever you want me to be. But I've got to know I'm welcome first, before I leave on Saturday."

Nothing from her. Her eyes were squint-hidden; he couldn't see them well enough to read them. In the background now, Mildred Bailey was singing "I Can't Get Started With You." Oh Lord, he thought, don't let that be prophetic.

"Think about it," he said, "will you do that? Think about it and give me your answer Saturday morning."

"Well, maybe I should think about it. Talk to Lonnie too, see what he says. But I guess I won't need to do either."

"Say it, then. Don't dance with me, Dacy. Yes or no?"

She said, "Yes."